PIONEER LONGING

THE O'ROURKE FAMILY MONTANA SAGA, BOOK FOUR

RAMONA FLIGHTNER

GRIZZLY DAMSEL PUBLISHING

DB
Without your amazing
insight and encouragement,
this book would not
be as it is.
Thank you for your
dedication and friendship.

CHAPTER 1

Missouri River, May 1866

Hell must feel like this, Eamon O'Rourke said to himself, as he felt he were on the verge of being baked alive. With a groan, he sat down and stared with abject longing at the river rumbling by. Although it appeared calm at the surface, he had seen its power as it ripped pieces of riverbank loose and smashed driftwood into the hull of the steamboat. He knew it would be foolish to attempt to swim or bathe in the rapid current, but he yearned for just such a respite from the heat on this early May day. Instead today's entertainment consisted of watching the steamboat captain discern how to maneuver the stranded vessel over a sandbar that stretched the width of the river.

"*Ugh*," moaned his younger brother and best friend, Finn, as he flopped onto his back beside Eamon. Less than two years separated them in age, and they looked and acted so much alike that they were affectionately called the twins. "I can't believe you're not upset that we're just stuck here."

After months in Saint Louis, his voice now only held a hint of his native Ireland.

Eamon crossed his long legs, a boot heel digging into the dirt as he rested on his back, his hat covering his face and protecting him from the harsh midday sun. "What is there to do, Finn?" He yawned. "I'd take a nap, but it's too hot. An' the women have congregated in the bushes, takin' all the shade."

"Aye, an' we're too sweaty after unloading all the cargo. I can only imagine what the women would say should we invade their space."

Eamon grunted his agreement. "I've no desire to loiter nearer the boat, or the captain would put us to work again," he muttered. "I've no patience for the man's ineptitude. Nor do I wish to drown because one of his harebrained ideas doesn't work."

The captain had hoped the steamboat could slip over the sandbar, if the boat were empty. However, that had proved a fruitless endeavor, and now tons of supplies and materials bound for Fort Benton lay scattered along the riverbank, as they waited to see if the captain had the ability to outmaneuver the river. The poorer men who slept on the ship's deck now acted like an extension of the captain's crew, working to tug the steamboat up the river with heavy ropes.

"Da will be upset if we lose our cargo," Finn said, as he sat up, resting on one elbow as he watched the ongoing struggle with the steamboat.

"Where is it to go, Finn?" Eamon asked, his voice tinged with exasperation. "We're sittin' here in the middle of nowhere. The Indians might attack, but, other than that, our cargo will arrive fine. As long as that man can figure out how to continue the journey upriver." Eamon also sat up to lean on his elbows, his hat now on his chest, as he stared at the moored boat and the captain waving his arms about in an ineffectual manner. "*Eejit.*"

"Ah, the captain's a nice man," Finn protested.

"*Nice* isn't goin' to get the *bluidy* thing movin'," Eamon said, sounding more like his father, Seamus. Eamon sighed and glanced around, his gaze pausing on a small group of women sitting in the shade of cottonwood trees closer to the riverbank. "I wish they weren't so unsociable. There's no reason they should hoard all the shade."

Finn groaned and laid on his back again. "I'd rather stare at the sky and try to find shapes in the clouds. Who needs to have another argument with the likes of Winnifred Mortimer?"

Eamon laughed. "You're upset she took an instant dislike to you. Every other lass has thought you charming." Eamon peered down the slight slope at the group he barely saw in the shadows. "Phoebe is nice."

"As nice as Lorena is boring," Finn said, as he sighed and rolled to his belly. He yanked on a piece of prairie grass and tore it into small pieces.

"She can't help preferring to read," Eamon said with a chuckle. "Don't you find it remarkable they're sisters? They barely look anything alike."

"'Tis odd," his brother muttered, as he stared at Eamon with intrigue in his gaze. "Makes me wonder if there isn't more to their story. How can they be sisters with the same parents if they only share eye color? Maybe they're like our brothers, Henri and Luc, or the younger lads."

Eamon nodded, thinking about his large family and the siblings he shared with Finn who were only half siblings. Three of his youngest brothers—Niall, Oran, and Bryan—had a different mother. And Lucien and Henri had a different father. However, all seven siblings who shared Seamus and Mary as parents considered their half siblings as full siblings, wholly accepting them into the sprawling O'Rourke family. "If there is a story, I doubt they'll ever share it with us.

3

Winnifred would kill you first. Lorena barely speaks to us, an' Phoebe ..." He shrugged.

Finn sighed. "Phoebe's too afraid of her own shadow around you." He smirked when Eamon stared at him in bewilderment. "Besides," Finn said, yawning, "I heard one of the sisters whining in their cabin that, if it were the last thing she ever did, she would ensure they were seen as respectable."

"*Hmm*," Eamon said, chewing on a piece of prairie grass, as he stared in the direction of the cottonwoods. "Which means something must make them disreputable."

Finn laughed. "Of that there is no doubt. Winnifred is proof."

Eamon rolled his eyes at Finn's dislike of the youngest Mortimer sister. They had met the sisters on the first night of their journey, and, during the subsequent weeks, Eamon had forged a friendship of sorts with the middle sister, Phoebe, while Finn and Winnifred relished each verbal sparring match. Lorena ignored them, preferring to read or to stare out at the river.

After a long pause, Eamon murmured, "I imagine many would claim one of the O'Rourkes is boring." He saw Finn tilt his head to one side as he picked up on an earlier comment before Finn speared him with a baleful stare.

"Who? An' which one of us? Ardan?" Finn shook his head. "He's responsible and the eldest. Kevin's not dull, not after he fought Declan in a saloon brawl for his wife."

They snickered. "Wish we could have seen that," Eamon said with an aggrieved sigh. "And now Declan's decided to separate from the family for another year. It makes no sense." He shook his head in frustration.

Finn shrugged and blew on his blade of grass, hoping to make a whistle. When he was unsuccessful, he focused on his brother again. "Dec will come around and will realize he wants to return home. He has to lick his wounds first."

"Fine, but you're the one tellin' Mum why her son isn't coming home," Eamon said. When Finn shook his head, Eamon groaned. "I wonder what's happened while we've been away? Do you think Niamh is finally happy with Connor?"

Finn snorted. "How could anyone be happy with him? If she's lucky, he's died."

"Finn!" Eamon hissed and then shook his head. "'Tis blasphemous to wish for another's demise." When his younger brother and closest friend shrugged unrepentantly, Eamon grinned at him. "Although I've wished for the same thing since she married the man. I'll never find myself in a situation where I have to marry a woman I don't know or love."

Finn rolled onto his back and dropped his bent arm over his eyes. "I'll never marry. Perhaps I'll start visiting the women at the Bordello." He yelped when Eamon hit him on his arm.

"You know Da would scalp you if you did."

"I wonder if wee Maggie has finally realized how much Dunmore cares for her?" Finn murmured.

"It doesn't matter," Eamon said with a huff of indignation. "She's too young. She's barely eighteen." He paused, as though envisioning his youngest sister. "We need time with her before she's taken away from us again."

"Aye, but she might have other ideas. Eighteen isn't too young to marry, Eamon." He stared wickedly at his brother. "Just because you're twenty-three, with no desire to wed, doesn't mean she won't want to."

Brushing off a sense of foreboding and an impending sense of loss, Eamon stood. "Come. Let's rile the womenfolk. It's been too quiet a day, and I'm bored."

Finn rose with alacrity. "Oh, yes."

〜

Phoebe Mortimer tucked a strand of blond hair behind one ear, giving up her attempt to keep her long hair tamed. She glanced at the expanse of prairie in the distance as the river gurgled nearby, silently asking herself why she cared what she looked like in such a wild place. Her sisters did not seem concerned, which was highly unusual for them, as appearances were paramount to them. Phoebe frowned as she realized the majority of the men on the steamboat had largely given them a wide berth. "It's as though we have the plague," she muttered to herself.

Although she yearned for more company than her sisters, Phoebe was thankful for their companionship. She had never realized how boring a river trip could be, nor how tedious the travel would become during the months-long journey from Saint Louis to Fort Benton. She rested on a tree stump under a grove of cottonwood trees, grateful for the shade on the blindingly bright day. Her youngest sister, Winnifred, had insisted the cool sheltered area was solely for the women, and the men had agreed after a little grumbling.

"Stop sighing like a you've lost your greatest love," Winnifred hissed, as she rested on the ground, her back against a tree trunk. Her long black hair flowed around her shoulders, as she worked out knots before braiding it again. "Be thankful I chased the men away, and we don't have to listen to their mindless boasting about embarrassing body functions."

Phoebe giggled and shook her head. "You're incorrigible, Winnie."

"You only protest about their presence because you're annoyed that the younger O'Rourke brother is as witty as you are," their eldest sister, Lorena, called out. She sat on a rock, rereading a novel, her red hair pulled back in a bun.

6

"At least he notices me," Winnifred said with a pouty snicker. "The other one barely gives poor Phoebe the time of day."

Phoebe flinched and looked down at her hands, now clenching her skirts. She forced her fingers to relax, as she feared she'd rend the cloth in her agitation at her sister's words. "I don't know what you imply."

"Protest all you want," her younger sister proclaimed. "I know you're bothered he's taken no notice of you, other than to talk about the weather or the progress we make each day."

Phoebe rose and walked to the edge of the shadowed space, fighting an urge to storm away from her sister's hurtful words. However, unable to forego her peacemaking nature, she murmured her agreement. "I've always known I was the plainest of the three of us," she whispered in a voice that didn't carry to her sisters. She smoothed a hand down her navy cotton skirts again.

When she heard the voices of the O'Rourke brothers approaching, she admitted to herself that they were the reason why she tried to appear put together. Since she had first seen them on the steamboat, she had felt an affinity with them. Upon meeting the brothers, her attraction to the older brother, Eamon, had grown. However, Eamon seemed interested in just a friendship, and she feared he only saw her as another sibling, not as a woman he would choose to court and to wed.

She shook her head in consternation, as she knew she should not be concerning herself with thoughts of marriage. She should be worried about locating her uncle and ensuring all the sisters were taken care of. Admonishing herself for her selfish thoughts, she turned with an impersonal smile to greet the brothers as they stepped into the shaded area. "Hello," she breathed.

"Miss Mortimer," Finn said with a smile.

Winnifred snorted from the ground. "You could be speaking to the three of us, not Phoebe."

"Aye, I could, but seein' as you're sitting on the ground on an ant hill, an' your other sister is engaged in a book, I thought I'd address my greeting to the woman who seemed sensible and friendly." Finn's blue eyes flashed with distaste as he stared at Winnifred. When she jumped up and patted at her skirts, belatedly realizing they were covered in red ants, he chuckled.

Eamon bit back a laugh, as he slapped a hand on his younger brother's shoulder. "Hello, Miss Phoebe," he said in his low baritone, his cobalt-blue eyes focusing on her for a moment. "'Tis lovely to see you and your sisters. We hope you don't mind us invading your sanctuary, but we found ourselves in need of company."

At Winnifred's snort of disbelief, Phoebe approached them and motioned for the brothers to join her sisters. She glared at her youngest sister, until Winnifred bit her lip and quieted. "We are uncertain how long we are to wait."

Eamon looked at the boat and shrugged. "I fear it could be a day or two, until they discern what's to be done."

"Must we sleep off the boat?"

Eamon shrugged. "I doubt they'd ask that of you, Miss Phoebe. Although I imagine we'll have to be careful, as we are more vulnerable to an Indian attack while tied up on the side of the river at night."

"Attack?" Phoebe gasped, paling.

"Eamon," Finn muttered, hitting Eamon's arm.

At Winnifred's proclamation that she could shoot better than any man present, Finn wandered off to bicker with her, leaving Phoebe and Eamon alone. "You are well, miss?" he asked. At her subtle nod, he whispered, "Do you need anything?"

She shrugged. "I need to be on my way to Fort Benton so

we can begin our journey into Montana Territory. We need to reunite with our uncle."

Eamon stared at her in confusion. "That's why you're travelin' upriver?"

"Yes. He wrote us last summer, when it was already too late to travel to the Territory, asking us to join him."

"He's your reason for travel?" At her shrug, he smiled. "I assumed you were mail order brides and already promised to men upstream."

She gasped and shook her head frantically. "Oh, no. No, no, no." Biting her lip to cease repeating the same word like a senseless ninny, she blushed as bright as the previous night's sunset. "I don't know how you could have come to that erroneous conclusion."

Eamon's lips quirked up into a smile, and he ran a hand through his inky-black hair, now longer than usual, as he mimicked his older brother, Declan. "My second-eldest brother, Kevin, met a woman on a steamboat last year. She was promised to my brother Declan, although neither knew it."

Phoebe gasped, her green eyes lit with interest. "What happened? Did he break your brother's heart?" Her gaze veered to her sisters and then back to Eamon, and she fidgeted under his astute gaze.

"No, Declan didn't know Aileen as Kev did. Declan didn't care for her as Kev did. In the end, Kevin married her, after rescuing her from the Bordello." When she gasped again, he winked at her. "So, you can see why I'd be cautious about meeting a woman on the steamboat."

Preening a little, Phoebe tilted her head back, hoping it showed off the fine length of her neck or the delicate curve of her earlobe.

"Besides, you remind me of my youngest sister, Maggie. 'Tis always nice to have good company on a long journey."

9

Fighting the urge to collapse at his feet in dismay, amid a pool of petticoats and lace-edged skirts, she looked away from him on the pretense of studying the men working on the steamboat. After blinking rapidly to clear her eyes of unwanted—and, she feared, unwarranted—tears, she motioned in the direction of the men laboring to move the steamboat over the sandbar. "It seems they need strong men to aid the captain's plan. Why don't you and your brother help?" she asked, clearing her throat to rid it of any huskiness, following her emotional response to him seeing her as a *sister*.

Eamon shrugged, his eyes lit with an inner warmth as he regarded her. "We offered, but, after we helped unload the supplies, he informed us that we'd done enough. Doesn't want to hurt his reputation by using men rentin' private cabins for such menial labor." He shrugged and winked at her.

Phoebe flushed at his wink.

"And then we realized he doesn't have a clue what he's doin', so we're hidin' away, in case he gets it into his head to put us to work again. With his muddleheaded ideas, I fear there'll be a disaster, and I have no interest in drownin' today."

Phoebe's gaze flit over him, taking in his broad shoulders and the muscles that rippled under his shirt with each movement. "I'd think you were used to menial labor." Stammering, she blurted out, "I beg your pardon. I meant no offense."

"None taken, miss. Aye, we're used to workin' hard. Da would have it no other way." His gaze was distant for a moment, before he smiled at her in a reassuring manner. "We might be successful now, but Finn and I work hard. As do all the O'Rourkes. None are lazy."

Phoebe stiffened, as though he had criticized her family. "Mortimers are hard workers too, Mr. O'Rourke."

"Aye, of that I have no doubt," he murmured with a soft chuckle. "I can imagine how much hard labor goes into reading a novel, over and over again."

Flushing, Phoebe fisted her hands at her side, as she took a step toward him, her shoulders back, challenging him. "Leave Lorena out of this," she whispered. "She's done nothing to earn such criticism from you."

He ducked his head. "I beg your pardon," he whispered. "I fear we are acting like Finn and your sister." He glanced in their direction, snorting with disbelief to see Winnifred standing on tiptoe, poking Finn in his shoulder, while expounding her point. Eamon focused on Phoebe, his stance relaxing and his blue eyes filling with regret. "I have no desire to quarrel with you, Miss Phoebe," he murmured. "I … Too often in our past we've been deemed less worthy because we are immigrants, willing to do whatever work we must to survive."

Phoebe took a deep breath and stared deeply into his gaze. "I don't understand what that life is like," she said in a soft voice. "But I do understand fighting against prejudice." She paused, as though debating whether to say more. "I forgive you, Mr. O'Rourke."

"Eamon," he whispered. "There are too many Mr. O'Rourkes to easily distinguish us, but I'm the only Eamon. Thank you, Bee." He smiled as she gasped at the use of a nickname. "Is it wrong for me to think of you as Bee?"

She swallowed. Finally she breathed, "I've only ever been Phoebe."

"You're much more than *only Phoebe*." He stilled as the steamboat whistle sounded. "Come. Let me help you back to the boat. I fear they've given up for the day, and we'll have to see what tomorrow brings."

Phoebe fought a girlish blush, as she slipped her hand through his offered arm, reminding herself that he was being a gentleman. And he only saw her as a friend or as another sister. Anything to dampen her growing attraction to this unattainable man.

~

Phoebe entered the small cabin that had room for the three sisters. Winnifred had the top bunk, while Phoebe slept below her. Lorena had a berth across from them, and she was already curled onto her side there, reading her novel. Phoebe had begun to suspect Lorena used a book as a barrier to interacting with her and Winnifred.

"Lo," Phoebe said, kicking at her sister's mattress to gain her attention. "Put down that stupid book. I know you've already read it three times on this journey alone."

Lorena stared at her in dumbstruck concern. "Are you ill?" Lorena whispered, setting aside her book. She rose, placing the back of her hand against Phoebe's forehead. "Were you in the sun?"

Phoebe rolled her eyes and then her shoulders, as she attempted to regain her composure.

Winnifred climbed into her bunk, where she rested on her side, her arm bent at the elbow and her head propped on her hand, as she stared at Phoebe in a mocking manner.

"I'm fine," Phoebe insisted. "I was hoping we could do something, other than watch you read."

Lorena flinched. "You know why I like to read." Her low voice held vestiges of a deep pain, and Phoebe gripped her elder sister's arm, before she could spin away to hide in her book again.

"I know, Lo, but can't you see what you're missing as you hide in your books? Can't you see we miss you?"

Lorena shrugged. "I'm sorry if you thought my presence

on this trip would help entertain you, Phoebe. I had thought you had found someone to assist you in that endeavor."

Phoebe dropped her hand and took a small step away, almost backing into the stateroom door in the cramped space. "I'm certain I don't understand what you mean."

Winnifred snorted and rolled her eyes. Her black hair was now completely freed of its confining braid and cascaded over her chest. "As if we didn't see you throwing yourself at the older O'Rourke brother today." When Phoebe blushed as red as one of the prized roses in their garden in Saint Louis, Winnifred chuckled. "You can lie to yourself, sister, but we know you."

Phoebe stood, battling a soft shivering, as Winnifred continued to talk, and Lorena watched Phoebe with sympathy. Fighting to keep her breathing slow and even, she shook her head.

"Yes, Phoebe," Winnifred proclaimed. "You know Mama always said you would make the worst gambler because you could never hide what you felt. Your eyes always gave you away." She played with the ends of her hair. "How does it feel to want a man who will only ever look at you as a bothersome little sister?"

"How can you be so cruel?" Phoebe gasped out, her composure falling to pieces at her sister's spiteful words.

Shrugging, Winnifred smirked at her. "You've always wanted to be Mama's favorite but failed. How that must have made you bitter toward us. Was that why you betrayed us? Was that why you forced us to sacrifice our happiness?" She glared at Phoebe with thinly veiled malice. "Because of you, Lo and I've had to suffer disappointments and rejections you can't fathom."

"If you mean Emory, you should be thankful that spineless puppy left before anything serious occurred," Phoebe

13

hissed, her agitation with her sisters warring with her loyalty to them. And to her mother.

Launching herself from the upper bunk, Winnifred nearly careened into Lorena but had the grace to land like a cat. "How dare you!" she screeched. "We were in love. We were to marry. But then you'd never understand what that means because you've always held yourself apart from anyone who's shown you the slightest interest. Instead you focus on the unattainable men who will never truly see you for what you are."

"How dare I?" Phoebe asked in a low voice that quivered with her suppressed emotions. "How dare you constantly remind me that I'm the unattractive sister. That no man has ever thought me worthy of pursuit. That I'm destined to die as the spinster sister. That Mama forever despaired of me. Thank you, Winnifred, for reminding me of all that, once again." She spun away to face the door and to avoid seeing their pity. For, if there was one thing she hated, it was pity.

"Unattractive?" Winnifred asked in a shocked voice.

"Unworthy of courting?" Lorena whispered. "How are you so foolish?" She had returned to her berth but rested on her side, watching her two younger sisters, rather than reopening her book, as though, for once, reality was more interesting than fiction.

"Why is it so impossible to accept the truth?" Phoebe gasped out.

"If it is the truth, that's fine," Lorena said in a low voice. "But it seems you've mangled everything in your attempt to prevent from being hurt. That's not life, Phoebe." She paused, as she rarely offered advice to her sisters or spoke more than a few words. "You'll have to accept what we are someday. And trust that, someday, a man will accept it too."

Winnifred snorted and rolled her eyes. "No, you have to

accept that no man need know what we are. A soft smile and a soothing voice will keep him happy and kill his curiosity."

"No man will accept what we are," Phoebe whispered, sniffling as she swiped at her cheeks, "and I fear you're bound to always be disappointed, Winnie."

Winnifred gave a huff of disagreement and climbed back up to her bunk. "If what you say is true, it's imperative we find our uncle and ensure he's well. For, if he's anything like Uncle Harvey, he'll be generous and take good care of us. I've never dreamed of living like a pauper."

"Nor I," Lorena whispered. She fingered the binding of her book.

Phoebe sighed and moved to her berth, ignoring the brewing headache and the ache in her heart. *Although her sisters had suffered disappointments in love, at least they had known such love*, Phoebe thought. Her suffering had been of another kind. Of another origin. And her sisters had no sympathy, as Lorena and Winnifred could only acknowledge what they had endured.

Phoebe let out a gust of breath and rubbed at her head. How she wished she could have hope in the future. However, she found such faith nearly impossible.

E amon stood, staring out at the river after supper that evening, his mind filled with images of Phoebe as they had chatted under the cottonwood trees. He grinned as he remembered her reaction to him giving her a nickname, resolving to only ever call her that when they were alone together. "Bee," he whispered to himself. Although he didn't know her well, he thought the name suited her, for she always seemed to be moving about, ensuring those around her were well.

He ignored the sounds of men talking, the scents of tobacco smoke and too many unwashed men in a crowded space. Fighting the memory of the first boat he'd been on when just four years old, he took a deep breath and looked around the steamboat, as though to remind himself he was on the mighty Missouri, not a cramped and decrepit ship heaving over the Atlantic Ocean. This ship had two levels, with the private cabins and fancy dining room on the upper level. Most of the men who paid only for deck passage were on the lower level, although a few had moved to the upper decks.

The lower deck was wider, with the majority of the cargo stacked in orderly piles. It was darker, with less air movement due to the high railing. Many men slept on top of the crates to cool off in a breeze. The upper deck was smaller, circling the dining room and cabins, while the pilot house atop was covered in a fine layer of boilerplate, in case of an Indian attack.

Eamon's mind returned to Phoebe. Although he knew Finn would disapprove, as his younger brother believed they should remain bachelors until they were at least fifty, Eamon couldn't stop thinking about her. Unlike the O'Rourke siblings, who bickered and argued but loved each other profoundly, Eamon sensed a deep resentment and tension between the Mortimer sisters. He sighed, wondering if Phoebe's desire to ensure peace and harmony was her way of pretending that everything was well in her world.

Against his will, he thought back to the years he had thought his mother dead. After their arrival in Montreal in August of 1847, his mum had given birth to his youngest sister, Maggie, in October. The following day, Da had been informed that both had perished from the horrible typhus outbreak. The family had never recovered from the loss of Mary O'Rourke. Colleen, his da's second wife, had made a feeble attempt to heal their broken hearts. When she realized she would be another casualty in the devastation wrought by Mary's death, Colleen had acted out, subtly and deviously, to hurt Seamus's youngest children.

Taking a deep breath, Eamon attempted to shut out his memories, but they forever lurked at the edges of his mind. He knew they would return soon to torment him again. A faint scent wafted over him, and he turned, smiling broadly to see Phoebe hovering nearby. "Bee," he breathed. His smile brightened at his nickname. "How lovely to see you this evenin'."

She took halting steps in his direction. "I feared you wouldn't wish to be interrupted. That I should leave you in peace. You seemed to be relishing your time alone."

He chuckled. "Nay, I wasn't. I need a distraction." He saw her flinch subtly at his words and frowned. "I missed speaking with you."

A smile burst forth, and her green eyes glowed with plea-sure. "How ... lovely," she murmured, mimicking one of his favorite words. She rested her hands on the railing beside his hand and breathed deeply of the cool evening air. "It's remarkable to me the evening can be so cool after such a warm day."

Eamon nodded. "Aye, 'tis nothin' like the city of Saint Louis. When I first arrived in Saint Louis last September, I thought I'd be roasted alive with the heat and humidity." His eyes sparkled as they chuckled together. "I can't imagine any work is completed in the summer months."

"Everything is a bit slower," she said by way of agreement. "We don't rush."

Watching her sagely, he heard a quiet warning in her voice. "I understand." He leaned against one elbow so as to better face her. "Even so, I like to think we are friends, Bee." At her pleased smile, he murmured, "Is all well between you and your sisters?" When she froze, he swore under his breath. "I beg your pardon, Bee. I shouldn't have …"

Squeezing his arm, she shook her head. "No, don't apologize. We had an argument before dinner. Nothing new but still hurtful." Phoebe bit her lip and shrugged. "My sisters are bitter at fate and look to blame others for what has happened. I think, deep inside, they hope I will be as miserable as they are. Which is why they insisted on this journey."

Shaking his head, Eamon furrowed his brows in confusion. "I don't understand. I know you're not mail order brides, and I know that you seek your uncle."

Phoebe faced him, everything around her ignored but Eamon. "Yes. I wanted to find a detective or to send a letter to Fort Benton, confirming his whereabouts. I did not believe it necessary for the three of us to travel all this way on a wild goose chase. I fear we will not have the resources to be successful and will find ourselves stranded in Montana Territory."

"Did he not send passage for you?" Eamon asked with a frown.

She shook her head. "There's no need to concern yourself about our welfare, Mr. O'Rourke." She took a deep breath of the cool evening air to calm herself, while speaking of unpleasant topics. As though unable to dampen the desire to share her inner thoughts with him, she blurted out, "Mama died last summer from a wasting disease." She smiled tightly at his murmur of distress. "Our uncle will be overjoyed at our arrival."

"How can you be certain?" Eamon asked, as he fought a frown and failed to hide the worry in his voice.

"He wrote to us. He wanted us to join him. And no man encourages three unwed nieces to travel to Montana Territory unless he misses his family. From what Mama told me, he's had great success since he left on his explorations before the War." She nodded and smiled with forced bravado. "I'm certain he'll be as kind as our Uncle Harvey."

When Eamon saw her spirit dim, he ran a hand over her arm in a gentle caress. "What's the matter, lass?"

"I just realized we've left all our friends behind. We'll know no one when we arrive."

Eamon reached forward, his fingers stroking hers. "Nay," he murmured, his voice low and soothing. "You'll always have friends in the O'Rourkes. You'll never be alone."

Phoebe stared at him, her eyes wide, mesmerized by him and his voice.

He leaned forward, watching as her eyes fluttered closed a moment before he kissed her softly. With one hand on hers, gripping the railing, he raised his other to hold her head, digging his fingers into her soft blond hair. Deepening the kiss when she moaned, he took a step closer to her, pulling her tighter into his embrace. With great reluctance he broke the kiss, his fingers stroking her silky cheek a moment.

"Why … ?" she stammered out, her chest rising and falling, as she stared at him with amazement.

"You're more than a friend, Bee," he whispered. As he heard footsteps approaching, he backed up to ensure a proper amount of space remained between them. "Or, at least, I hope you will be one day." He forced an easy, carefree smile, as he looked over her shoulder. "Finn, you found us," he said, the joy in his voice not reaching his eyes. Frustration radiated from him.

Finn approached, stepping between them, as he looked out at the river under the faint moonlight. "Miss Mortimer," he said with a deferential nod.

"Sir," she whispered, before she cast a final glance in Eamon's direction and scurried away.

Finn rolled his eyes. "She's afraid of her own shadow," he muttered.

Eamon nudged his shoulder and shook his head. "No, she's not. She's just partial to me and not to you." He winked at his brother. "Come. Let's find a poker match to watch." They strolled away from the railing, although Eamon's thoughts remained filled with Phoebe and holding her in his arms.

CHAPTER 2

"Tell me more about your uncle," Eamon murmured, as he sidled up beside Phoebe, while she stood outside on the upper deck after supper a few days later.

She took a deep breath, his bay rum cologne mixing with the mossy scent of the river and the ever-present wood smoke from the steam engine. She inhaled deeply again, hoping to impart the scent on her memory forever. They had managed to free themselves from the sandbar two days ago and had continued their steady travel upriver. Although she had seen Eamon with his brother at each meal, he had sat a fair distance down the table, while he spoke with well-to-do businessmen traveling to the Montana Territory. She had tried to convince herself that he was acting as a responsible businessman, drumming up future sales at his store. However, she had difficulty fighting her disappointment that his increased interest in her had been so short-lived.

It felt like, in each waking moment of the past days, her every thought had been of his kiss. Of feeling his strong arms holding her close. Of feeling cherished. Her nights were no better, for now they were filled with dreams of him. Of forging a future with him. Silently she berated herself for her overactive imagination, wishing she could find a way to temper her attraction. Unexpectedly she understood her sisters' disappointments with a greater acuity, for Phoebe didn't know what she would do if Eamon reverted to being solely a friend. Or worse, a disinterested acquaintance.

This evening, she slipped out of the dining room before dessert, desperate for a few moments to herself. She knew she was safe for a little while longer, as the drinking and poker playing wouldn't begin in earnest for another hour or so. By then, she'd be safely ensconced in her stateroom with her sisters.

Tonight the air was still, as the temperature dropped after a warm spring day. The boat swayed in the current, securely moored in the middle of the river, and an owl hooted on the distant shore. The half-moon cast its rays over the rippling water and the steamboat. Phoebe sighed, half elated at Eamon's presence and half disgruntled she would have no time to herself.

"Hello, Mr. O'Rourke," she murmured, as she kept her back to Eamon and continued to stare out at the water.

"You know I've told you to call me Eamon. Should you call out a greeting for a Mr. O'Rourke in Fort Benton, you would get many responses."

She fought a smile, the corners of her lips tipping upward. "And you know it's improper for me to do so."

"Come on, Bee," he teased, as he nudged her with his shoulder.

At the use of the nickname he had given her while under the cottonwoods, her breath caught, and she prayed she was in the shadows to hide her reaction, as she felt her cheeks heat.

When she remained quiet, he huffed out a breath.

Leaning with his back against the railing, he faced her. "What's your uncle like?" he asked again.

She let out a long breath before saying, "I don't remember him well. He left to adventure when we were girls, although my mama said he was one to avoid a conflict. He also had gold fever." She grimaced, as though she were being disloyal to a man she barely knew. "We all feared that the War Between the States was coming long before it started and that all able-bodied men would be needed to fight, if such a conflict arose. Mama always thought my uncle hightailed it west years before the conflict so he wouldn't have to fight."

"So he's a coward," Eamon muttered, his expression filled with concern.

"I think he's more of an opportunist. Although he was always my mama's favorite brother. And she extracted a promise from him that he would care for the three of us, if something happened to Mama before we were wed."

Eamon frowned. "Thus you're traveling upriver to find a man you barely know?" His brows furrowed in confusion. "I still don't understand, lass. Why wouldn't you have him come to you?"

Phoebe closed her eyes to avoid any censure or criticism in his gaze. "I know that seems more sensible, but Uncle hasn't returned to Saint Louis in years. In his letter, he said he refused to travel to us and to be forced to suffer the indignities of so-called good society." She swallowed as Eamon stared at her with concern, as she intimated she and her sisters weren't worthy of such regard or care from the unknown uncle. "In the letter, he advised that we were to travel to him as soon as possible, or we were in jeopardy of losing our inher ..." She flushed and stammered. "Or our futures were in jeopardy." She forced a smile. "We took a vote, and I was outnumbered."

"I would have thought your eldest sister would have

insisted on the three of you remaining in Saint Louis. She seems sensible too."

Phoebe sighed. "Because she seems meek and studious, she has the appearance of being the most grounded among us. But she's actually the most fanciful. All those books have made her quite a romantic."

Eamon grinned at her, the light from a nearby lamp enhancing his chiseled good looks. "Have you ever been accused of such a thing?" When she gaped up at him, he whispered, "Of being a romantic?"

She shook her head, reminding herself how he first thought of her as a sister and then as a friend and could hope for nothing more. That she could not envision a white dress and an eager groom awaiting her approach. "Of course not. I'm the practical sister."

He stared at her a long moment, to the point she fought squirming, and then he shook his head. "I think that's what you tell yourself as you battle disappointment. I think you want to be just as fanciful, just as daring as your sisters."

"Life is rarely kind to those who dream," she whispered.

He made a small grunt, almost of pain, at her words. "How I wish you were wrong." Eamon turned to lean on his elbows, looking out at the river in quiet companionship with her.

Whereas, before his arrival, she had yearned for time for silent contemplation, now she prayed he never left her side. A momentary serenity filled her, and she wished for it to never end. The sounds of the men bickering as they played poker and of the captain calling out to his men faded into the background, as she closed her eyes and relished the peace of this moment. Never before had she thought being in the presence of another person could bring her such tranquility.

Eamon pushed away from the railing, abruptly disrupting the quiet interlude, a strange look in his gaze. "I must return to find Finn. I fear he'll find a poker match and beggar us before arriving to Fort Benton."

"Of course," she murmured, watching as he scurried away from her. With a long sigh, she attempted to recapture the previous moment's peacefulness, but his absence proved such a desire unattainable.

~

Minutes later, cursing as the door to the miniscule stateroom he shared with Finn slammed against the wall, Eamon entered and shut the door with another *smack*. Finn rested on the upper bunk, reading a five-and-dime novel, while Eamon paced around the small room.

"Leave and come back if that's all you're going to do," Finn snapped. "Watching you from up here gives me vertigo."

Eamon rolled his eyes but opted to kick off his boots and to shuck his outer clothes,. before flopping onto his back on the lower bunk. "What I wouldn't give for a proper bath," he muttered.

Finn peered at him from above, his head upside down. "You're in such a state because you want a bath?" He yelped when Eamon batted him on his head, so Finn returned to resting on the upper bunk, muttering under his breath the entire time.

"Of course not." Eamon sighed and tried to settle into the bed.

"She's not your sister, Eamon," Finn said in a soft voice.

With a growl, Eamon launched himself from the bed, barely avoiding hitting his head on the wooden frame of the upper bunk, potentially knocking himself out cold. He resumed his pacing and nodded. "I know. But she sees me that way. And she's young. I'm young. Too young to consider marryin.'" He rubbed at his head, sending spikes of black hair standing on end.

Finn sat so his legs dangled off the edge of the upper bunk, partially hunched over so his head didn't hit the ceiling. "Why would you be thinkin' about marriage now? A few days ago, you thought you'd never marry."

Eamon walked the few paces to the small window and stared outside. Immediately he thought about the time he had spent with Phoebe. All that she had said, but also all she had alluded to. Instinctively he knew there was much more to her than a well-put-together, controlled woman. For some reason, he was intrigued and wanted to know more about her.

"I thought the sisters were like Aileen. Mail order brides." He met Finn's amused gaze. "But they're not. They're in search of an uncle who they haven't seen for years, although I'm uncertain he's an uncle to pine over."

Finn rubbed at his head. "Unlike Mum and Maggie."

Eamon looked at his brother over his shoulder and turned to lean against the windowsill. Grasping at the distraction, he said, "Do you think Mum will still be there when we return? Or will she have disappeared again?"

Finn hopped down and stood with his hands on his hips and his head tilted to one side, studying his brother as though he were a foreign creature he'd never seen before. "Are you addled, Eamon? Did someone bash you over the head, which caused you to spout nonsense about marrying and fears Mum will be gone again?"

Eamon swore and crossed his arms over his chest, his shoulders hunching. "I'm not addled. I know exactly who *you* are—my meddlesome brother."

"Mum will be there," Finn said in a low voice, his words emerging like an avowal. "She wouldn't leave again, Eamon. She wouldn't." When Eamon continued his pacing, Finn

26

added, "She never intended to leave us in the first place. It was all a horrid misunderstanding between Da and the French-speaking nun."

For a moment, Eamon was reminded of the boy Finn had been during the months after their mother had died. The confusion and fear Finn had felt every day as he woke to find Mum absent and to feel the resurgent grief at the understanding she wasn't coming back. The responsibility Eamon had felt in equal measure to soothe his brother, while Eamon's own heart broke into just as many pieces. "Aye, she'll be there. She has to be."

Finn nodded, as though the possibility of her absence were not worth contemplating.

After a long moment, while Eamon smiled as he stared at the brother he adored, he said,. "You know that I won't marry because, if I do, our adventures will cease."

Finn nodded emphatically, any worry forced away. "Aye, an' there's still too much livin' to be done before we bind ourselves to a woman." He moaned, arching his arms overhead to touch the ceiling of the cabin as he stretched. "Can you imagine chainin' yourself to a woman like Winnifred?" He shivered dramatically as he dropped his arms. "Within a month of marriage, she'd be the death of any man unfortunate enough to marry her."

Eamon chuckled at his brother's antics. "Aye. We'll be busy enough as uncles for years to come."

Finn gave an appreciative sigh. "Uncles. That sounds perfect. You can love the babes with all your might and then hand them back when they start actin' up."

Eamon laughed again and tumbled into his bunk to sleep. Although he knew his charming brother Finn had reason for not wishing to marry anytime soon, an ache settled deep inside Eamon at the thought of being alone for years to come. His mind instinctively returned to the time he had spent with Phoebe tonight, and he relaxed, as though she were beside him.

Although she thought herself levelheaded, he knew she must have moments where she was passionate and outspoken. He wished he were the man she turned to, the man she shared such intimate thoughts and ideas with. Instead he feared he would forever be on the periphery of her life, watching as she blossomed under another man's attentions.

Finn had thought Eamon muddleheaded to express doubts about their mum, but he harbored a deep-seated fear she would have left again, while they were away during the winter. Her disappearance and reported death eighteen years ago—when they had first arrived in Canada, after fleeing Ireland and the horrible potato famine—had affected him greatly. Even though he had acted as though he barely remembered her, her absence had acted like a wraith, forever present but out of reach.

He had tried to be the strong big brother for Finn, shielding him from bullies and mean words, when they did menial tasks to earn a penny. However, the woman his da had married, Colleen, was miserly in her love. She had felt betrayed because Seamus would always love the memory of a dead woman more than the woman alive and warming his arms.

From the moment Eamon, as a boy, had seen both Seamus's misery and then Colleen's, Eamon had vowed to never feel more than a fond affection for a woman. Any stronger emotion only led to heartache and pain. He'd learned at an early age such suffering was never worth the risk.

He sighed and thought of his brother Declan, who hadn't learned the lesson of their mother's absence, and now Declan was miserable. With one last long sigh, Eamon resolved to overcome any attraction he felt for Phoebe. He resolved that he and Finn would be the carefree bachelor brothers forever.

Nothing was worth the despair Declan felt. Nothing was worth the agony their father had suffered for almost eighteen years. Nothing was worth the pain and rejection of love where another didn't love you back. Before he slipped into sleep, Eamon said a silent prayer that his brother Declan would find his way free of his torment.

A week later, Phoebe paused, hitching her normally smooth stride as she noted Eamon standing by himself at the railing. Although she saw him at each meal, he had merely smiled at her in an impersonal manner and spoken with men traveling to Fort Benton. Finn had largely ignored Winnifred, and her sister was irate at being snubbed.

With a deep breath for courage, Phoebe approached Eamon, pasting on a friendly smile. "Hello, Mr. O'Rourke."

He stiffened at her sidling up next to him but then nodded in a deferential manner. "Miss Mortimer," he murmured. After a long moment of stilted silence, he cleared his throat. "We appear to be making good time."

Her head bobbed up and down, as she stared at his profile when he refused to look at her. Tearing her gaze from him, she stilled her repetitive movement and looked out at the river. "Yes. I hear we should arrive by the first part of June. Only a little over a week from now."

Eamon chuckled. "Captain's irate we won't be the first ship to arrive, but we've lost too much time caught up on sandbars and cutting firewood."

She shrugged. "As long as we arrive safely, it shouldn't matter if we are the first or the tenth." When she saw him staring at her with a slightly disapproving look, she flushed.

29

"Although I'm certain I shouldn't have an opinion on the matter."

"Whether you do or don't, it won't make us arrive any faster, Miss Mortimer." His jaw clenched tight for a long moment before he relaxed. "I hope you are having a pleasant journey with your sisters."

When he turned to leave, she gripped his arm. "Please. What have I done to offend you?" She bit her lip at the pleading in her tone. When he stared at her with unrelenting coldness in his gaze, she shivered.

"Why, you've done nothing, Miss Mortimer."

Her hold on his arm tightened to prevent him from wandering away. "I don't believe you. You've been unfriendly. I know I'm not the sort of woman a man would desire to marry, but I'd hoped we were friends. I thought we might be more." She grimaced at her last words.

"You're wrong," he rasped, his blue eyes flashing with anger and a deep emotion before he expelled a long breath, easing his tension. "You're wrong," he repeated in a calmer, emotionless voice. "I believe we just had a friendly conversation. I could never want for more."

"Never want for more," she whispered, parroting his words back, as though attempting to make sense of them. She shook her head repeatedly. "I don't understand. I never meant—" When he placed callused fingers over her soft lips, her eyes rounded like saucers, shock and confusion in her vivid green eyes.

"Please, Miss Mortimer. Don't embarrass yourself. Or me."

She gasped and took a step away from him. "Never," she choked out. "I beg your pardon." She twirled around, racing away from him, until she careened into her stateroom door. Her hands grasped at the doorknob, shaking so violently that she couldn't get the handle to turn. Finally she pushed her way into the room, falling to her knees when she entered the tiny space.

Looking around, Phoebe let out a relieved sigh that neither of her sisters were present to witness her humiliating entrance. She kicked the door shut and crawled to her berth, resting on her side, her knees pulled up to her chest, like she were a child. The last scene with Eamon played as though on eternal repeat. Cringing at the apologetic, pleading woman she had been, she wished she had been strong and confident. Captivating. Intriguing. Anything other than she was. For she knew no man would find her appealing.

Ever since she was a girl, she recalled hearing those around her talk about how terrible it was that she was so plain. That thank heavens she had the Mortimer eyes, for at least that gave her an alluring trait. That it was a shame she didn't have Lorena's charm or Winnifred's wit. What a tragedy that she was so frightfully boring. *Boring*, the most dreaded word, besides *pity*, in Phoebe's vocabulary because it had been bandied about with such alarming frequency in relation to her since she could remember.

Unlike Winnifred, who had sharp cheekbones, a husky voice, and the confidence to match her becoming figure, Phoebe had always known she was homely. Her blond hair was more dull than lustrous, her skin marred with freckles, and she had been afflicted with a crippling shyness until recently. Her willowy frame had too often been referred to as having all the grace and beauty of a stick.

Although she would never say a disparaging word against her mama, she knew her mother had always despaired of her, while rejoicing in Winnifred and Lorena. As her mama had proclaimed time and again, they were the daughters who were destined to shine and to make brilliant matches, not Phoebe. No, Phoebe was meant to remain at home as the spinster sister, caring for her mama as she aged. As her mama had said, with a regretful pat to Phoebe's cheek, no man would truly desire such a woman as Phoebe.

Curling onto her side, Phoebe admitted to herself that she had created fantasies in her mind about Eamon, hoping that he would prove untrue all that had been said about her in the past. That she was desirable. Attractive. That someone would want to marry her.

"I should have known better," she whispered to herself, her breaths emerging in a sob. "He barely wants to be my friend. He only said what he did because he desired a kiss. Like all men wanted from my mama, he just wanted to use me."

She curled farther into herself, wishing that she were far away from Eamon and that she never had to see him again. Deep inside her, a fierce determination sprouted, and she promised herself she would mimic her sister Winnifred. Although she might never have her youngest sister's natural confidence or poise, Phoebe vowed she would become the woman she had always envisioned she could be: strong, self-assured, and admired.

Eamon be damned.

～

Eamon let out a stuttering breath and swore softly as he watched Phoebe race away from him. He fought every instinct to reach for her and to haul her into his arms. To comfort her and to soothe away the harm and the pain he had wittingly caused. However, he remained motionless, watching her until she dashed around a corner and out of sight.

"Feck," he muttered, as he turned to blindly face the river again. Rather than the riverbank and the prairie in the distance, he saw Phoebe's devastated gaze as he treated her callously. The hope fading in her gaze, replaced by mortification and confusion. "'Tis for the better," he reassured himself, as he gripped the railing.

"Talkin' to yourself again?" Finn teased, as he nudged Eamon's shoulder. When Eamon didn't return a wisecrack comment, Finn frowned and studied his brother. "What's the matter, Eamon?"

"I hurt Phoebe's feelings," he said in a low voice, as he didn't want anyone to overhear their conversation.

"Apologize for the misunderstanding." Finn shrugged, assuming nothing more needed to be said.

Eamon sighed and made a face, as he looked out at the same scenery they had stared at for weeks on end. "No, Finn, I hurt her on purpose." He met his brother's shocked stare. "I didn't want her to have any romantic notions about me."

His brother gazed at him with an astute assessment. "Is it that, Eamon, or the other way around?" When Eamon stared at him impassively, Finn said, "I fear you've foolish notions in your head about some pact we made." When Eamon swallowed, Finn nodded. "And fears you've yet to overcome."

"Finn, I don't need your meddlin'," Eamon snapped.

Chuckling, Finn crossed his arms over his chest and one foot over the other as he leaned against the sturdy railing. "Of course you do. What is a younger brother for?" His smile broadened at Eamon's exasperated expression. "Eamon, we've been best friends since I have a memory. We've done everything together. Gone everywhere together. But there is a time for you to go your own way."

Eamon shook his head, his grip on the railing so tight that he knew he could give himself splinters. "I can't, Finn. I just can't." His eyes gleamed with anguish. "I can't risk caring for a woman and losing her."

Taking a deep breath, Finn studied his brother. "You

already have, Eamon. Now you have to see if you're brave enough to fight to win her back."

Eamon closed his eyes, as the truth of Finn's words seeped into him. Although he knew he should race after Phoebe, find her, and apologize, he wanted time. Time to ensure what he felt was more than a momentary infatuation due to confinement on a ship. And, for that, he would need to be patient, until they docked in Fort Benton. He only prayed that she didn't hate him too much by then. And that she would remain in town long enough for him to make amends.

CHAPTER 3

Fort Benton, Montana Territory, June 1866

"Lads!"

Eamon turned in the direction of the bellow and waved madly at his da. He saw Finn do the same. Soon they jumped free of the steamboat and onto shore. "Da!" Eamon yelled, as he rushed to his father and wrapped his arms around him. They rocked back and forth, before his da released him and repeated the same with Finn.

"Oh, 'tis a fine day to have my lads return home," Seamus said, his bright blue eyes sparkling with delight. He glanced over Finn's shoulder expectantly. "Declan?"

"Ah," Eamon stuttered, as he shared a long look with Finn. "He decided to remain in Saint Louis. Thought it better to have an O'Rourke in the warehouse there than for one of us to ferry up and down the river each year."

Seamus O'Rourke stood nearly six feet tall, his hands on his hips. His beard now had a sprinkling of black in it and was mostly gray. The hair at his temples and his sideburns were slightly grayer than when they had left in August of the previous year. However, for the most part, he didn't appear to have changed since they had left nine months ago.

"Declan's not comin' home?" he breathed. "Not for another year?" He rubbed at his temple and shook his head. "I want the lad home." He glared at the river, as though he could convey the message downriver to his absent son. "I wanted the whole family together again."

Eamon shrugged. "I didn't know how to convince him, Da. Not after …" He broke off and shook his head. "'Tis a story that should be told the one time. With Ardan and Kevin present too."

Seamus clapped a hand on each of his sons' shoulders. "Aye, an' we must focus on unloading the cargo and stocking the warehouse. Many men will be arrivin' this year, an' I mean to earn a fair profit off them." He paused as he watched a group of attractive women disembark the steamboat. "I hope you had the sense to make their acquaintance while you were on board."

"Da," Finn said, with an exasperated roll of his eyes. "The youngest one would make anyone daft."

Seamus studied his son with an assessing look, before focusing on Eamon, who observed the women with a thinly veiled intensity. "Aye, but they are the ones who make life worth livin'." He paused, waiting for Eamon to speak, but he seemed transfixed, as he watched the sisters laugh when they stumbled over a rut in the rough road. "I fear the lasses won't last long here without attractin' unsavory attention."

Eamon jerked at his father's murmured comment, his jaw tightening with frustration. "They are nice enough, Da, but not our concern. Did you bring the wagon?"

After staring at his son another long moment, he nodded. "Aye. We have a hard day's worth of work ahead of us, if we're to move all our supplies into the warehouse. Kevin will work there with Niall and Lucien, while you lads take over the running of the store again."

"Where's Ardan?" Eamon asked.

"At the café. With his wife," Seamus said with a satisfied smile. "He and Deirdre married after you left. They'll be one of your first deliveries, as she needs supplies to feed the mass of men who'll be comin' through town."

As they worked to load the wagon with the first batch of stock, Seamus said, "You never said why such pretty lasses decided to travel to such an uncivilized place."

Eamon hefted a heavy barrel, gasping when he set it in place in the back of the wagon. After catching his breath, he said, "They came here to meet their uncle. Said he wrote them, and they were to come find him, if he didn't make it home last fall."

Seamus gaped at him and then shook his head. "Those fine lasses are related to Uriah Chaffee?"

Eamon looked to Finn, who shrugged. "I can't remember ever askin' after the uncle's name. Should it matter?"

"Feck." Seamus looked at the half-packed wagon and motioned for them to continue packing. "We'll bring the first load to Kevin, and then we must find those women. For, if Uriah is their uncle, they are in for a rude awakenin'."

Phoebe paused upon exiting the steamboat, her breath catching at the sight of the wild frontier town. She and her sisters had donned their finest clothes, as they had hoped to find their uncle or to solicit the aid of someone in their quest to locate him. Her hand slid down the soft silk of her emerald-green dress, the fabric shimmering in the bright sunlight, hoping the sheen of polish and sophistication would hide her uncertainty as they began their foray into town. Her boots created divots in the moist earth, and she clung to her fan as though she were a fine society lady about to make a call, rather than a newly arrived woman with no friends in a town more uncivilized than she ever could have imagined.

She moved from the boat landing, as men grumbled at her to get out of the way, and she heard the sound of men unloading the heavy cargo. However, she stood transfixed at the sight of patched-together clapboard buildings, some whitewashed, most faded to a dull gray by the harsh environment, with bold lettering overhead proclaiming their purpose.

Ignoring the numerous saloons, she saw the *O'Rourke and Sons* store nearly across from her and then a hotel a short distance down the boardwalk. A laundry, a café, and a barbershop were intermingled between saloons. At first glance, there appeared to be a surplus of saloons, although she saw the men from her steamboat swarming into them, like hungry locusts. "Parched locusts," she muttered to herself.

Urging her sisters to move across the street filled with deep ruts, she avoided the even deeper potholes filled with mud, horse and oxen dung. She sighed with relief to step onto the boardwalk but jumped backward when a man with rancid breath, wearing tanned hides for clothes, with greasy hair past his shoulders, leaned toward her. He reached for her, as though she were fair game, and she batted at him with her fan, suddenly thankful she had worn her best clothes and had a weapon of sorts. When he grunted in surprise, she scooted away from him.

"Hey, where you goin'?" he called out. "The Sirens always enjoy what I got to give 'em."

Phoebe glared at him over her shoulder as she prayed her sisters were smart enough to walk ahead of her toward the hotel. "I have no idea what a Siren is, sir. But you would be advised to stay well away from me. And from my sisters."

She trotted away as fast as possible, entering the hotel on Winnifred's heels. A man who appeared to be in his midthirties sat on a stool behind the desk, perusing a newspaper, and he hopped to his feet at their entrance. "Ladies," he said with a broad smile. His chestnut-brown hair hung to his shirt's collar, and his mustache curled around his mouth. "How might I help you?"

"We would like a room," Phoebe said, taking control of the situation before Lorena froze at the thought of speaking to the stranger and to stop Winnifred from flirting or becoming insolent in her discomfort. Phoebe never knew how her youngest sister would react when she was uncomfortable.

"Excellent. I'm glad you arrived when you did. I have very few left. Fort Benton is quite popular this year."

Phoebe jumped as a gunshot sounded, and thereafter men hooted and hollered from the attached saloon. "Is it always this … lively?" she asked.

"Oh, no," the hotel proprietor said with a reassuring smile. "It's often much worse."

"Worse?" Winnifred gasped. "How are we expected to sleep?"

"You adapt," he said, as he reached behind him to extract a key. "If you'd like to follow me?" He turned and smiled at a man dressed in a colorful suit as he made his way downstairs. "Enjoy your outing, sir."

"Uncle?" Phoebe asked, as she gaped at the man's large paunch and jowls.

"How did you get so fat?" Winnifred blurted out, causing Phoebe to stifle a snicker, before she nudged her youngest sister in the side to quiet any more impertinent comments.

The man paused, his turquoise waistcoat nearly bursting

from the pressure to keep him clothed, and turned his beady eyes on the three sisters. At first, he appeared annoyed, as though he were about to be exploited. After staring at the girls from head to toe, a satisfied gleam sparkled in his eyes.

"You are Uriah Chaffee," Phoebe said, as she took a step closer to the man she barely remembered, but whose picture had sat on their mantel since his departure over a decade ago. Although much heavier than the lean man with a naively hopeful expression, his coloring was similar to their mother's, and Uriah was the spitting image of their beloved uncle, Harvey, who had died three years ago. "You are our uncle."

He blustered, puffing out his chest. "I could be uncle to many young women. For I am a successful man, and many would wish for such an alliance. Who was your mother, girl?"

"Are you claiming our mother wasn't respectable?" Winnifred snapped. "Your own sister?"

Uriah shrugged. "You know her better than I do."

Phoebe poked her finger into his chest. "How dare you disparage our mama's memory with such vicious and vile speculation? She was your sister too! Your sister, Marilda." She took a deep breath and cast a quick glance over her shoulder to find the hotel proprietor watching their interaction with deep interest. "You're the one who wrote us, asking us to join you here, so we could be a family again. Why else would we leave our comfortable home to travel here?"

Uriah had the grace to look momentarily chagrined. "Oh, dear girls, I can barely believe you're standing in front of me! Dear Marilda's girls. How is it possible, after all this time, to finally be reunited?" He smiled, although it appeared more feral than welcoming. "Come. Have you seen the joys and delights to be found in this wonderful little town? I've discovered it to be of my liking. Now that you are here, it will truly feel like home."

He chuckled as they jumped at the hoots and hollers of men in the Levee Saloon next door. After a moment, he brightened as he looked at them. "Why don't we delay your perusal of a boring hotel room? I'll show you around this fine little town."

Phoebe looked at her sisters, and they shook their heads. Phoebe wavered, not wishing to offend him when they had just found him, although she yearned for a long walk, a proper bath, and a fine meal. With a resigned sigh, when it was apparent he would not accept their refusal, she muttered, "Fine. I'll go with you. My sisters will remain here to settle in."

He looked them over and smiled. "Fine. One at a time will increase …" He broke off what he would have said and motioned for her to follow him. "Come, dear girl. I have a desire to show you this intriguing town."

Phoebe smiled reassuringly at her sisters and accompanied him outside.

~

Eamon followed his da, leaving the first wagonload of goods with Kevin. As luck would have it, two of their good friends, Dunmore and Cormac, were present at the warehouse, and they offered to help move their supplies, so Seamus and Eamon could search for the Mortimer sisters.

Eamon's long strides matched his father's, and he looked around the town that had come to life with the arrival of the steamboats. "Cormac doesn't appear as sullen as usual, Da."

Seamus came to an abrupt halt, staring in wonder at his son. "You don't know," he breathed. "*Jaysus*, all the time apart with no ability to communicate. How are we to survive another entire year without Declan?" He shook his head at the miserable possibility. "Connor died, lad. He was killed at

41

the Bordello in October." Seamus waved down the board-walk to the house of ill repute at the far end of town. "He left Niamh a widow and wrote an infamous will. Those in town over the winter were entertained by the O'Rourkes' misfortunes."

Eamon goggled at his father. "What misfortune? The man's dead! After all our prayers, he died?" When Seamus hissed at him to keep his voice down, Eamon took a step closer to his father and lowered his voice. "I'd think Cormac would be more saddened by the death of his only living brother."

Seamus shook his head. "I can't explain it all here, but no. There's much you don't understand." A smile burst forth. "But the important news is that he and Niamh married in December."

Eamon burst into a broad smile, before sobering. "Was she forced to marry him, Da?" He paused as his father stared at him intently. "Or is Niamh finally happy?"

"Oh, Niamh's ecstatic, as you'll see well enough at the family dinner your mum's prepared for tonight." He clapped a hand on his son's shoulder and ushered him down the side-walk. "Come. Let's find these women and keep them out of mischief. If we're fortunate, we'll have time to sneak to the café for one of Deirdre's treats."

They entered the hotel, and Eamon stood beside his father, content to watch his father interact with the towns-folk. His da had always commanded respect, and he marveled at how he earned it with charm and wit, rather than malice. He had seen too many men during his time in Saint Louis attempt to use brute force and fear to prove themselves worthy of esteem. He shook his head as he real-ized that he'd been raised by a master charmer and that he only ever needed to emulate his da to have success.

"Foster," Seamus called out, as he entered the hotel. "How's business?"

"I've only one room free. I should look into expanding," Aaron Foster said with a proud tilt of his head. "If we're fortunate, this is the first of many prosperous years to come."

"Aye," Seamus said. "If what my lads have told me comes true, many ships will come up the river this year." He glanced outside, as though he could see the river past all the wagons and the cargo on the levee. "And 'tis a good water year. They should make it to Fort Benton, rather than havin' to stop at Cow Island."

Aaron Foster nodded. "Yes. I hope you ordered plenty of supplies."

Seamus shrugged in a noncommittal fashion and focused on the proprietor. "I heard a trio of sisters came to stay with you."

Frowning and staring at Seamus at his perceived impertinence, Foster crossed his arms over his chest. "I fail to see that it's any business of yours."

"My lad, Eamon, befriended them on the boat. When he informed me that they were lookin' for their uncle, I was worried he meant Chaffee." His friendly cajoling disappeared when he saw the flash of panic in the other man's gaze. "Tell me they have yet to meet the man."

"Ah, I wish I could, Seamus, but he was descending the stairs as I was about to show them their room."

"Are they well?" Eamon asked, his cobalt-blue eyes lit with concern, as he took a step closer to the desk, joining the conversation.

"Two of them are. One, the blond, accepted her uncle's offer to see the sights of the town with him."

Seamus rocked back on his heels, frowning. "The sights of this town? You know as well as I do, the only thing to see is one saloon after another an' which man can piss farther." He shook his head.

The hotelier choked on a snicker. "Yes, and that's the daytime activities."

Stilling at the quiet warning in the other man's voice, Seamus murmured, "What do you know? What aren't you telling me, Foster?"

"I hear rumors, working at the hotel and so near my saloon." He glanced over Seamus's shoulder and nodded, satisfied no one was interested in his conversation with the shop owner. "Chaffee is keeping interesting company. He's made friends with that man, Bell, who just opened up a new saloon a few doors down from me and next to your café." He paused. "Called the Daybreak, it's intent on luring customers away from the Sunrise Saloon. I've heard they are interested in competing with the Bordello."

Eamon took a step closer and glared at Foster. "Why would that have anything to do with Phoebe?"

"Ah, a lovely name for a lovely young woman," Aaron said. "Many would be willing to part with their cash or gold dust for time with such a lass."

Seamus grabbed Eamon's arm to prevent him from vaulting over the hotel desk and pummeling the man. "No, son," he rasped. He glared at Foster. "How could you have allowed her to leave with the man?"

"How could I not have?" Foster countered. "I'm no relation. Besides, if he is her uncle, he has more right to determine what is appropriate for her than I do."

Studying him, Seamus whispered, "What's he have on you?" When the proprietor remained quiet, Seamus swore under his breath and pushed his son outside. When they stood on the boardwalk again, he murmured, "Calm down. You won't help the lass if you act like an *eejit*, attacking anyone who offends you." He took a deep breath. "We have to keep cool heads if we're to rescue your lass. An' we have to find a way to protect the other ones too."

Phoebe walked beside her uncle, casting furtive glances in his direction, as he seemed to be showing her off to the men who gazed at her with lascivious stares. She ducked her head, wishing she had worn her drabbest clothes and that she had a shawl to cover her shoulders and bosom, as she had no desire for these men to stare their full of her in her finery.

She looked away from the bustling levee and the mounds of barrels, crates, and other supplies left to be distributed to shops in town and delivered throughout the growing Territory. Instead she focused on the land across from the ever-flowing river, dreaming of boarding a small vessel and floating away from the man beside her.

Wishing she had found a way to convince her sisters to ignore her uncle's letter months ago, encouraging them to travel to Fort Benton, she fought a profound sense of unease. Silently berating herself for her desire to placate him and to accept his tour of the town, she focused on her surroundings.

A spit of land jutted out on the opposite side of the river before rising into cliffs that towered over the river and the small town. Although they were majestic and beautiful, at this moment, the cliffs made her feel caged in. As though they were contriving to keep her in a dangerous place. If possible, she would stand here, staring at the river and cliffs until suppertime.

"Stop your dawdling," her uncle hissed, as he grabbed her arm and towed her down the boardwalk. He jerked her upright when she stumbled, ignoring her cry of pain. "A friend of mine is eager to meet you."

Gasping for breath as she trotted beside her uncle, while he walked at an unforgiving pace, she saw an attractive woman, dressed in navy satin, watching her with concern. She sent her a pleading look but had to focus on the uneven boardwalk or risk falling. When her uncle pulled her into a saloon, she dug her heels into the boardwalk. However, she was no match for his strength, and she toppled forward, landing with a *thud* on her hands and knees in the darkened interior.

Laughter and conversation halted at her precipitous arrival, and she looked up in horror to find every man in the room watching her lewdly. After pushing herself up, she brushed at her skirts, wincing at the splinters in her palms.

"Uriah!" a man boomed from the shadows. "How delightful to see you. And how marvelous you've arrived with such an eager lass."

Phoebe took a step backward, squealing when she stepped into a man who had sidled up behind her. She moved away from him, forcing herself to take deep breaths in an attempt to calm her panic. She feared what would happen were she to lose consciousness. "I am not eager, sir. I have been manhandled into coming into this den of iniquity. I am most eager to depart."

The man laughed. Rather than soothing her fraying nerves, it sent the hair on her arms on edge and a shiver down her spine, for no sympathy was in his tone. Instead, amusement at her predicament shone through. He stepped from the shadows, and she swallowed. Unable to hide her reaction, her eyes rounded, and she felt lightheaded. She dug her nails into her hands so she would not faint.

The man was a giant at well over six feet tall. He had a large muscular chest that rippled with movement, and she had no doubt he could pick her up with one arm. His long mahogany-colored hair was tied back, and his brown eyes held no sympathy.

Phoebe thrust her shoulders back, meeting his stare, as she forced a bravado she did not feel. "You have no right to detain me here."

"Uriah?" the man asked.

"She is my niece," Uriah murmured. "None will come to protest."

"Excellent," the giant said, as he reached for her. His hand slid down the silky material of her dress to rest on her waist. He smiled at the panic she could not hide in her gaze as she swatted at his hand. "Tonight, we'll make a fortune off you."

"No," she gasped, looking around the room for someone to show her mercy. None were to be found, and she shrieked as she was tossed over the giant's shoulder, carried away to an upstairs room.

CHAPTER 4

"She can't have disappeared into thin air," Eamon muttered, as he stared up and down the boardwalk. His gaze searched for some sign of her beautiful dress, of her shiny blond hair. Of her mesmerizing green eyes.

"Nay," his da said. "Somethin's afoot, but I don't know what it is. Too many newcomers are come to town, and I don't know them all." He sighed, as he rubbed at his head. "I understand the desire to earn money, but I don't understand the desire to harm innocents in the pursuit of profit."

Eamon watched the Daybreak Saloon, his mood souring the longer he studied it. The most disreputable men seemed drawn to the establishment. "Why'd we need more saloons?"

"Ah, lad, you know there will always be work helping those who are thirsty," Seamus said. He paused. "One person in town always knows what's going on. The Madam. Come. Let's visit her."

Eamon gripped his father's jacket, stilling his da's movement to the Bordello. "Da, you always told me that I was never to enter such a place."

"Aye, and you're not. But this is a special circumstance.

And we must do what we can to help your lass." He paused as he studied his son, who appeared embarrassed by his words. "She is your lass?"

Eamon shrugged. "I don't know what she is, Da. I like her. She's nice. But I know I'll never marry."

"Never marry? What sort of nonsense is this?" His da gazed at him with concern. "You'll wed and have fine strong lads, like you."

Flushing under his father's praise and words of confidence, Eamon whispered, "I have no faith in constancy or forever, Da. And that's not fair for a woman. She would want more. Deserve more."

Seamus made a sound of displeasure before pulling his son into motion. "'Tis a conversation for another day. For now, we must find your Phoebe. For she's your friend, if not your future wife." Ignoring his son's sputter of protest at the use of the word *wife*, Seamus knocked on the Bordello door. It was early yet for many visitors, and he was not here as a patron.

Ezra, the Bordello's protector, answered the door with his billy club in his hand. When he saw Seamus, he relaxed. "'Bout time you showed up. The Madam was about to send for you." He motioned for Seamus and Eamon to go down the long hallway to the Madam's private office.

Eamon peered at the infamous interior in awe. Comfortable chairs were scattered around the room in dark nooks and crannies for men to acquaint themselves with a Siren, before joining her in her crib upstairs. A bar to one side of the room provided libations, as the customers listened to a piano player, chatted, flirted, or waited their turn. Eamon could envision just such a scene, imagining the room during its busy business hours, rather than empty and rather forlorn during the midafternoon lull.

"Madam," Seamus said, with a deferential smile at the

doorway to what appeared to be an office. "'Tis always a joy to see you."

"Seamus." Her smile was one of a familiar friend but not one of shared intimacy. She stood nearly a foot shorter than Seamus and Eamon, her brown hair tied back in an intricate knot. Her brown eyes, which usually sparkled with mischief, were filled with worry as she beheld her friend. "I see you've brought one of your sons with you." She motioned for them to enter her office and shut the door behind them.

Eamon looked around the comfortable room at a desk piled high with paperwork, which faced the door, while two comfortable chairs angled toward a potbellied stove sat in a corner of the room. He focused on the Madam again, silently marveling at his da's friendship with her.

Slapping Eamon on his shoulder, Seamus looked at him with pride. "Aye. Eamon returned today from Saint Louis. I've yet to hear of his escapades while away from the family." He waited until Eamon had nodded his respects to the Madam. "Nora is a good friend of the family and a close friend of your mum's." He ignored Eamon's confused stare, for Nora had not been on intimate terms with the O'Rourke family when Eamon had departed for Saint Louis in August.

She motioned for the two men to sit, with Seamus sitting in his customary comfortable chair and Eamon on a wooden desk chair she had pulled out for him. She nodded. "It appears the adventures on the steamboat have proven more entertaining than what occurred in Saint Louis." When Eamon stared at her guilelessly, she said, "Your young friend is not as fortunate in her relations as you, dear boy."

"How do you know this?" he asked, nodding his thanks as she handed him a glass of whiskey.

Nora passed another to Seamus before settling into her chair. "I find the Bordello to be confining at times, and a daily stroll helps clear my mind. Especially when I have a problem to consider. During today's walk, I was intrigued to notice a well-dressed young woman being towed down the boardwalk by Uriah. She seemed displeased by his behavior but helpless to prevent his mistreatment."

Eamon inched forward in his chair, his whiskey forgotten. "Do you know where she went? We've visited all the saloons, but none report seeing her."

Nora nodded, as though contemplating the ethics of each saloon owner. "I imagine they would claim that. But then Mr. Bell has never been one to allow scruples to interfere with profit."

Eamon shared a long look with his da and then asked, "I —we—heard a rumor he wishes to compete with the Bordello."

Nora tilted her head back and laughed, highlighting her long elegant neck, encircled by a simple gold chain. "He will attempt, but he will not succeed. You will never succeed when you abuse a woman to force her to do what you desire. She will rebel and will find a way to flee." Nora made a motion to encompass her establishment. "The Bordello is successful because the Sirens know Ezra will protect them, a decent meal always awaits them, and they can leave whenever they choose. They are in control."

Before Eamon could rise and race to the Daybreak Saloon to challenge the owner, Nora shook her head. "Mr. Bell is at least twice as strong as you and would have you resting beside your worthless brother-in-law by midnight," she murmured, referring to Connor Ahern, Niamh's first husband, who lay dead in a grave on a small hill overlooking the town. "A man like Bell doesn't understand strategy. He knows only brute strength."

"What do you recommend, Madam?" Eamon asked.

She studied him a long moment. "I've heard a rumor. That Chaffee and Bell are hoping to offer a series of auctions for their customers. It seems more than one sister arrived today."

Eamon paled at her words. "No one could be that cruel."

Nora gave a mirthless chuckle. "Oh, my boy, you have no idea how cruel the world can be to an unprotected woman."

Phoebe pounded on the door again, to no avail. Either no one heard or no one cared. She turned around the small confining space, wishing for a window. However, she had been locked in a cave-like room with only a candle for light. She had no idea how much time had passed, nor when they would come to retrieve her.

Shivering at what could befall her, she rose to pace. With an aggrieved roar, she slammed into one of the walls, pausing when she heard a cracking noise. She listened intently, but no one approached, so she hit the wall again. The noise intensified, and soon she panted and sweated as she attempted to make a hole in the wall. She sat down, resting on her back, her legs in the air, and used her booted feet to kick at the wooden planks. After she was truly sweaty and sore, a rending sound echoed through the room as a board gave way.

Rising, she poked her head though the hole and realized she had kicked through the outer wall. With renewed determination, she kicked and pushed at surrounding boards until a large-enough space for her to crawl through had been created.

As she heard the sound of the giant approaching her room, tears coursed down her cheeks. His voice called out to her, "Kitten, it's almost time for you to come out of your den. The men ..." His voice broke off, as though he had been interrupted.

Galvanized by this momentary reprieve, she stripped the cot and placed a blanket over the rough patches of wood. With a prayer, she pushed herself out of the small opening, crying out as a shard of wood cut into her thigh.

Flying through the air, she thought she'd never land. Then she thought she'd die upon landing. When she crashed with a *thud* onto the roof of the next-door single-story barber shop, it cracked and groaned but did not collapse. Her breath left her in a *whoosh*, and she gasped in short painful gulps of air in an attempt to gain her breath back. Black spots danced in her eyes, and she blinked in an attempt to clear her vision. With more tears coursing down her cheeks, she crawled to the rear of the building, staring down at the back alley one story below.

Gathering the remnants of her courage, Phoebe crouched and gripped the edge of the roof so she could swing herself down. She swallowed a shriek as her skirts caught on something on the roof. She swayed back and forth, tearing herself loose. Finally she closed her eyes and dropped free, landing on the soft earth with a moan.

Although she wished she could lay here and rest, she knew the giant and her uncle would be after her. Rising, she ignored the pain in her right thigh, the blood seeping from her wound, saturating the cloth, and stumbled down the alleyway behind Front Street. The sky was a pale pink, and she tried to find joy in seeing another sunset rather than focusing on her terror and pain. In the distance, she saw a two-story house, and she used it like a beacon, praying someone kind lived in such a place.

~

E amon had returned to the large two-story O'Rourke family home with his da, with every intention of rounding up his older brothers to immediately journey to the Daybreak saloon with him. Instead he sat at the large kitchen table and prayed for patience. After a quick hug for his mum and sister Maggie, he had asked his mum to postpone the welcome home dinner for a night when he felt like celebrating. She had taken one look at him, cupped his cheek, and nodded, her relief at having him home evident in her gaze.

Little had changed in the large O'Rourke home since his departure last summer. The two-story structure with kitchen built on the back exuded a sense of hominess and welcome. The kitchen—with a large stove, a sink, and a countertop area to one side—had a massive table against the opposite wall, where the O'Rourkes gathered for meals. A back door led to the summer garden, a chicken coop, and the privy. The main house had two more large rooms on the main floor. A living room with another stove and a large room that had been Niamh's before her marriage. Upstairs were four bedrooms.

Now Eamon sat at the kitchen table, as anxiety and determination filled him to take some action, rather than continue to talk and plan. Eamon knew they would need to pool all their funds in an attempt to outbid the men who had more money than sense. A quick glance outside the kitchen window revealed it was close to sunset, and they should return to the saloon soon. "We can't miss the auction," he said to the men gathered. He relaxed marginally as his father nodded in agreement.

Glancing around the table, Eamon gave a sigh of relief to have his family around him. Finn glowered and appeared as serious as Eamon had ever seen him, while his oldest brothers, Ardan and Kevin, were somber in their intensity. His brother-in-law, Cormac, sat at the table beside Ardan, while their friend Dunmore had joined them too. Eamon's chest filled with fiery determination at the sight of the strong men who would be at his back. He refused to fail Phoebe.

"I think you're missing an important piece," Dunmore murmured in a lull in the planning. His blue-green eyes shone with concern, as he tapped a finger on the tabletop. A stagecoach driver, Dunmore would leave in a day or two to deliver men to Virginia City or Helena. For the rest of the season, he would be busy and rarely in Fort Benton. Although focused on the topic at hand, his gaze often flit to Eamon's youngest sister, Maggie, who worked at the stove. Their mum had slipped out of the room, ostensibly to prepare a room for Phoebe.

Eamon frowned as he studied the man who was closer to his brother Kevin's age at twenty-nine, with Kevin now thirty-one. "What do you mean, Dun?"

"I understand your focus is on the lass stuck at the saloon, but her sisters are in as much danger. They must be removed from that hotel." He paused as he stared at the men around the table, who were like family to him. "You know what Chaffee is like."

Eamon shook his head, as Finn's jaw ticked with anger. "That's the problem. Finn an' I have no idea what he's like. If we did, we would have warned the Mortimer sisters. We would have discovered who the uncle was and would have ensured the sisters were safe before they disembarked the steamboat."

His eldest brother, Ardan, gazed at him with patient understanding. Ten years older than Eamon, Ardan was the spitting image of their da as a younger man. Tall, broad shouldered, with thick black hair and a beard to match. His cobalt-blue eyes shone with love and determination.

"Chaffee is a man with no principles, who delights in the torment of others. Especially if it brings him a profit. He was thrilled at the pain he caused Niamh by aiding Connor in writing a vindictive will." When Eamon nodded his understanding, Ardan asked, "Where will the sisters go now? Is there room here?"

"They could have Niamh's old room," Cormac said. "The addition is finished at our house, and Niamh and Maura don't need it here."

Seamus nodded. "Aye, that would be fine. And, if there's need of more room, you've rooms in your home above the café, Ardan." Ardan nodded his agreement at the plan, and Seamus continued. "Finn, I want you, Dunmore, and Cormac to go for the other lasses. They know you, Finn, and won't be as terrified by a group of strangers arrivin' to take them away. The rest of us will go to the saloon."

Eamon looked at the pile of money in the center of the table. "Do you think it's enough, Da?"

Seamus shrugged. "I'll offer what I must as collateral. The lass won't be abused tonight, Eamon."

Gratitude and pride swelled within Eamon, as he noted the determination in everyone's faces when they nodded in agreement with his da.

Maggie, working quietly at the stove, turned toward the back door, and stared intently.

For a moment, Eamon was distracted by his sister Maggie. "What is it, Mags?" he asked.

"I thought I heard someone knocking at the back door. Or banging into it." She shrugged, as though not hearing anything more. "I must have been mistaken."

Eamon rose and squeezed his sister's shoulder. "I'll check," he murmured and opened the door to poke his head out. With a grunt, he fell to his knees to catch the body tumbling toward him. "Da!" he bellowed. "Da!" He eased the body up, cradling Phoebe in his arms. "Oh, sweet *Jaysus*," he breathed, "what did they do to you, lass?" He turned to face his family, ashen and terrified, the *drip-drip-drip* of blood on the floor the only sound in the thunderstruck room. "Dear God, what do we do?" he breathed.

"Bring her to Niamh's room, Eamon," Maggie said in a commanding voice, as she dried her hands on a towel after washing them. "Dunmore, boil water and tear clean cloths into strips. Cormac, find the doctor. If you can't find him, or he's no longer sober, find the Madam. Find Nora. Finn and Da, save the other sisters. Ardan and Kevin, get your wives." She ushered Eamon into Niamh's old room, now mainly used as a playroom for her daughter, Maura. However, a bed remained pushed against one wall, with a bureau on the wall beside the door.

Eamon settled Phoebe on the bed, a towel under her legs. "Oh, look at her sweet hands," he whispered, holding them up to kiss. He swore and spun from the room. After a moment, he returned with tweezers to pull splinters from her palms and fingers.

"No! No!" Phoebe gasped in a weak voice. "I will not be a pawn."

"Of course you won't," Eamon whispered, as he ran a hand over her head. "You're at the O'Rourke house, Phoebe. We'll care for you. We'll ensure you're well."

Her wild and crazed gaze calmed at his voice, and she settled on the bed. "My sisters," she panted out.

"We'll ensure they are safe. Soon you'll hear Winnifred bickering with Finn. It will be like old times. I promise you." Maggie watched him with a curious look. "Like the time we spent on the steamboat."

"Eamon, hold this cloth to her leg, while I ensure she has no other injuries," Maggie instructed. She waited for Eamon to press a towel to Phoebe's jagged wound and then ran her hands over Phoebe, searching for grimaces as she pressed against bones. "It's difficult to tell with her fully dressed, but it appears her only wound, besides bruising, is on her leg. As far as I can tell, she has no broken bones." Eamon sighed with relief and sat beside Phoebe as Maggie continued her ministrations.

Phoebe arched and cried out as Maggie pulled at her skirts, attempting to free the linen from the gash on her thigh. "Make it stop. Make the pain go away," she pleaded, turning her head to the side. Some of the cloth of her skirts had dried and stuck in the wound.

Eamon fell to his knees by her bedside, resting his head next to hers to whisper words of support and encouragement in her ear. If words of love slipped out, he ignored them and refused to call them back. Right now, his focus was on Phoebe and her recovery.

When Aileen and Deirdre burst into the room, Maggie asked them to make willow bark tea and to bring her honey. She thanked Dunmore, who entered with cloth and water, and she smiled as he set up a makeshift worktable for her. Without asking, he brought in more candles and lamps, illuminating the room, and then remained, awaiting further orders from her.

"How can you be so calm?" Eamon asked in an aggrieved voice.

"You can fall to pieces, Eamon. I can't. It would do Phoebe no good if we were all running around with no purpose." Dabbing a piece of cloth into the water, Maggie moistened the linen stuck in the wound and eased it free. She looked up and smiled as their mum entered the room. Soon the two women worked in concert to clean the wound of any wood and cloth pieces. Then Maggie took the honey from Dunmore and trickled a small amount inside the wound. "I can't promise anything, Eamon, but this may help with the infection."

He blanched at the word, understanding the implications of the worst-case scenario, and then nodded. When Maggie motioned for him to ease Phoebe to sit up, Maggie handed him a mug Aileen had given to Dunmore. "Convince her to drink this. 'Tis a bit bitter," she murmured.

Eamon looked deeply into Phoebe's pain-filled eyes. "Come, love. Drink this up. 'Twill help with your pain, and then you can sleep for a while. You've earned your rest." He coaxed her into drinking all of it before she collapsed onto the bed, white faced and panting from the exertion of sitting up.

Maggie looked over her shoulder. "Are any of the other lads around?" When Dunmore returned with Ardan and Kevin, she motioned for Eamon to remain where he was at Phoebe's head. "Continue talking with her." She took a deep breath and spoke directly to Phoebe. "Phoebe, I have to sew your leg shut. If I don't, you have a worse chance of infection." She rested a hand on Phoebe's shoulder. "'Twill hurt."

Phoebe tensed, leaning as much as possible into Eamon.

"Why not wait for the doctor or Nora?" Ardan whispered to Maggie.

She shook her head. "They'd be here by now if they were coming. I've cleaned the wound, and it needs to be closed." Taking a deep, determined breath, she said, "It's no different than sewing, Ardan."

"You're a brave lass, and I'm proud of you, sister," Ardan said. "Tell us what you need us to do."

Ardan and Kevin climbed onto the bed to hold Phoebe down, while Maggie instructed Dunmore to hold Phoebe's injured leg. "With any luck, she'll pass out soon after I start," she whispered.

Eamon focused wholly on Phoebe, ignoring everything

his sister was doing. He trusted Maggie would do what was correct and prayed she could truly help Phoebe. He rested his head next to Phoebe's, swiping away the tears that fell. "*Shh*, love," he murmured. "You'll be all right. We'll care for you. We'll nurse you back to health. You have nothing to fear now. The O'Rourkes have taken you in." He continued to stare into her eyes, talking in a soothing voice, as she arched and screamed in pain at the first suture. Tears fell unheeded down his cheeks as her agony filled gaze fixed on his, until her body went limp, finally succumbing to the pain. When he saw she was unconscious, he dropped his head down, his shoulders shaking as he sobbed for a few moments.

All through the long ordeal, he whispered words of love and encouragement to her, wanting her to hear his voice, if she heard anything at all. In the background, he heard his mum encouraging Maggie, his brothers quietly talking to each other as they sat on the bed, in case their strength was needed again, and Dunmore's soft words of praise.

Maggie worked tirelessly, using splashes of her father's fine whiskey to clean the gash as she progressed down the long wound. After nearly an hour, she tied off the last stitch and rose, almost falling to the floor, as her legs had fallen asleep. Dunmore caught her, and she rested in his arms a moment before wriggling to free herself. She flushed as he eased her onto a chair.

"Eamon," Maggie whispered, "I've done what I can."

"Thank you, Mags," Eamon whispered, using the nickname Kevin had given her after her return the previous summer. "I can never thank you enough."

After tapping her feet and regaining circulation, Maggie rose. She murmured to Dunmore, "Can you find me a little more clean cloth?"

After he departed, she returned to look at the jagged,

61

angry line down Phoebe's right thigh. She looked at her mum. "I think more honey is needed along the stitches."

"Aye," Mary said. "Anything you can do to fight infection." She handed Maggie the bowl with the honey, and Maggie spread a liberal amount down the length of the wound. Then, after Dunmore returned with more cloth, she and Mary bound the wound in long strips of clean cloth. "There," Maggie whispered, as she washed her hands and dried them. "I've done what I can."

Eamon tilted his head up and stared at his sister with profound gratitude. "Maggie."

She ruffled his hair and eased from the room for a moment.

Eamon continued on his knees by the bed, his focus wholly on Phoebe. He wanted to be present when she woke. A soft hand ran over his back, and his head jerked up, meeting his mother's concerned gaze. "Eamon," she whispered, "we'll do all we can to save your Phoebe."

He swallowed, no longer protesting that Phoebe wasn't his. Or that he didn't care for her in such a manner. All he knew was that he was desperate for her to recover. And he would have bartered with the devil himself for her to never know the pain she had suffered to arrive at their doorstep. "Thank you, Mum." He moved his head into her soft caress and then rose at the sound of angry voices in the living room. "Will you stay with her for a moment while I'm away?"

He poked his head inside the living room to find Lorena and Winnifred standing in one corner with Finn, while Da stared at them like they were exotic creatures. He listened as Winnifred proclaimed, "You might believe you have the right to manhandle us and to kidnap us, but I'll find our uncle! I'll inform him of what you've done, and he'll punish you."

Any amusement Eamon felt evaporated at Winnifred's words. "Oh, will you now?" he snapped, as he entered the room, covered in splotches of Phoebe's blood. "Do you think your uncle cares what happens to a niece he intended to auction at a saloon and brothel to the highest bidder tonight?"

Winnifred's eyes rounded, the green brighter than usual with her shock. "No. He wouldn't be so cruel. He wanted us here to … to …"

"Aye, he does. I have no idea what your sister suffered, but she lived through hell to escape whatever he had planned for her. If you care for her at all, you'll remain here until she can speak with you. For, if you seek out your uncle, no O'Rourke will come to rescue you a second time." He waited for her to deflate at his words, thankful she took him at his word. Despite his warning, he suspected Finn would have found a way to convince them to aid Winnifred, if needed. Although she annoyed Finn, they had an odd relationship, and Eamon knew Finn would never want to see Winnifred harmed.

"I don't believe you," Winnifred said with a defiant tilt of her chin, her bravado returning.

"I don't lie," Eamon snapped. His mouth firmed, and his blue eyes flashed with anger. "Come," he barked, as he motioned for Winnifred and Lorena to follow him into the sickroom. He entered it to find Maggie working on Phoebe's hands, using the tweezers he'd dropped by the bedside. His mum brushed at Phoebe's hair, while Aileen and Deirdre were in the kitchen. Dunmore maintained his sentry in the corner.

"Maggie, Mum," he murmured, "Winnifred and Lorena doubted Phoebe's injury. They believe their uncle to be a good man." Dunmore snorted in disbelief in the corner.

Maggie looked up with shock at the women hovering in the doorway a moment before refocusing on her task. "Then you're fortunate you weren't the one to be suffering in this bed," she muttered. "Daft fools, you are." She bent over

Phoebe's palm as she attempted to free it of a sliver, smiling at Dunmore as he moved closer to hold a candle for her to have better light.

"Phoebe," Winnifred gasped.

Eamon grabbed her before she rushed to the bedside and undid all of Maggie's work. "No," he gasped, as she wriggled in his arms. "She's injured, and you will not harm her further."

"What did you do to her to force her to sleep?" Lorena whispered.

"Nothing," Maggie said, as she gave a triumphant chirp at freeing a deep splinter. "She passed out from exhaustion and pain." With a quick glance, she murmured, "And, I suspect, from blood loss. She was bleeding heavily when she arrived."

"What did you do to her?" Winnifred demanded, stomping her foot in aggravation at being denied freedom to move as she pleased.

Eamon towered over her, as though a demonic creature with wild black hair and blue eyes blazing. "Everythin' in our power to save her. She has a gash down her leg that my sister worked tirelessly to clean and to sew shut. We're not your enemy. Your uncle is. A *bluidy* infection is." He was breathing heavily, as he battled deep emotions.

Winnifred collapsed into a chair, as Lorena watched them in horror. "What are we to do?" Winnie wailed. Her green eyes were filled with desperation. "Where are we to go?" Her hand swiped down her fine skirt, as a tear leaked out. "We may have fine clothes, but we're one step away from destitution."

"Our uncle was to save us," Lorena murmured. "I suspect he had a different definition of what that entailed."

Eamon nodded. "I don't know the man, but my da does, and, if my da says he's not a good man, then he's a scoundrel."

Winnifred firmed her shoulders. "Will you allow Phoebe

to remain here tonight as she recovers?"

Eamon shook his head, as he stared at her in wonder. "Of course not." He met her dejected gaze. "She'll stay here until she's fully recovered. As will all of you. You're not safe with your uncle wandering this town."

"You can't tell us what we can and cannot do," Winnie snapped. "Where we may and may not go."

Eamon quivered with rage. "No, I can't. But I can assure you, Miss Mortimer, our time and energy will be focused on Phoebe and her recovery. Not on spoiled women who defy their better judgment merely to be spiteful." He took a deep breath. "'Twould be better for everyone if you'd remain here, or in the company of an O'Rourke, for the foreseeable future."

Winnifred shared a quick glance with Lorena and nodded, although she failed to lose any of her mutinous defiance as she glared at Eamon.

Mary O'Rourke had remained quiet as her children spoke with the two Mortimer sisters, but she rested a hand on Eamon's arm as she stood beside him and felt him quivering with rage. "I'm Mary O'Rourke, an' I couldn't be more pleased to welcome you to my home. I'm certain Seamus and the lads will ensure your trunks are delivered here soon, and you'll feel right at home before you know it." She smiled at them with compassion. "I fear 'tis not how any of us would have liked to have met."

She paused as she saw the sisters staring at Phoebe lying prostrate on the bed. "Why don't you have a moment with your sister and then join us in the kitchen? I imagine you haven't had a chance for dinner."

Everyone in the room, except Maggie and Eamon, left the sisters with Phoebe.

Eamon exited Phoebe's room for a brief respite at Maggie's urging. Although he had no interest in supper, she had convinced him to eat to keep his strength up for Phoebe's sake. He collapsed, with his gaze glazed, as he stared at bread crumbs on the tabletop.

When the back door burst open, Eamon jerked into alert battle readiness. Noting a panting Cormac, Eamon relaxed and let out a long sigh. "Where have you been?"

Cormac shook his head. "All over town. To every saloon. I think I was led on a wild goose chase, searching for the doc." His eyes shone with frustration. "I never found the man, and Nora was having a crisis at the Bordello."

"Aye?" Seamus asked, as he took Mary's hand. "What bothers the lass?"

"That idiot Bell got it into his head she was harboring the injured Miss Mortimer." He paused a moment. "Phoebe?" At Eamon's nod, Cormac continued. "That Phoebe would rather be a Siren than a Temptress." Cormac grimaced. "That's what Bell plans to call his … ladies at his saloon." He was hesitant to speak about such subjects with women present. "He was on the verge of causing a riot in the Bordello. Damn fool wanted to go through every crib to ensure Phoebe wasn't there, and the men weren't happy at bein' interrupted."

"He'd doubt Nora's honor?" Mary murmured, arriving at the important point, while skipping over the more salacious details of Cormac's trip through town. "*Eejit.* She'll never forgive him. An' never forget." She ran a soothing hand over Seamus's shoulders that had tensed at the news his friend was experiencing difficulties.

Cormac nodded. "Thankfully the men in the Bordello didn't take kindly to Bell interrupting their … endeavors. But Nora couldn't leave." His gaze was filled with regret as he looked at Eamon.

Eamon smiled at his brother-in-law. "'Tis all right, Cormac. You tried hard enough. And it seems wee Maggie learned plenty while I was away." He paused. "Or she has the confidence now to do what she's always loved. She was a fine healer tonight."

Cormac heaved out a relieved breath. "Thank God. I had visions of Miss Phoebe bleeding to ..." He coughed, rather than finish his sentence, wincing as he saw Eamon pale. "Sorry, Eamon."

Glancing in the direction of the sickroom, Eamon looked as though he fought a natural inclination to march back into the room to sit by Phoebe's sickbed. He rocked back and forth in his chair but remained seated, his mum moving to him, resting a hand on his shoulder. "I don't know what to do." He stared at his mum for guidance and aid, his gaze lost and worried.

"Grant her sisters time with her," his mum said. "You'll have plenty of opportunity to sit in the chair beside her bed. Always have faith she'll recover, Eamon," she murmured, "but understand 'twill be a slow, long recovery."

"I hate that she suffered," he whispered. "I ..." He closed his eyes, blocking out the chaos of the kitchen, the various conversations, the scraping of chairs and clattering of plates and silverware as food was served. "I failed her, Mum."

Cupping his cheeks, she crouched over him, waiting for him to meet her gaze. "No, you didn't, my brave son. You spent the entire day searchin' for her. You planned to go to the saloon tonight, and you never forgot her sisters." She ran a hand over his hair. "You have to accept your Phoebe is intrepid and found a way to save herself. She did no' wait for you."

Chagrined, he met her steady gaze. "I wanted her to see me as a hero, as I swept in to save her," he breathed.

Mary's smile was filled with love and understanding. "I

know, my lad. All men want to feel that way." She sobered as she looked at him. "That would have been momentary. Now you have a chance to show your steadfastness, which is far more valuable to any woman of sense." When he stared at her in confusion, she said, "When you sit by her, talk with her, keep her company, and encourage her as she recovers, those acts of kindness will be worth a hundred moments as a hero, my boy."

"Truly?" he whispered. "I thought women liked the extravagant display of care."

Mary chuckled and patted his legs. "Not a woman of substance," Mary reassured, kissing him on his forehead.

Eamon sat, deep in thought, his gaze trained on the sick-room. He bided his time to return, waiting for the sisters to emerge.

~

Maggie bustled around the room, tidying it up after the events of the evening, as she watched the sisters. They had approached the bed but had not reached for Phoebe's hand or murmured soothing words, as Maggie had expected. She shared a confused glance with Dunmore before shrugging. Although there was no need for him to maintain his vigil with her, she appreciated his presence. "One of you might as well sit here," Maggie finally said in an exasperated tone, as she motioned to the chair by Phoebe's head. "Talk with her. Urge her to heal."

The mouthy, spirited one who Maggie believed was the youngest, collapsed into the chair with a dramatic sigh. Her black hair was escaping its pins and hung down her back in coils. "Only you, Phoebe," Winnifred muttered, "would manage to embroil yourself in such a scandal on our first day in town."

Maggie froze, watching to see what the eldest would say. When Phoebe groaned, Maggie moved to her side, swiping at her forehead and squeezing her bandaged hand gently. "All is well, Phoebe. Your wound has been cleaned and bound. You're safe." At the words *you're safe*, Phoebe relaxed.

With a snicker, Winnifred said, "For now. I can't imagine we'll be welcome here for long." She rolled her eyes. "I don't know what we were thinking, traveling to the middle of nowhere."

Maggie continued to hold Phoebe's hand, as she spun to glare at the two healthy Mortimer sisters. "And I suppose you blame your injured sister for that too? Or is it that you merely like to spew your resentments at her when she's unconscious and unable to defend herself?"

Winnifred stiffened, her back straight and her chin held high, as she beheld a fierce Maggie. "Who are you to presume to comment on my relationship with my sister?"

Her gaze filled with scorn, Maggie shook her head. "You're a fool. You have yet to understand how few people in this world will love and cherish you without asking for anything in return. A sister is such a person." She stared at the two women with derision. "Until you can treat Phoebe with respect, please do not return to the sickroom. Phoebe has enough to contend with without having to battle your contempt as well."

She continued to hold Phoebe's hand as the sisters rose and stormed from the room. With a sigh, she sat with stooped shoulders, closing her eyes in defeat.

"You are magnificent, Miss Maggie," Dunmore said in a low, reverent voice.

Her head jerked up, meeting his devoted gaze. "Dunmore."

"Someday ..." he whispered, before slipping from the room, leaving Maggie alone with Phoebe.

69

E amon emerged from Phoebe's sickroom the following morning, bleary-eyed and in desperate need of a cup of coffee. He had largely ignored the noise from breakfast and sat in a dazed stupor as a full plate was set before him. He heard his mum murmur, "Eat, love," as she caressed his shoulder and moved back to the stove.

Glancing outside, he noted it was a bright sunny day, with birds chirping. Maggie and his oldest brothers were all present, including Kevin and Ardan, but their wives were noticeably absent. Eamon did as his mother bid. After wolfing down his breakfast, he drank his coffee and gathered his courage. Luckily the youngest boys and the two Mortimer sisters were not here, as Eamon addressed Declan's absence.

After focusing on his father, mother, and eldest siblings, he sighed. "Thank you for helping Phoebe last night. I know yesterday's events interrupted our homecoming." When his da murmured he shouldn't be daft, Eamon blurted out, "I know you're worried about Declan." He cast a furtive glance at Finn, but his brother kept his head bowed and didn't meet his gaze. "Finn an' I are too." He shrugged, the dark circles under his eyes enhancing the despair in his gaze. "We couldn't force him to come home, Da."

Seamus sat in silence for a long moment, his blue eyes sparkling with confusion and hurt. "Why would my lad prefer to remain away from his family? What was done to make him shun us?"

"No, Da," Eamon stammered, shaking his head to clear it from the fog of fatigue and to focus on his parents' misery. "No." Rubbing at his temple, he whispered, "He fell in love."

Mary sighed and fell toward Seamus, her expression softening with joy. "Oh, how lovely. Do you like the lass? Is she good to Declan? When will they marry?"

Eamon watched as his father ran a hand down his mum's back, a soothing and yet warning caress. Eamon firmed his shoulders and shook his head. "She doesn't love him, Mum," he whispered. "She broke his heart, ran off with another man, and abandoned him in Saint Louis."

Mary gazed from Eamon to Finn and back again, her brows furrowed, and her eyes overflowing with devastation for her son. "I don't understand. How … Why didn't she love him?"

"Mary," Seamus soothed, "we know the lad to be a wonderful man, but not everyone will love him."

"For him to love her, she must have led him on," Mary demanded.

Eamon took a deep breath and cast a pleading glance in Finn's direction, but Finn resolutely stared at the tabletop. "Ah, I believe she did." He cleared his throat, a flush rising up his neck. "There's the wee matter that she was carrying his child when she ran away to New Orleans."

"What?" Seamus whispered in a lethally soft voice, all the more potent for its soft intensity. When his son nodded,

Seamus slammed his hand onto the table. "And you left your brother alone to deal with such heartbreak and deception?"

Firming his jaw, Eamon spoke in a clipped voice. "We didn't leave him, Da. He wanted nothin' to do with us. Told us, if we were his brothers, we'd leave him be."

"Leave him be in a city where he knows no one?" Mary demanded, her eyes flashing with anger. "You know he was striking out from pain."

Finn hit the table with his hand and looked up. "What did you want us to do, Mum? Fight him? Force him to accept our help, so he'd resent us forever? Make him sneak away in the middle of the night and never see him again?"

Seamus paled. "Never see Declan again?" he breathed, as he stared at his two recently returned sons, the gravity of the situation settling in, finally understanding their solemn expressions. "No, never that."

Eamon sighed and shook his head, attempting to blink away tears that threatened to fall. "Aye. He swore ..." After pausing to clear his throat once more, he rasped, "He swore, if we remained in Saint Louis, if we interfered in any way, we would be dead to him. That he would no longer be an O'Rourke and that he'd never return to Fort Benton."

Seamus stood abruptly, his chair clattering to the floor, as he spun to face away from his family. "Feck," he hissed. He slammed his hand against a wall once and then again. "Feck!"

For long moments, only the sound of Seamus's agitated breathing filled the room. "I'm sorry, Da," Eamon finally whispered, his shoulders stooped, as though in failure. "I didn't know what to do. I had hoped, by returnin' here, we were doin' the right thing."

Seamus turned back, his eyes lit with grief, fear, and regret. "Aye, you did, lads. I'm proud of you. Rather than act like a hotheaded fool, like your da, you ensured there's a chance he'll return to us. An' I find I desperately need that

73

hope." He righted the chair and sat, tugging Mary closer, so she could cry on his shoulder. "Did he send a letter or anythin' to us?"

Shaking his head, Eamon felt a wave of fatigue wash over him. "No," he murmured. "I've never seen him so out of sorts, Da. 'Twas as though he were possessed. All he could think about was finding her. Racin' after Magnolia was his only purpose."

"Why was he so angry at you?" Ardan asked, finally entering the conversation. "It makes no sense, Eamon. We fight, aye. We bicker. But we never make such threats against family."

After taking a slurp of coffee, Eamon focused on his eldest brother, who sat beside their second-eldest brother, Kevin. "Declan thought he'd finally found what you have. He dreamed of returnin' to Fort Benton, triumphant, with a gorgeous bride by his side." He ducked his head. "Magnolia was beautiful, aye, with a doll-like fragility. She had long gold curls that seemed frozen in place and blue eyes as bright as a crystal, but there was a coldness to her that Declan couldn't see."

"Wouldn't see," Finn interjected.

"When he first noticed her, I told him that I didn't much care for her. I said I thought he could do better. That he should find an Aileen or a Deirdre." Eamon's flush brightened at that admission.

"Oh, Eamon," Mary murmured.

"That seemed to spur him on, as though he were intent to prove Magnolia as good an' kind an' loveable as Deirdre or Aileen." He paused, as though considering his brothers' wives. "He could never see her calculatin' smile or her fightin' a grimace, when he spoke of our family, or that she only was pleased when he gave her a gift."

"She was after his money, never Declan," Finn said.

"What happened?" Maggie whispered, her cheeks wet from silent tears. Although she didn't know her elder brother Declan well, she had liked him during the few months she had known him before he departed for Saint Louis. When she saw Eamon frown with worry at her presence, she waved a hand in the direction of the sickroom. "Dunmore is with her."

Eamon relaxed and murmured, "One evening, Finn and I brought a friend home for dinner. An Andre Martin from New Orleans." When Finn huffed out a breath, Eamon nodded. "We thought him friend. He was captivated by Magnolia, but she barely spared him a glance."

"We were planning our return trip," Finn added, "talking about the supplies we had bought, about running the store and warehouse, and about life here."

Eamon rubbed at his head, his thick black hair disheveled and in need of a trim. "Within a week, she'd left Declan a letter and had run off with Andre. Declan blamed me for her defection. Screamed that, if I'd accepted her an' been more friendly, she never would have run away. That, if I'd never brought Andre Martin home, she would never have left with him."

"Bull," Ardan muttered, as Kevin grunted in agreement.

Finn nodded. "Aye, she admitted to me one evening, when I sat beside her, flirting and flattering her, of her disappointment that Declan had such a large family, and she couldn't hide her distress that Declan would not inherit a great sum of money."

Mary gasped, her grip on Seamus tightening. "All she wanted was money?"

The two brothers nodded grimly. "Aye," Eamon breathed, "I believe so."

"Seemed appalled," Finn continued, "as though Declan

had deceived her, when she found out no grand house awaited him here, with servants and carriages."

Maggie sputtered, as she shared an amused smile with her mother. "What would we do with carriages and servants?"

Seamus huffed out a breath. "Well, if you ask me, the lad had a lucky escape, except for his child."

"If it is his child," Mary muttered.

Nodding in agreement at his wife's sage words, Seamus said, "An' nothin' is to be done for him, except wait and hope he comes home. Although 'tis unlikely 'twill occur until next year." After a long moment of silence, he looked at his recently returned sons. "You did what you could, an' no need to feel guilty because you couldn't talk a stubborn O'Rourke 'round to your way of thinkin'. He'll find his way right at some point." After a long silent moment, he focused on Maggie. "Love, how is our patient?"

At the sudden change in topic, Maggie froze before relaxing. "She appears to be doing well, although I'll need to change the bandage today and to look for any signs that the wound's festering. I fear, no matter how diligent we were in trying to prevent infection, that she could still suffer from one."

Eamon paled at Maggie's frank words. "What can I do?"

At his whispered question, Maggie reached forward and squeezed his hands, now gripped together on the table. "Sit by her. Read to her. Continue to spend time with her. She will soon tire of those four walls, and your presence will be soothing."

"Aye," Ardan said. "When Deir hurt her ankle, she appreciated the time I spent with her."

Eamon focused on his eldest brother a moment. "How can you be away from the café for so long?"

With a shrug, Ardan smiled. "Family always comes first, and Deirdre understands that. She wanted to shut the café for a day, but I insisted she remain open. 'Tisn't worth losing a day's worth of profits or giving another the idea to open a competing business."

Finn rolled his eyes. "'Twouldn't matter if they did. None could match Deirdre for her delicious food."

Looking around the room, Eamon frowned. "I haven't seen Niamh since our return. Is she angry with us?" He referred to his eldest sister, whom his father had married Cormac in December.

Mary smiled. "No, love. She's to keep her feet up. The babe is causin' her trouble."

"Babe?" Eamon said, as he and Finn whooped with joy. "We're to be uncles again?"

"Aye," Seamus said. "The babe is to be born sometime this month."

Sharing a confused look with his brother, Eamon asked, "But how? She just married Cormac six months ago."

"Ah …" Da cleared his throat. "The babe is Connor's." He nodded as his sons gaped at him.

"Connor's?" Finn gasped, as Eamon stared at him, slack-jawed.

"How does Cormac bear it?" Eamon asked at almost the same time.

"He loves Niamh," Kevin said in a sure, strong voice, as though nothing more needed to be said.

After a long moment, those gathered then rose and restarted their days. Ardan shouted his goodbyes as he headed for the café; Kevin spoke to Da a moment before departing for the warehouse, and Finn rose to go with Kevin. Eamon remained at the table, shamelessly eavesdropping on the conversation between Maggie and Mum.

Maggie had risen to return to the sickroom but stopped. "Mum, what about the other sisters? They didn't come down for breakfast?"

Mary sighed and rubbed at her forehead. "Bryan whispered to me that they had hoped their breakfasts would be served to them in bed." She fought a chuckle as her children goggled at her in indignation and stupefaction.

"You can't be serious, Mum," Maggie breathed. "Do they think we don't already have enough work, caring for their injured sister?"

Mary took a sip of tea, hiding a smile behind her teacup. "What do you suggest, love?"

Shrugging, Maggie stretched her arms overhead. "I'd have them make their own food, if they can't make a meal on time. It's not like they're working."

"Working," Mary murmured, her gaze filled with mischief a moment before focusing on Eamon. "Do you have any ideas?"

Eamon shook his head, absently noting Maggie sidling out of the room to return to Phoebe. "No, Mum. But they seem spoiled and unaware of their change in circumstances."

"So it seems." His mum settled in to enjoy the momentary quiet. Soft morning air from the open windows cooled the kitchen after the mass of bodies dispersed, the warm stove dying down a bit too, while a robin trilled outside, and a floorboard overhead creaked.

Eamon sat in the sudden silence of the empty kitchen, his mind racing as he relived scenes from the previous night.

"Are you well, my Eamon?" Mary asked, resting a soft hand on his arm.

He jerked, as he had expected her to leave the room too. "Mum," he whispered. "You're here." His unfocused gaze settled on her, taking in her earnest expression as she studied him. Rather than the middle-aged woman with wrinkles around her eyes, gray mixed in her auburn hair, and plump cheeks, he saw the thin woman with laughing hazel eyes who had picked him up and had swung him around when he was a boy.

Rather than the large kitchen with the fine stove and the immense table, he saw a crowded room with a kettle over a peat fire. However, he realized joy flourished in both places because of her presence. "Mum," he whispered again, suddenly fighting tears.

"*Shh*, Eamon, love, you're all right," she murmured, as she pulled him close, urging him to rest his head on her shoulder, as he had done as a young boy.

He sniffled, and her scent filled his senses, recalling all the times she had held him. "I forgot," he whispered, his arms suddenly binding tightly around her. "I made myself forget."

Running a hand over his head and down his back, she *coo*ed at him, as though he were a wee babe in need of comfort. "What did you forget?"

He leaned away, scrubbing at his face, as he flushed at the evidence of his grief and also his relief at her presence. "You. I made myself forget you."

Blanching, Mary held herself ramrod straight. "I don't understand, Eamon. Why?"

"It hurt too much to remember," he whispered. He ducked his head, ashamed at being so weak. After a long moment, he looked up to see his mum sitting in front of him in silent misery, a stream of tears coursing down her cheeks. "Oh, Mum, I'm sorry."

She shrugged. "I don't know what I could have done, Eamon. I never wanted to be separated from you or your siblings. Or your da. I wanted the life we had." She sniffled, pulling a handkerchief from her pocket and swabbing at her face. "But fate had other ideas for us. An', by the grace of God, we're together again, aye?"

"Aye," he said with a smile. "But you have to understand, I have difficulty believing in *forever*. And *always*."

Mary smiled, cupping his face. "Believe in *now*. Believe in *tomorrow*. For, if you believe in tomorrow, you'll find your forever and your always."

Eamon sighed, pulling her close again. "I've missed you, Mum."

"As I've missed you, my Eamon."

~

Two days after Phoebe's escape from the saloon, Eamon jerked awake, sitting up and gasping as his bedroom door slammed against the wall, interrupting his much-needed nap. He had spent the past two nights by Phoebe's bedside. Eamon studied the door in a sleepy daze, as it careened forward to hit the person in the doorway. "Winnifred?" Yawning, he stretched and tried to shake off an overwhelming fatigue. "What's the matter?"

"My uncle is here. He's spouting his thousand-dollar words."

Shaking his head again, Eamon rubbed at his eyes. "It wouldn't matter if they're million-dollar words. You're here, and he can't make you leave." He stared at her intently, as this was one of the only times he could remember seeing her so out of sorts.

Biting her lip, she murmured, "That's not what he says."

With a growl, he motioned for her to leave, rising when the door closed to tug on clothes. He rushed from his room to barrel down the stairs, following the sound of raised voices. He slipped into the kitchen, shutting the door behind him in an attempt to protect Phoebe from hearing her uncle's voice. A man he didn't recognize, but who he assumed was the uncle, stood with his back to Eamon, and waved his arms around in a grandiose manner, bellowing at his da. Kevin and Ardan stood near the stove in front of their mother, while Finn glowered at the man as he stood behind their da.

Eamon nodded to his brothers, moving to stand beside his da. "Why are you here?" he demanded, the question barely intelligible as he yawned again.

"And who are you to question me or my presence here?" the rotund man in garishly colored garments asked. His saffron-yellow waistcoat clashed with the green of his suit, and Eamon stood momentarily stunned by the man's horrible fashion sense.

"I'm an O'Rourke," Eamon said, as though that were all the justification he needed.

"Why should that matter?" the man asked, puffing out his chest and straining his already precariously fastened buttons. He waved his hand around to indicate everyone in the room. "They're all O'Rourkes, and they're as useless as you are." He pointed at his chest, tilting his head back with pride. "I am Uriah Chaffee, Esquire. I am a man of law. I am a man of importance. What is an O'Rourke? Nothing!"

Eamon stood even taller at the man's proclamation, suddenly wide awake and irate. "You have a lot of nerve, barging into our home and insulting us. You have no right to be here."

"I have every right, when you have kidnapped my nieces," Chaffee hissed, absently swiping at drool on his chin. "You have no right to keep them here against their will."

"They aren't here against their will. They're here to evade you and your evil plans," Eamon said, as his brothers murmured their agreement. "Phoebe is battling for her life because she was so desperate to escape your scheme to use her to earn you money that she nearly died in the attempt."

"Lies!" Chaffee bellowed, his eyes bulging with his anger. "How dare you impugn my honor?"

Shaking his head, Eamon said, "A man who would force his nieces into prostitution has no honor."

Sputtering and beseeching, Chaffee looked around the kitchen, searching for someone sympathetic to his plight or his version of the story. "I had no idea Mr. Bell had such nefarious intentions for my poor niece. I thought he would offer her a job as a … as a …"

Seamus chuckled. He stood tall with his arms over his chest, but no humor lit his startling blue eyes as cold as a glacier. Instead they reflected his disdain and his disgust. "I can imagine what sort of work you hoped he would offer your niece," he murmured. "No estimable man would ever consider forcing a woman he cared for to work in a saloon, much less in a brothel."

"Oh, but it's acceptable for an O'Rourke to work at the Bordello?" Chaffee demanded.

"You know—as well as everyone else in this town—that she works on off-hours as a seamstress for the Bordello Sirens. And during these busy summer months, she works at home. The Madam is very careful to guard Mrs. O'Rourke's safety and reputation," Kevin snapped.

Glaring at Seamus and then Eamon, Chaffee snickered. "You O'Rourkes will always alter every rule, every social convention, to suit your needs, won't you?" He put his hands on his hips. "I cannot be blamed for accepting aid to help feed and clothe those worthless women when they showed up unannounced and unwanted. Who would want three unskilled women to care for?" He ignored the gasp of indignation in the hallway behind him, as Lorena and Maggie hushed Winnifred. Rolling his eyes, he made a motion to indicate that the O'Rourkes would and that their inclination to help their womenfolk was a sign of their feebleness.

Eamon stood shoulder to shoulder with his father. "We might bend the rules, aye, but we never have and never will accept harming the safety of those we love. 'Tis an unpardonable offense." He paused as Chaffee rolled his eyes again.

"Do you think I care about you spouting your platitudes and theories about familial love and loyalty? I've never been bothered by such sentimentality, and I certainly won't start now. How do you think I've had such success in my life? If I had allowed myself to be bogged down by feelings for my poor, pathetic sister, I would never have left Saint Louis. Thankfully she was more realistic than you lot and grabbed at every opportunity that came her way."

"You are reprehensible," Seamus said in a low voice that sent shivers down Eamon's spine. It was the voice every O'Rourke child dreaded hearing, for it signaled their da's deepest disappointment. However, this time it was laced with loathing, a tone Eamon had never heard before.

"So sue me!" Chaffee said with a cackle. "Oh, wait. You can't because I'm the only lawyer in town." His laughter intensified as he reached forward and poked Eamon in the chest with a pudgy finger. "Here's your problem, O'Rourke. *I* am their uncle. *I* am their family. *I* am perceived as the one to safeguard them. Not you and your ragtag family."

Eamon tried to unclench his tight fists, while he reined in his temper. "Say what you want now for you are not welcome in our home ever again."

Uriah gasped and puffed out his chest at Eamon's edict. "As their only living male relative, the law will perceive me as their legal guardian. Thus, what I wish for them is what will happen. And I will sue you because you are preventing me from caring for my beloved nieces as I see fit. If you believe that spineless sheriff will see things any differently, you are a fool." Uriah leaned back on his heels, as though he had just declared checkmate.

Eamon stared at Seamus and paled at Uriah's words, the only outward sign of doubt.

"You mean, you'll mangle any an' all laws an' their inter-pretations to suit your needs," Seamus said, as he glared at Uriah.

With an insolent shrug, Uriah sniffed and looked around the O'Rourke kitchen, as though it were fit only for street urchins. "I'll return in a few days' time. I would hate the added expense of doctor's bills for Phoebe after she so fool-ishly injured herself." He pushed past Seamus and Eamon, the floorboards heaving as he stormed from the room to exit the kitchen door.

After their unwanted visitor left, Seamus spoke, clasping Eamon's shoulder and looking at the other O'Rourke men in the room. "Now that 'tis summer, and the roads are passable again, we must look into findin' our own lawyer. I'll speak with Dunmore about fetchin' a real attorney from Helena or Virginia City to aid us in riddin' this town of Uriah for good."

Ardan nodded, his strong arms crossed over his muscular chest. "Aye, Da, but 'twill be a challenge to convince a man to leave the profitable towns to return here. Let's hope Dunmore is persuasive."

Eamon stood in shock at the uncle's visit, listening to his family chatter around him, his mind racing with one overar-ching thought, *How could he keep Phoebe safe?*

❦

On the fourth night of his vigil, Eamon sat on the chair beside Phoebe's bed, the book in his hands slipping to his lap and then to the floor with a soft *thud*. He jolted softly but did not awaken from the noise. He arched forward until his head rested on the mattress beside Phoebe, his arms and hands cushioning his head like a pillow. With a satisfied sigh, he began to slide into a deeper sleep. He had assured Maggie that he would watch over Phoebe, reading long into the night before fatigue caught up to him. Now he relished dreaming about a time when Phoebe was better, and they could dream about their future.

Bolting awake, he stared in confusion at Phoebe to see her thrashing on the bed and reaching for the bandage covering her right thigh. "No, Phoebe, no!" He grabbed her hands, holding her as still as possible, as she shivered and heaved. In the dim candlelight, he saw the flush on her cheeks and the sweat on her brow.

Clamping both wrists together in one of his hands, he raised his free hand to touch her face. "Feck, you're burnin' up." Glancing around, he saw he was completely alone, and he heard no noise in the house to suggest anyone was nearby to help him. With a resigned sigh, he bellowed, "Maggie!" After a moment, he yelled her name again, saying a prayer of thanksgiving when he heard the *thump* of footsteps upstairs, then Winnie complaining—as always—and the clamoring of many feet on the stairs.

"Maggie," he breathed, as his sister burst into the room. "She's on fire." Unable to hide the fear in his gaze, Maggie nodded. "And she's tryin' to undo her stitches."

"Aye," Maggie said, tugging down the blankets to look at the bandage. She frowned to see it soiled. Turning to the door, she called out orders. "Boil water, bring me clean cloths, and find ice." When she didn't hear footsteps scurrying to obey her orders, she called out, "Go!"

Finn and Niall poked their heads in, and Maggie bade them hold Phoebe down. "'Tis like before," Maggie said to Eamon. "You talk to her, while the lads hold her down."

Phoebe kicked out, hitting Maggie squarely in her chest, sending her sprawling to the ground.

"Mags!" Eamon called out, as Finn helped pull her up. "Are you all right?"

85

"Ouch," Maggie breathed, as she rubbed at her chest. "I'll be fine, but now you know how strong she is. And she doesn't know what she's doing. The fever rules her."

Mary entered with a bowl of water, and she and Maggie washed their hands before cutting off the soiled cloth. "Oh my," Mary breathed, as she looked Phoebe's reddened scar. "What should we do?"

Maggie shook her head, staring at it. "I don't know. Get her fever down. Let's see if she'll drink any more willow bark tea."

"Isn't the fever protecting her?" Niall asked. At fifteen, he was the eldest of Seamus's younger sons from his second wife, Colleen. Although he had Seamus's black hair, he had his mother's green eyes.

"To a point, Niall, but then it could kill her," Maggie said, ignoring Eamon's flinch at her blunt talk. "We need ice. Hopefully Da found some."

"Finn and I'll get the bathtub ready," Niall said, as he ran from the room, eager to help.

Henri and Bryan entered, balancing a huge mug of willow bark tea between them. "We have the tea!" Bryan called out, his green eyes shining with pride as he aided his older brother in his time of need. At eleven, he worshipped his older brothers and rarely had the opportunity to help them.

"Good lads," Eamon said, his voice nearly choked with deep emotions as he saw his family pulling together to help Phoebe. "Thank you."

"Anything for you, Eamon," Bryan said, as Henri nodded his agreement.

Eamon eased Phoebe to sit up, holding her upright, an arm under her shoulder as he balanced on the small part of bed beside her. "Come, love. Drink your tea. 'Twill help your pain and make it all better." He continued to coax her, as he urged her to take small sip after small sip. When she had drunk half of the large mug, he handed it to his mother, who set it on the bureau.

A clatter at the back door heralded Seamus's return, and he called out, "I have ice!"

"Oh, thank God," Mary said, as she gripped Eamon's shoulder.

After they had moved the bathtub into Phoebe's room, Seamus poured the bags of ice into it. Water was added, and soon Maggie attempted to shoo Eamon from the room. "You can't see her without clothes, Eamon. 'Tisn't proper."

"And do you think you're strong enough to lift her into and out of the tub, with or without Mum?" He shook his head. "An', no, Da is not helping if I can't." He looked from his mum to Maggie and back to his mum again. "Phoebe is ..." His voice broke. "Don't deny me, Mags."

Maggie stared into his eyes a long moment, before nodding her agreement. "Fine, but you're the one who'll have to tell her what you did." She rubbed at her chest. "I've no desire to be walloped again."

Eamon chuckled, suddenly grabbing her into his arms for a quick embrace. "Thank you, Maggie. For everything."

She kissed his cheek and stepped back. "Always, Eamon. 'Tis what family does." She looked at Phoebe and motioned for the door to close behind the men, now leaving. "Come. Let's help her."

Eamon stood back as he watched his mum and sister work to free Phoebe of her sleeping gown. When Maggie motioned for him to approach, he lifted her into his strong arms, hating her cry of pain as he jostled her injured leg. "Forgive me, love," he crooned. "I'd never mean to hurt you, but we have to get you better." At Maggie's urging, he lowered Phoebe slowly into the cold water, holding her in place, even though his hands felt like icicles, while she thrashed and fought to escape.

"Cold!" she screamed. "Why are you torturing me?" A few tears leaked out, and he saw Maggie frown in concern.

"Mags?" he whispered.

"You must get her to drink," Maggie said in a soft voice. "Have her finish this tea." She handed him the mug of cold willow bark tea. "I'll get more water."

Eamon focused on Phoebe, urging her to drink. When she had swallowed all of the tea and nearly an entire glass of water, he saw Maggie give a satisfied nod. "Why, Maggie?"

"She should have cried tears, but few came down her cheeks. It's a bad sign, and she needs more fluids." Maggie squeezed his shoulder. "Trust me."

He stared at his sister intently for a moment. "I do, Mags. With her life."

Running a cloth through the cold water, he ran it over Phoebe's head again and again to help cool her. Finally Maggie instructed him to extract her from the water and to cover her in a large bath sheet. After wrapping her up tightly, he sat on the chair with Phoebe on his lap, as a nightgown was eased over her head. Mary dried her hair with a towel, placing another on her pillow, before Eamon settled her again on the bed. He watched as Maggie and his mum rubbed alcohol and then honey down the wound again and afterward bound it with fresh clean cloths.

"Why did you do that, Maggie?"

She shrugged and flushed. "I've read that alcohol can clean a wound and that honey can help with infection. I fear, if I open the wound, it will never heal, but hopefully this will help a little." She shrugged. "I'm doing the best I can, Eamon."

He gripped her shoulder and gave it a gentle squeeze. "Of course you are. You've done more than the doc, who spends too much of his time in the saloons." His gaze roved over Phoebe, who had tumbled into sleep. He feared she wouldn't remain restful for long. "Go get some sleep, Mags and Mum. I'll sit with her."

Mum nodded and quietly left. Maggie smiled. "Bellow when you need me."

~

The next four days were an exercise in faith, stamina, and patience. Phoebe vacillated from deep sleep to thrashing about to whimpering, as she pleaded for her agony to end. Her fever spiked in the middle of every night; her selfish baby sister quick to bemoan each middle of the night awakening. Eamon slept throughout most days and sat beside Phoebe all night. Although her sisters had demanded they be given an equal opportunity to keep vigil, Maggie had insisted they not be allowed into her patient's sickroom without an O'Rourke present at all times. Their protestations that it was an affront to their honor to be doubted in such a manner, and their requests for time alone with Phoebe were denied by Maggie with great relish. Much to Lorena's and Winnifred's chagrin, what Maggie declared necessary for Phoebe's recovery was seen as gospel in the O'Rourke household.

For his part, Eamon had argued that Winnifred and Lorena should spend time with Phoebe when she was least likely to do them any physical harm. Maggie had agreed, rubbing at the bruise on her chest. Thus, the sisters spent their time with Phoebe during the daylight hours—with Maggie or Mary watching over them with a vigilant eye.

During those long days, the O'Rourkes struggled to keep their thriving businesses open, while also caring for Phoebe. Eamon had heard his exhausted Da murmur to Mum that he'd never before been so thankful to have so many children. Maggie worked like a woman possessed, reading everything she could find to discover something to help with the fever and to stop any infection. Madam Nora had sent a basketful of books to Maggie, although few offered any practical suggestions.

Eamon spent every night with Phoebe, regaling her with stories of his youth with Finn. He embellished tales, hoping, if he said outlandish things, she'd scold him. However, she never responded, and he feared she would never come back to him. The only time he evoked a response was when he coaxed liquid into her. She fought him then but eventually drank whatever tea Maggie had brewed, instinctively under-standing he wouldn't stop until Phoebe had finished the drink.

Finally on the fifth night of her fever, nearly a week and a half after her injury, Eamon sat holding Phoebe's hand. He'd talked himself until he was hoarse, and he found he had no more stories to tell her. He wanted to look deeply into her eyes as he talked with her. To hear her laughter, to hear her scold him, to have her squeeze his hand.

He ran his fingers over her hand again. It was cool to the touch, and she was not shivering, as she had done on the previous nights, heralding the return of her fever. Instead she continued to sleep deeply. With a stealthy softness, he caressed her forehead, letting out a sigh of relief to find it cool to his touch.

He dropped his head forward, resting it on the clean blankets and sheets by her side, thankful again for his mum and Maggie, as they had cared for Phoebe with such love and steadfastness. They had cared for her as though she were one of their own. When he felt a gentle hand stroke over his head, he tilted his head to the side. "Mum," he whispered. "You should be in bed."

She made a small sound as she stepped up to his side, wrapping her arms around his broad shoulders. "As should you, my lad. But you're keeping vigil over your love, and I wanted to make sure you were well."

"I fear she'll never awaken," he whispered. "That she'll forever be just out of reach." He swiped his head on the blankets to hide his tears.

"Oh, Eamon," Mary murmured, her hand dropping to run through his hair. After a long moment of silence, she knelt by his side, so she could meet his devastated gaze. "Don't give up hope."

He continued to speak in a low voice. "What if she *does* awaken and wants nothin' to do with me?" He closed his eyes, as he voiced one of his deepest fears. At her murmured voice indicating her confusion, he took a deep breath as he gathered his courage to meet his mum's gaze. "I wasn't kind to her the last few weeks on the steamboat."

"I don't understand, Eamon. Whyever not?" She continued to stroke a hand down his arm and back, soothing him as he quivered beside her. "No one watching you these past days could doubt your devotion to her."

"I'm ashamed, Mum." He met her comforting, loving gaze. "I was afraid. That I could care for her, as Da did you, and that I'd lose her."

Mary cupped his cheek, gazing at him with a deep tenderness. "And then your worst fear almost came true."

He shivered and swallowed, fighting a sob. "Who's to say it still won't?"

Mary raised her gaze from him to Phoebe, an assessing, astute gaze. "From what I can see, and from what the past nights have wrought, it appears Phoebe is finally recovering. 'Twill take her time to overcome her injury and the infection, but I know she will." She paused as she again stared at her son with understanding and motherly concern. "You must understand. If your da had treated me as you say you treated Phoebe, I wouldn't have been keen to forgive him. Or to trust him again. You'll have to be patient, constant, and brave as you fight for her."

"I've been fighting for her!"

She ran a hand over his head again. "Ah, love. I know that. You know that. But I doubt she'll remember that, since she's been delirious from her fever, while fighting off the infection." She paused. "And she may have a different view of why you're actin' as you are. Women don't think like men." She kissed his forehead and rose with a groan. "Oh, I'm too old to think I'm young enough to wander about in the middle of the night."

Eamon reached out and grabbed her hand. "Thank you, Mum. I don't know what I'd do without you."

She sniffled, her eyes glistening with tears. "Just as I'd be lost without you, my Eamon."

CHAPTER 6

The following evening, Eamon sat in a daze as the entire family, including the two healthy Mortimer sisters, were seated at the table. After they had missed the first breakfast with the family and had gone hungry, they hadn't failed to miss a meal. The table was crowded, as even Niamh and Maura had joined them this evening, and Niamh had given Eamon a hug, whispering in his ear to stay strong and to never lose hope. She sat beside Ardan and Deirdre, her arms over her belly. Although Cormac was away on a trip, delivering goods to Helena, her gaze continued to dart to the door, as though hoping he would appear.

Maggie and Mary set bowls of stew on the table that were passed around until each person had a bowl in front of him or her, while slices of bread were passed around too. After everyone was settled, Seamus said a quick prayer over their hearty meal, always including his thanksgiving for the return of Mary and Maggie, followed by a prayer for the return to health for Phoebe and for Declan's safe return. At his "Amen," the younger boys heaved out sighs of relief, as they slurped up their stew.

When everyone had eaten his or her fill, Seamus cleared his throat. The youngest boys nodded, understanding that was their cue to rise and to leave the older O'Rourkes to their discussions. However, Seamus waved them to remain seated. "Nay," he said. "I believe everyone should listen to this discussion, as it very well might affect all of us." He smiled as his youngest, Bryan, gave a triumphant *whoop* to be included in the grown-ups' discussions.

"What is it, Da?" Eamon asked. He fought to focus on the discussion at hand, when all he wanted to do was return to check on Phoebe. Or collapse into his bed for a few hours of sleep.

"As we are all aware, Uriah Chaffee, the uncle, visited and made threats against Phoebe, Winnifred, and Lorena." He nodded in Winnifred's and Lorena's direction, as they sat in nervous silence beside Finn and Lucien. "He is their uncle and believes he has the right to act as their guardian, even though they are fully grown women, and he has nefarious intentions."

He paused, sighing as he rubbed at his temple. "This is where 'tis challengin'. I know nothin' about the laws governin' such things. I focused on my rights as a store owner." He shook his head in chagrin, as though he had been shortsighted. "However, there is little we can do, as he claims to be a lawyer, and he knows enough hundred-dollar words to impress the townsfolk."

Winnifred gave an indignant huff. "He might be our uncle, but he has no right to believe he can control us. After all, we are of the age of majority and have been living on our own for the better part of the year, after our mother died."

Seamus looked at her with patience and a fair dose of pity. "So you say, lass, but I fear Uriah was correct in one assertion. I met him again today, and he proudly claimed our sheriff would do little to interfere in a family matter. Few men will intervene in such a private affair."

Niamh shook her head. "Nay, I fear none will." She leaned against Ardan who wrapped an arm around her shoulder and pulled her close, as she battled her memories from her first marriage, wed to an abusive man. "The sheriff was aiding Chafee last fall as he attempted to take my daughter from me."

Winnifred ignored Niamh and stared around the table in horror, her eyes widening to see the O'Rourkes nodding, as though accepting their father's word. "And you'll not challenge him? You'll allow Phoebe to return to him to be used as he pleases? You'll allow him to harm Lorena and me?"

Finn focused on Winnifred with a mocking smile, his blue eyes sparkling with mischief. "Until now, you seemed to believe we were lying about how horrible your uncle is. That we'd treated *him* poorly and that we were cruel to keep you separated from him. Now you desire our protection? You are fickle, Winn."

She glared daggers at him. "Don't call me that! I've had the good sense to realize what he is. An opportunist who will never cherish his nieces."

Eamon watched his brother lean forward to continue sparring with the youngest Mortimer sister, but Da murmured his name, and Finn sat back. His silence fueled Winnifred's rage more than anything he could have said, as she continued to rage at Finn.

"Winnifred," Seamus said in a firm voice, his commanding tone causing her to freeze in place, her words sputtering to a halt. "Cease sparring with Finn. He's not your adversary."

Mary ran a hand down Seamus's arm, and he focused again on his family around the table. Seamus spoke with

95

quiet authority. "I have spoken to Dunmore and Cormac. They are attempting to find a lawyer who would be interested in working here, rather than in the more profitable towns of Helena or Virginia City. As of now, Dunmore's been unsuccessful. I continue to hope Cormac is more persuasive."

Niamh sighed. "He'll do what he can, but he won't extend his journey to find a lawyer." She rubbed at her belly. "Not when he wants to be here when the babe is born."

Seamus nodded, a glint of delight in his gaze, as he beheld his eldest daughter. "Aye, thus we have to forge our own plan." He addressed Winnifred and Lorena. "From what I can determine, the only way to ensure you are safe is to bring you under the shelter of the O'Rourke family." Seamus nodded, as Winnifred gasped and Lorena paled. "One Mortimer sister, if not more of you, must marry an O'Rourke."

"Never," Winnifred hissed, glaring at Finn. "I'll never marry an O'Rourke."

"As if I'd offer," Finn taunted.

"And the others are too young," Lorena whispered in horror, as she looked at the younger O'Rourke boys, the eldest nearly ten years her junior.

Seamus chuckled, a wry humor in his voice as he addressed Winnifred first. "We're not that vile, child." Glancing at Lorena, amusement lighting his gaze, he added, "And, yes, the lads are too young for you." He looked to Eamon, his gaze assessing, as Eamon sat in rigid stillness. "Eamon?"

Eamon looked at his da and nodded. "Aye, I'll marry Phoebe. I would have married her with or without an injury. With or without the threat from her uncle." He spun to glare at Winnifred who snorted in disbelief. "Think what you will, Miss Mortimer, but 'tis the truth."

"Have fun convincing Phoebe of what you proclaim. She has a long memory, almost as long as mine, and you'll be miserable because of it."

Sighing and pinching the bridge of his nose, Seamus spoke in a commanding voice. "There will be no strife. There will be no arguments. From the moment Eamon and Phoebe wed, Lorena and Winnifred will be members of this family and will be cherished and protected as such." He gazed at the two sisters. "Your uncle will have no right to interfere in your lives as you will be under our protection. As long as you live here—and are with one of us—he won't dare to approach you or to harm you. Should you go about town alone, however, you do so at your own peril."

Lorena spoke up. "You presume he has honor, sir. What he allowed to happen to Phoebe proves he doesn't. He won't acknowledge your desire to safeguard us."

"Which is why you must always have an O'Rourke with you."

Winnie snorted, rolling her eyes, but a quick stare from Seamus had her sitting straighter.

Then Seamus smiled at his eldest sons, shaking his head ruefully as they looked eager for an opportunity to thrash the man. "No, lads. No violence. We must outsmart him with his weapon of choice—words."

"What if he crosses the line?" Eamon asked.

Seamus took a deep breath. "As long as he's aware of the limit of our forbearance, if he crosses it, then he only has himself to blame."

Eamon nodded his agreement. "For his sake, I pray he's more sensible than he's shown himself to be."

~

Jolting with the sound of a bowl slamming on a table, Phoebe fought to quell any reaction to what occurred around her. However, she knew she failed at the triumphant sound of a woman's voice.

"Ha!" Maggie nearly shouted. "I knew you were faking being asleep all this time." She pulled back the blankets, stripping Phoebe of everything but her nightshirt.

Gasping, Phoebe flailed an arm out for some sort of cover, flushing when she met Maggie's triumphant smile. "Fine, I'm awake." When Maggie continued to stare at her with disdain, Phoebe's flush brightened to the color of peony pink. "I didn't want to speak with him. Why should I have to? And who are you to be so bossy?"

"I'm about out of patience with Mortimer sisters spouting nonsense," Maggie said with a long sigh, as she pushed a lock of auburn hair behind her ear. She lost her battle, and a smile emerged when she saw Phoebe wince at her comment. "I'm Maggie, the youngest O'Rourke sister. And you should speak with Eamon because he's nearly driven himself to the grave carin' for you," Maggie said, her hazel eyes flashing with frustration. "Or because he nearly talked himself hoarse in an attempt to keep you company. He was terrified you'd wake and feel alone. He never wanted you to feel alone."

Phoebe pushed to move around the bed, gasping in agony and going bone white. After collapsing back onto the pillows, she took deep breaths in an attempt to calm the searing pain. "Oh, when will the pain improve?" she rasped, her hand going to her leg to massage it. However, she stilled the movement, knowing touching her wound would only intensify the now-throbbing ache.

"I don't know," Maggie murmured. "I've done what I can to aid you, Phoebe. But I'm not a formally trained healer. I swear though that I did my best."

Phoebe gaped at the young woman, who looked so much like Eamon. However, rather than Eamon's startling blue eyes, she had beautiful hazel eyes. "Where was the doctor?"

Clearing her throat, Maggie shrugged. "Busy at the saloon. I thought …" She firmed her shoulders. "I made the decision that you would be better off with me than with a man who had too much to drink."

Phoebe continued to gape at Maggie. "How many other patients have you tended with wounds like mine?"

Flushing, the younger woman shrugged. "None."

Phoebe nodded calmly, as she looked from Maggie to her leg covered by her gown. "May I look at it?"

Maggie agreed, washing her hands in clean water from the ewer and then easing up Phoebe's leg to slip off the bandage. "It's time to change the bandage anyway."

Phoebe ignored Maggie, her gaze roving over the jagged scar along her leg, followed by her fingers gingerly inspecting the wound. It was inflamed and puckered, but the skin around it was cool to the touch and only slightly stung with soft pressure. She frowned as her fingers came away sticky.

"Honey," Maggie murmured. "I read that honey could help with infections, and I was desperate to help you. I didn't have any of the other remedies, like silver powder, and I refused to …" She shook her head, as though she couldn't say any more.

"Refused to … ?" Phoebe asked and then blanched. She made a chopping motion with a hand, her breath leaving in a *whoosh* as Maggie closed her eyes in agreement. "Oh, never, please God never."

"Aye, that's what Eamon said. He begged and bartered with God, so you'd never suffer such a fate." Maggie sighed. "I feared his refusal would cause you to die, but it seems he was right."

99

Taking a deep breath, Phoebe lifted up slightly to help Maggie as she rewrapped her leg. Then Phoebe washed her hands on a washcloth to rid her fingers of the honey. "Why am I so tired?" she moaned, as she fell back against the pillows. She opened one eye to stare at Maggie. "I'm not pretending now."

Smiling, Maggie sat on the chair beside her bed. "No, I believe you. You're recovering, Phoebe. And you will for some time. Be patient."

"My sisters?" she asked, as she fought sleep. "Were they here at all?"

Gripping her hand, Maggie squeezed it. "Yes. Every day they chattered away worse than a pair of magpies—Lorena reading from a book and Winnifred complaining about her mistreatment from Finn and how she plans on revenge for your uncle." Maggie smiled. "I rather liked how inventive she is."

"Lorena's the fanciful one," Phoebe whispered with an indulgent smile.

"I'd say they both are." Maggie met Phoebe's gaze, pausing as though attempting to read the unspoken question held within. "You were never alone. Someone was always with you. And your sisters were dedicated to you." When that did little to ease Phoebe's worry, Maggie said, "They are living with us now. We won't let your uncle near them. We O'Rourkes are protective of those we've taken in."

Phoebe let out a sigh of relief, tumbling into a deep sleep.

~

M ary sat on the bed in the tiny room she shared with Seamus. She looked around the cramped space, smiling at the small signs of a shared life. Random buttons on the bureau to repair several shirts, a pebble from Maura from her recent ramble by a nearby stream, a comb with a few strands of Seamus's black and gray hair. A shawl draped over the back of a chair and a pair of thick socks at the base of it. She rose to take off her necklace and stilled when she saw a rock on the bureau that she didn't recall seeing before. Tracing the top of it, she stared at its familiar color but couldn't discern where or how she had seen the rock before.

"So, you've seen it then," Seamus murmured, as he came to stand beside her.

Mary sighed with pleasure, leaning backward to rest against him. Her head turned to nestle into the crook of Seamus's neck, and she gave a small purr of pleasure as his hands caressed her shoulders and down her arms. "Shay," she murmured, before turning to press into his chest, her arms folded over her chest, as though protecting herself from harm. "Hold me." Her breath caught as Seamus's arms banded about her, hugging her securely to him.

"What is it, *a ghrá?*" He kissed her head, his tender embrace eliciting a shiver. "You're well, my love. You're safe."

"I know," she whispered. "All is right in the world when I'm in your arms, my Seamus." She paused, as she unfurled her arms to wrap around his back and to tug him incrementally closer. "Eamon," she choked out.

"Ah, love, he'll be all right," he soothed. "He and Phoebe will find their way and will be happy. As our other lads are, as our Niamh is."

Mary sniffled and tilted her head up, so she could meet his worried gaze. "Aye, I know they'll find their way true soon enough." She paused as she shook her head, unable to prevent her eyes from filling with tears again. "Nay, my darling, 'tis that he's accepting I'm home. He doesn't look at me with distrust or fear any longer." She ignored the tears coursing down her cheeks as she gazed deeply into her husband's beautiful blue eyes. "When he burst into the kitchen the first night he returned from Saint Louis, a fraction of his tension eased when he saw me standing beside Maggie. As though he didn't believe I'd truly be here."

She turned her head into Seamus's hand, as his thumb swiped at her tears on one cheek. "I wanted to run to him, to hold him, and to ease him of his burdens. But he's a grown man, not my little Eamon." Regret filled her gaze as she bit her lip. "I am tired of feeling so bitter for all the time I lost with my children. Why did I have to be denied all those years, Seamus?"

"Oh, love." Seamus cupped her cheeks, lowering his head so their foreheads touched. "Ah, *a ghrá mo chroí,*" he breathed, calling her the love of his heart in Gaelic. "There's no reason. There's nothing to ease the pain of all the lost memories. But you have time now to make more memories." His smile filled with encouragement, he said, "Eamon's discovering that he can have faith and not be betrayed by it, thanks to you and your constancy, Mary."

She fell forward, clinging to Seamus again. "I'd be lost without you, Seamus. Promise me that you'll never do anything to risk being taken from me."

"I promise I'll do everything in my power to keep our family safe and to return to your arms every night." He kissed her head and eased away to unbutton his shirt and to prepare for bed. Mary slipped off her robe and slid under the covers, shivering as the evenings remained cool, even though the days were warm.

After Seamus curled around her in bed, she sighed as she slid her foot over his calf and used his chest as her pillow. "I'll never take such moments with you for granted." Her eyes drifted shut as he kissed her head. "What is that rock on the bureau?" Her fingers played through his black and gray chest hair, before he clasped her hand, tangling their fingers together.

"Do you recognize it?" he asked, his cheeks flushing.

Twisting so she could gaze into his eyes, she nodded. "Aye, but I don't know why I do. 'Tis just a rock."

"Nay," Seamus said in a low, nearly reverent voice. "'Tis not just a rock. 'Tis a small piece of stone from our land in Ireland." His eyes gleamed with the anguish that continued to resonate nearly twenty years after leaving his farm behind.

"Oh, *a chuisle*," she whispered, her hand rising to stroke through his hair and then his beard. She saw his eyes flash with deep emotions at her term of endearment for him, *my heartbeat*, in Gaelic. "Oh, my darling. I never knew you carried it with you."

He ducked his head, as he kissed her fingers. "We had so little space in the bags we brought with us. I should never have used any of the space for it." His eyes gleamed. "But I needed something from home."

"A talisman," she whispered, as tears spilled down her cheeks.

"Aye, and a reminder that I would again build all that I had lost."

Mary pushed up until she sat with her legs on either side of Seamus's waist, leaning forward so she bracketed him with her arms on either side of his head, her hands caressing his cheeks, and her hair forming a curtain, blocking out everything but the two of them. "Nay," she said in a fierce, low voice. "You did not lose anythin', Seamus. 'Twas taken from us. By misfortune and greed and bad luck. You did everything you could for us. And you still do." She kissed one eyebrow and then the other, before moving to kiss his cheeks.

His arms wrapped around her, pulling her down to rest

on his chest, her head on his shoulder. "Oh, Mary, I was lost without you," he breathed. "Let me love you."

"Please, my darling," she said, as she arched into his kiss. "Reassure me that you're here and never to be taken from me." Words were soon unnecessary, as they lost themselves to each other's touch, rekindling their passion for each other.

CHAPTER 7

Two days later, Phoebe grimaced as she moved, a razor-sharp pain shooting outward. With slow, deep breaths, she repositioned her leg and then relaxed as she struggled not to cry. She was exhausted. From fear. From uncertainty. From overwhelming emotions. From the lagging effects of the fever. She sniffled and turned her head to the side in case one of the sharp-eyed O'Rourkes watched from the doorway. She would not have them think of her as weak or pathetic.

Praying that Eamon would grow bored and leave her be, Phoebe grappled with her contradictory emotions. Her soul called out to him, and yet she dreaded seeing him. She resented his attentiveness now, when he had refused to show her such concern when they were on the steamboat. When she was a healthy, whole woman, he had spurned her. Now that she was an invalid, he was solicitous and caring. Anger and bitterness built, allowing her to stifle her tears.

At the sound of his voice, her gaze flew to his, and her defenses scattered.

"Hello, sunshine," Eamon whispered, as he stared at Phoebe with tenderness. "How are you feelin'?" His gaze roved over her, as though attempting to discern how she was without her telling him.

Tugging at the bedcovers, she pulled the blankets up to her chin. "Fine, Mr. O'Rourke," she whispered. After a confused, searching stare, she dropped her gaze to the floor. "There's no need to spend your time worrying about me."

"Phoebe," Eamon murmured, moving to sit in the chair by her bed. He touched her hand gently. When she jerked away from his soft touch, he stilled, any joy in his gaze leeching away. "Phoebe?"

She laid in the bed, shaking her head over and over again as he stared at her. "No," she whispered in an emotion-laden voice, filled with sadness rather than elation at his presence. "No, you do not have the right to all of a sudden care for me. To … to pity me because of my circumstances. I am strong. I am capable." Her voice broke. "I'll find a way to be fine. Without you."

She shivered and shook like she was in the throes of a fever again, but, after a few long minutes, her excess emotions eased, and she rested against her pillows, exhausted.

"I have never doubted your strength," he whispered. "I've never doubted your ability." He reached forward and cautiously rested his hand beside her blanket-covered hip. "I could never admire you more than I do, Bee."

"Don't call me that," she gasped out. "Not now. Not after the way you wanted nothing to do with me on the steamboat." She swiped at her wet cheeks, her chin quivering and her gaze mutinous, angry at herself for betraying any emotion.

He gripped her hand, stilling it from waving about in agitated circles. "You're wrong, love," he said in a soft cajoling voice. "I avoided you because I feared what I felt for you. I had promised myself to never care for a woman, and then there you were. I was terrified."

Refusing to gaze at him, she stared at the bureau with the chipped ewer and pitcher on top. "I don't believe you. Not after seeing your family these past days." She turned her head and stared at him with an emotionless gaze. "Why can't you be honest and admit what you truly feel?"

With a gaze filled with uncertainty and puzzlement, he shook his head. "You're not making any sense."

"You pity me. You pity me!" she yelled at him again, before she swallowed a sob and covered her face with her free hand. "And I hate you for it."

He froze at her whispered words. "No," he gasped, gripping her hand harder, tugging on it, as though to extract her love with as great an ease. "No, Phoebe. That's the last thing I feel. And, I pray, the last thing you feel about me."

"I'll never believe you," she sobbed. "I'll never trust your motives, ever again."

Letting out a stuttering breath, he whispered, "Please don't say that, Bee. Please. For we are to marry. And I can't imagine a lifetime of mistrust between us."

With tears pouring unheeded down her cheeks and chin, she gaped at him. "Why would you say such a thing? You know I will never marry you. Never."

Eamon dropped his head forward, resting it on the bed by her hip. He bounced it a few times and took a deep breath, as though attempting to find the words that eluded him. Finally he looked up at her, any teasing replaced by a resolute earnestness. "We will marry, Phoebe Mortimer. To protect you and your sisters from your conniving uncle. We will try to be happy. That is all I can promise."

"No," she whispered, staring at him as though he had the plague. "No."

Rising, Eamon dropped her hand and backed away a step. "Yes, Miss Mortimer. We will wed."

"You would force me into a farce of a marriage?" she whispered, her gaze filled with betrayal and pain as she stared at him. "I thought I knew what sort of man you are …" She broke off, as she attempted to swallow a sob.

"You know who I am, Bee," he rasped, flinching at calling her *Bee* rather than *Miss Mortimer*. Eamon closed his eyes for a long moment and then opened them again to stare at her with dulled determination. "Within a few days' time, the priest will visit, and we will have a quiet ceremony. For this isn't only about you but those you love. And I know you aren't the sort of woman to leave your sisters vulnerable to your uncle. I know you wouldn't want them to suffer as you did." He paused as he watched tears drip off her chin. His hands twitched as though he wished to swipe them away and to offer her comfort, but he remained across the room from her. "We will find a way forward."

She watched as he spun on his heel, leaving her staring at him in shock. How was she to argue against his logic, when it seemed his goal was to protect her and her sisters? How would she ever survive a marriage of convenience, when there was love felt only by one in the union?

∾

"Why are you such a baby?" Winnifred hissed. "I thought you were more adventurous, Lo. You did vote to come here."

Lorena tripped as Winnifred tugged her along beside her. "I was as desperate as you, Winnie." She gasped as she barely righted herself before tumbling into a pile of muck. She wrenched her arm free of her sister's hold and slowed her pace, forcing her sister to slow her march to the nearby creek. "Phoebe's the stalwart one. She would have found a way to survive with ten cents."

Winnifred snorted with disgust. "Shows her poor heritage, and I don't mean Mama."

Lorena sighed with relief as they arrived at the creek, finding a small shaded area and sitting on two large rocks. "We all have questionable antecedents, Winnie. And Mama's family isn't without blemish. Look at our uncle."

Settling beside her sister, Winnifred asked, "But is he truly that awful?" She waved her hand as though disregarding any argument Lorena could make. "I've spoken with him a few times, and he seems rather charming. And repentant for the way the O'Rourkes provoked him into speaking against us."

"Provoked?" Lorena asked with a quirk of an eyebrow. "How did they do that? It sounded to me as though he proffered those sentiments on his own." When Winnifred remained mutinously quiet, Lorena said, "He called us *worthless* and *unskilled*, Winnie."

"I'm certain he didn't mean you or me," she said with a shrug. "How could he have?"

Lorena studied her youngest sister, as though truly seeing her for the first time. "I see," she murmured. "How did you speak with him?"

"He loitered near the privy, and we spoke a few minutes," Winnifred said with a triumphant smile. "The O'Rourkes believe they can control us, but they are mistaken!"

Staring at the sky, as she studied the large puffy clouds, Lorena took a deep breath. Rarely in the past five years had she allowed herself to feel any deep emotions. However, anger and resentment toward her youngest sister had begun to stir. "Did you never consider that the O'Rourkes are generous in their concern for us and their desire to protect us from a man like our uncle?"

"Did you never consider that their actions prevent us from receiving our rightful inheritance?" Winnifred snapped. "Uncle is running out of patience, and he doesn't have to give us the money he's set aside for us."

Lorena sat in deep contemplation, her silence enraging her youngest sister.

"You may desire to remain a pauper, living off their kindness, but I dream of more." Winnifred pushed herself to stand, freezing in place as she looked toward town.

Lorena sat up straight, peering over the prairie grass to see Finn O'Rourke approaching. "For once, be nice."

"Ladies," Finn said. He smiled at Lorena and stared with unconcealed animosity at Winnifred. "How unfortunate you didn't inform any of us that you planned on a walk. Maggie was quite worried about you."

"We're not your prisoners," Winnifred snapped.

"No, but we would like to ensure you are well, regardless of your lack of gratitude," Finn said. "Although I hear the rooms above the Daybreak are quite … entertaining. Perhaps I should escort you there, so you could peruse them and choose one of your liking?"

"You vile man," Winnifred sputtered.

He shrugged. "Be careful, Winn. One of us will seek you out only so many times before we lose patience. Then you'll discover who truly is vile." He paused. "Come. 'Tis time for the midday meal, and we're starving." He heaved Lorena to her feet, winked at her, and ignored Winnifred's moaning the entire walk back to the house.

Phoebe sat propped up on pillows in the comfortable bed, although she had tired of the four walls a few days ago. She yearned to go outside, to explore the town, to watch the chickens peck in the ground. Anything but sit cooped up in this room, as the world carried on without her. Eamon had poked his head in a few times to ensure she was well but had refrained from speaking with her, as though understanding they would only argue.

Now her sisters sat with her, and she yearned for quiet. Or the cheerful chatter Maggie always provided. Instead a sullen silence interspersed a pointed pecking that left her feeling as though she were bleeding inwardly. She sighed at her thoughts, for they were becoming fanciful. She feared this was what boredom provoked in her.

"You'll have to forego any dream you have of walking down an aisle," Winnifred said, as she sewed. "He'll have to walk toward you." She snickered.

"I fear you won't have the wedding gown of your dreams, Phoebe," Lorena murmured, true regret in her gaze. "I've heard the seamstress wife is working on repurposing a nightgown as we speak."

"Just think. You'll have a marriage of necessity," Winnifred said with a giggle. "The one thing we promised each other we'd never have." She muttered a curse as she poked herself with her needle. "Do you remember the oath we took as girls, about the marriages we would have?"

Lorena bit her lip, shaking her head, as though to quiet Winnifred. However, Winnifred was in a mood to poke at her sister.

Nodding, Winnifred said, "Remember? We proclaimed we'd only marry men who were madly in love with us. Who were rich. And who would never expect us to have children." She smiled smugly as she stared at Phoebe. "It seems you'll fail on all three parts of the vow, dear sister."

"Why is any of that amusing?" Phoebe asked, as she stared at her two sisters. "If I marry him, it's to save you too."

Winnifred rolled her eyes and made a *tsk*ing sound.

"You've always been too dramatic, Phoebe. I thought that would be Lorena's role, as she fills her mind with fantasy stories. Now that I've thought about it, I'm certain our uncle never meant to harm you as you claim. You're exaggerating everything, as you always do."

Phoebe flushed beet red with incredulity and anger. "You seriously believe that I'd tear a whole in a wall, climb through it while ripping a gash in my leg and launch myself onto the neighboring business's roof one story below if I hadn't thought I was to be sold as a prostitute that very evening?" She shook her head, as though she didn't speak the same language as her sister. "I can't believe you'd doubt what I went through. What I knew I needed to do."

"We know you were disappointed Eamon was ignoring you on the steamboat. Now you have his attention again." Winnifred looked at her with a calculating expression.

"I did not go through all this to garner his attention!" She took a deep breath. "It's like you find my injury a source of entertainment. I had thought you'd be concerned that I almost died."

Winnifred rolled her eyes. "You've always embellished the truth about everything, Phoebe. We were concerned. We are concerned, but you're fine now. Well, almost fine."

"Your fever broke, so that's good," Lorena murmured, her gaze flitting to Phoebe over her book. Lorena appeared taken aback by Winnifred's comments, but she refrained from defending her middle sister from Winnifred's verbal barrage.

"What does that mean?" Phoebe looked from one sister to the other and back again, before slapping her hands on the covers beside her hips. "If you know something, it isn't fair not to share it with me."

Winnifred shrugged. "Isn't this like the time you knew Emory was going to leave me, but you said nothing? You let me spin my dreams and act a fool, rather than warn me." She smiled balefully at her sister. "Payback is always so unpleasant."

Closing her eyes as she prayed for patience, Phoebe spoke through clenched teeth. "I feared he would leave. I didn't know he would. I had hoped he was more honorable."

"Don't lie!" Winnifred shrieked. "He left because you told him the truth. It was my choice whether or not I told him everything, not you."

A tear trickled down her cheek, and Phoebe paused before speaking. "I never told him anything, Winnie." She met her sister's spiteful look. "I never liked him. I'll admit that. But I never told him anything."

Winnifred glared at her, her sewing forgotten on her lap. "Even now, even after almost dying, you can't do me the courtesy of respecting me. Of telling me the truth."

"I am telling the truth." Ducking her head, Phoebe closed her eyes. "I promised," she whispered. "I can't break my vow." She bit her lip and prayed for the strength to swallow back the words desperate to burst forth. However, she'd sworn on her mama's deathbed that she would take her secret to her grave, and she refused to break her promise.

Winnifred rose, her black hair hanging loose down her back. "Well, I can't break my vow to tell you what you're clearly not ready to hear yet. Lo?" Winnifred spun on her heel and left the room, Lorena following after her.

Phoebe sat on the bed in a dazed stupor, as she thought about her sisters' increasingly antagonistic visits. At first, they had seemed genuine in their distress about her injury. Then the sly comments had begun. And the insinuation that she hadn't been truly averse to the plans their uncle had for her. She shivered at the implication.

At the knock on the door, she pasted on a calm expression and forced a smile. "Maggie," she murmured.

Maggie stared at her with a penetrating gaze. "Your

sisters seem unsettled." At Phoebe's snort, Maggie smiled. "I have a cup of tea and a few cookies for you. Mum always said everything's better with tea and cookies."

Suddenly fighting tears, Phoebe nodded and motioned for Maggie to come in. After shutting the door, Maggie set the cup and plate on the small table beside the bed. "It's rose hip again. I want you to drink at least two cups a day to help fight infection."

Taking a sip, Phoebe sighed. "I don't mind it. It isn't nearly as bitter as the willow bark."

Maggie laughed. "Oh, you'll have more of that too, as I can see you are still in pain." She sat with a sigh. With a calculating smile, she looked at Phoebe. "Do your sisters cook?"

Phoebe ate her cookies and finished her tea, settling against the pillows and feeling much more relaxed than when her sisters had been present. "Cook? No."

"Can they use a knife to chop vegetables?"

Shrugging, Phoebe nodded.

"Excellent," Maggie said. "We're busy here, and Deirdre's overrun at the café. Their help will be most appreciated. And I'm certain they won't mind washing a few dishes here and there."

Phoebe covered her mouth, as a peal of laughter burst out. "You can't be serious. You think to have my sisters work?"

Maggie nodded. "Aye. All O'Rourkes work. One way or another. If you're young, and you study, that is your work. But, in the summer, we all pitch in and work hard. 'Tis the busy season and how we earn enough to survive for next year."

Watching the younger woman with admiration mixed with a healthy dose of envy, Phoebe said, "It must have been remarkable to grow up in such a loving family." When

Maggie froze, Phoebe wished she could recall her words. "I didn't mean to be impertinent."

Sighing, Maggie relaxed. "You're not impertinent. I assumed Eamon had told you about Mum and me." She paused as Phoebe continued to stare at her in abject befuddlement. "Mum and I were separated eighteen years ago from the family. A day after I was born." While Phoebe stared at her in astonishment, Maggie shrugged. "Da thought Mum and I had died. Mum thought he'd abandoned us. He remarried. Mum married Francois." Maggie shivered at the name. "Somehow we met up again here. And we've been a family again for a year now."

"But you're so self-assured, so secure in your place in your family."

"They accepted me as theirs the moment they saw me. They'd prayed for me every night in my absence," Maggie whispered, her voice tear thickened. "They never forgot me —or Mum—and 'twas like a miracle we were returned to them. And Da has never stopped giving thanks every night, as he says grace."

Tears leaked out as Phoebe stared at Maggie. "I don't know what it is to be part of such a family." She ducked her head, as though she were the most disloyal daughter and sister. "I've always known I must earn my mother's or my sisters' love. And I've never done a very good job of it."

"Earn it?" Maggie asked, her brows furrowed in confusion. "You don't earn love, Phoebe."

Phoebe sat forward, gasping in pain as she sat a bit too far forward and put pressure on her wound. With a hand to her leg, she held the other one out as she attempted to make her point to Maggie. "Of course you do. You dress properly, speak well, always are polite, and never have too strong an opinion. Appearances—and the family's reputation—must never be blemished."

Maggie gaped at her. "But then you're just a puppet if you act like that. Who are you if you don't speak your opinions? Who are you if you can't show you're mad or happy or sad?"

Clearing her throat, Phoebe played with the covers. "You have a chance to be loved."

Maggie gripped her hand, stilling the nervous fiddling with the blankets. "No, Phoebe, you never have a chance to shine if you act like that." Her gaze was filled with entreaty. "Spend time with my mum. Listen to her wise words. You'll understand that not everything you learned as a girl was what you should believe."

Phoebe nodded and then whispered, "Is there something you aren't telling me about my wound?" At Maggie's bewildered look, she said, "My sisters acted like I didn't understand something about my injury."

Maggie sighed and squeezed Phoebe's hand. "I feared they'd heard me talking quietly with Mum last night." Her gaze was filled with apologetic pleading. "I worry that you'll have a limp."

"Forever?"

At the breathed question, she nodded. "Yes, forever, although I hope with time it won't be as pronounced. I fear the muscles didn't knit together as well as I would have liked and that the infection harmed your recovery. We won't know until you walk freely, which will be in a few more days."

Phoebe's hand covered her wound, rubbing up and down the blanket, as though willing the flesh to heal. "I don't know what else I could have done," she said in a low voice. "I was terrified. Perhaps I was foolish and should have accepted my fate."

"Never," Maggie said in a firm, confident voice. "You are so brave, and your actions inspire me. You're not the only one who has demons to battle, Phoebe. And who fears being caught." With that, Maggie rose, picking up the plate and tea mug, as she returned to the kitchen.

Phoebe rested, suddenly wishing she could return to a simpler time, when her sisters still liked her and when Phoebe didn't have to worry about marrying a man who only tolerated her.

~

Maggie fixed herself a cup of tea, sitting with a groan in the empty kitchen. She eased onto the bench with her back against the wall, resting her head against a cool plank. Rather than worry about Phoebe, her mind wandered to imaginings of walking to the nearby creek to soak her feet, the birds serenading her. Against her will, her mind envisioned the return of Dunmore and her wholly inappropriate desire to leap into his arms when she saw him. She fought the rush of anticipation at that last thought as she knew she should consider him simply a friend. However, she had trouble ignoring his patient, fervent stares.

The door clattered open, and she jolted upright, grabbing her cup to prevent it from spilling. "Winnifred. Lorena," she muttered as she woke from her daydream. "What's the matter?" she asked around a huge yawn.

Winnifred pulled out a chair to sit at the table, while Lorena slipped through the kitchen to go to their shared room upstairs. "We're bored." She rolled her eyes as she watched her sister's retreat to read in their shared bedroom. "At least I am."

"Bored?" Maggie asked. "I'm sure Mum wouldn't mind help with the washing and cleaning and cooking. Nor would I."

"As if I would do that sort of work," Winnifred said with a

snort. "You seem to have an odd notion about who I am, Maggie."

Instantly alert, Maggie shook her head. "No, I fear you are completely mistaken about who you are. And about how far you can push those who would shield you from your evil uncle."

Winnifred sat in silence a long moment, swiping at sweat on her forehead with her handkerchief. "Now that I've had a little time to consider everything, I have to wonder if he is truly as awful as you claim. He did come here to claim us. He does want us."

"Have you always been delusional?" Maggie asked. "Phoebe seems lucid, but you …" She shook her head, as though she pitied poor Winnifred and her lack of intelligence.

"I'm as smart as anybody," Winnifred snapped.

"If you are, then you'll have the sense that God gave a goose and not attempt to reconcile with your uncle. Didn't you hear him say he has no use for worthless, unskilled women? He was speaking about you."

Winnifred shrugged. "I've come to realize he didn't mean me. *I'm* not worthless. I've got skills."

Frowning, Maggie studied her. "Although the implication is your sisters are? What kind of horrid person are you?"

The youngest Mortimer sister rolled her eyes at Maggie. "I'm smart enough to know I wouldn't have injured myself as Phoebe did, forcing everyone to focus all their time and energy on me."

Maggie watched her keenly. "No, that's the problem. Our focus isn't on you, and you resent your sister. Do you believe your uncle will treat you better than he threatened to treat Phoebe? Do you believe yourself more cunning and able?"

Winnifred stared at the ceiling, refusing to reply.

Maggie rose and moved to the stove to brew another pot

of tea. At the pounding on the back door, she frowned. "Speak of the devil." When the door creaked open, she gasped and grabbed the first weapon she found, hiding it in her skirts. "Mr. Chaffee, you know you were barred from this home. Please leave," Maggie said, standing tall with chin high.

He snorted. "Don't attempt to dissuade me from taking what is mine. I know my nieces are eager to reacquaint themselves with me." He speared a glance in Winnifred's direction. "Or are you not as eager to claim your inheritance as I believed you to be?"

Winnifred paled before regaining her bravado. "My desire to reside with the O'Rourkes shouldn't diminish your regard for your nieces. Or your desire to aid us."

"My regard for you?" Chaffee parroted with a huff of derision. "If Marilda had instilled any familial loyalty in you, you wouldn't have accepted the O'Rourke charity and wouldn't be on the verge of turning yourself into a pauper!"

Winnifred took a stuttering breath, edging ever-so-slightly in her uncle's direction.

"You can't possibly be charmed by this man? He's as smooth as an irate hedgehog." Maggie turned to Uriah with a huff, shaking her head in disbelief. "As I said before and as I say again, you are not welcome here. You have no right to be here. Get out."

"I have a right to speak with my nieces! I have been cruelly denied their company." A button from his cranberry waistcoat burst free with his agitated breathing.

"Or you've been denied the profits you thought yours," Maggie snapped. She screeched when Uriah reached for Winnifred, thrusting her aside. Acting with instinct, she raised the rolling pin high, letting out a roar as she clobbered him on the back of his head.

She watched as his eyes rolled back, and he fell to his

knees before landing on his belly. With rounded eyes, Maggie stared from him to Winnifred and then back again to the man laying lifeless on the kitchen floor.

"Did you kill him?" Winnifred screeched. "What will we do if he's dead?"

"Celebrate?" Maggie asked, as she kept the rolling pin in her hands. She shook as the adrenaline left her. She careened until the kitchen counter supported her weight. "Why would you mourn such a man?"

"How dare you judge him?" Winnifred hissed. "He's our only family. He ... came here because he wants us."

"Delusional," Maggie muttered, gasping as the back door burst open. She raised the rolling pin over her head to prevent an attack. "Dunmore," she gasped, dropping the pin to the floor with a clatter and throwing herself into his arms. "You're here."

Wrapping his arms around her, he closed his eyes to relish the short time she took momentary comfort from him. "Yes, darlin', I just returned and heard a scream. Scared the bejesus out of me." He eased Maggie away, keeping his strong hands on her shoulder. "What happened?"

By this time, Kevin and Niall had entered too. "Mags." Kevin yanked her from Dunmore's arms into his. "Tell me that you're all right."

"I'm fine. Uriah came here wanting the Mortimer sisters. Mum's with Niamh. The house was empty except for us." She shivered as she thought of all that could have happened. "I didn't have anything more than the rolling pin."

As Chaffee groaned, Kevin kissed her head and released her. He, Dunmore, and Niall picked him up, wrenching his arms and evoking more groans of dismay. Maggie heard her brothers informing him that this is what happened to men who attempted to abuse women as they dragged him from the kitchen.

"What will they do to him?" Winnifred asked.

Maggie spun to stare at her. "Nothing. Because they are honorable." She paused as she marshaled her anger. "Consider that, Winnifred, as you determine who you wish to be loyal to." She sat at the table again, as Winnifred left in a huff. Rather than spend any more time contemplating Winnifred and the confounding Mortimer sisters, Maggie's mind returned to the moment Dunmore held her. To the feel of his strong arms around her. To the sense she was cherished and safe. Oh, how she longed to feel that way again.

CHAPTER 8

The following day, Eamon sat at the table for the midday meal, smiling his thanks as his mum placed a bowl of stew in front of him. She then placed a loaf of thinly sliced brown bread, so that there would be plenty for all. Maggie set a crock of fresh butter on the table and sat beside him.

"She's improving, Eamon," Maggie murmured.

He studied his sister and frowned. "Aye, but I fear you're ailing. You're working too hard, Mags. Between caring for Phoebe and helping Mum feed all of us, you're exhausted."

Maggie shrugged, as she picked up a slice of the still warm bread. "Phoebe doesn't need much care now, and I'll start sleeping more again." Her gaze flit to the sisters, sitting in sullen silence a little ways down the table.

"Are they bothersome roommates?" he murmured. At her shrug, he nudged her.

"They like to complain. About everything. Especially Winnifred," Maggie said, as she widened her eyes for emphasis. "And I'm tired of hearing them bellyache when they do nothing." She clamped her jaw shut as she focused on Winnifred speaking to Lorena in a carrying voice.

"It's stew again, Lo," Winnie said. "And that horrible peasant bread." She sniffed at the food, as though it were only fit for the pig trough.

"I've had it," Finn snapped, snatching their bowls of stew and standing up. He turned to the sink area and set down the bowls with a clatter. "All you do is complain and find fault. Never do you show appreciation. Never do you give thanks for what's been offered you." His blue eyes gleamed with ire.

Eamon cast a glance in Da's direction, noting that, although Ardan and Mum attempted a conversation, Da listened intently to Finn and Winnifred's argument. Lorena sat with her head down, as though attempting to become invisible.

"How dare you?" Winnifred hissed. "I have every right to express how I feel."

"Do you?" Finn asked. "Do you ever feel thankful? Grateful?" He motioned to all the O'Rourkes in the room. "To all of us for taking you in. For makin' room for you in our home and for sharin' our food with you. We already have plenty to feed without havin' to worry about two ungrateful brats from Saint Louis."

"Ungrateful?" Winnifred gasped. "Ungrateful? How dare you accuse me of that when my pathetic sister, lying in her bed, is the one who has wreaked such havoc on your family."

Eamon stiffened at Winnifred's rasped words. Maggie gripped his arm, in an attempt to keep him from lashing out at the youngest Mortimer sister. "Give Finn a chance. Let's see how this goes," Maggie whispered.

"Do you have any idea what desperation is?" Finn asked, as he rested his hands on the table and leaned forward, his face near hers across the table. At her mutinous expression, he shook his head. "I thought you were entertaining on the ship, and arguing with you was a fun way to pass the time. I thought there was more to you than your limited view of the world, where everything bad that had ever occurred had been done deliberately to hurt you. Little did I realize how wrong I was."

"How dare you mock my pain?" Winnifred snapped.

"And how dare you mock the food we share with you? How dare you call the delicious bread Mum labors over 'peasant bread,' as though it were somethin' you'd never deign to eat? How dare you turn up your nose to *any* food?"

Winnifred rolled her eyes and crossed her arms over her chest. "Is this where you go on and on again about having survived starvation? The story does get a bit old." She shrieked and jumped as Seamus slammed his hand down on the table, causing everything on top of it to rattle.

"Enough!" Seamus roared. "I've had enough, and it seems my family has too." He met Winnifred's insolent stare. "You've had time to rest after your journey, far more time than my lads who went to work the day they arrived. You've acted like little princesses."

He shook his head when Winnifred acted as though she would dare to interrupt him. "Nay," he said in a low voice, his blue eyes gleaming with a deep coldness. "Nay, you are no princesses. You are no better than any of us. I've accepted you into our family because of your relation to Phoebe. My family has attempted to show you the same charity, which you have scorned and ridiculed in equal measure. I've had enough!"

"Da?" Eamon asked in a low voice, as he shared a worried glance with his siblings. Rarely did Da raise his voice, and, when he did, they knew he had been pushed too far.

"You," Seamus growled in a low voice, pointing to Winnifred and Lorena, "you will work and earn your place here with us, or you will not have a place here. You will act like members of our family."

"You promised to protect us," Lorena said, breaking her silence.

"Aye, an' I will. We will. And your part of this arrangement is that you will work and be respectful and grateful." He paused as he looked at the two sisters, his gaze roving between the two of them, one defiant, the other desperate. "Every member of our family works hard. And so shall you. Either here or at the café but you will work." He shook his head at any attempt at a discussion. "Starting tomorrow."

Eamon shared a shocked glance with Maggie before watching his future sisters-in-law sit in stunned silence. "Da has a way of quieting them down."

Maggie snickered and nodded. "Especially the youngest one. She's delusional in her belief that her life has been challenging. I fear life has many more disappointments in store for her due to her insolence."

～

Eamon sat on a crate in the warehouse after the store had closed, staring into space. He had spent a portion of the day working with Finn and Niall in the store, but he had been relegated to stocking shelves due to his surliness. Now that the store was closed, he had time to think through his interaction the previous day with Phoebe. His feet tapped and kicked at the crate, and he muttered to himself as he considered what he should have said, rather than what he did.

He jerked when Finn nudged his shoulder. "What's the matter, Eamon? You're out of sorts, and you're never discourteous to customers." He whispered the last bit as neither of them wanted Da to hear how Eamon had barked at a customer asking for advice on whether to buy a pickaxe. Eamon would generally have charmed him into buying three, rather than advising him that he'd be better off taking the next steamboat back to Saint Louis.

Eamon rubbed at his head and leaned forward, as though he had just suffered a severe body blow. "Phoebe doesn't want to marry me."

"What?" Finn gasped. "Now I'm convinced lunacy runs in that family." He rolled his eyes. "Winnifred isn't the only daft sister."

Eamon half smiled, as the ongoing feud between Finn and Winnifred had only worsened since the sisters had moved into the O'Rourke home. He looked up as his two eldest brothers joined them. "I never realized what hell it was to care for a woman and not have her return your feelings."

Ardan stared at him a long moment, as he and Kevin settled onto crates as well. "Phoebe cares for you, Eamon, but she's afraid. I've learned that, when Deirdre's afraid, I have to determine why and do what I can to rid her of that fear. Telling her that she's bein' foolish only enhances her fear."

Kevin nodded. "Aye, although I don't know why you're havin' trouble. You've always managed to enchant the lasses."

Ardan smiled in understanding. "Those other times you were just teasin', but this time it matters, aye?" When Eamon stared at him in silent misery, he looked at his brother with quiet understanding. "You've always found a way to live a charmed life, Eamon, finding joy even during the bleakest moments. You'll find your way through this."

Eamon rose and began to pace. "I don't want to charm her into marryin' me," he grumbled, his accent thickening to mimic that of his eldest brothers. "I want her to be as eager to wed as I am. To yearn for a time we are husband and wife." He turned away from his brothers.

Finn shrugged. "What are you waiting for? Tell her, and

all will be well." Finn motioned with his arms, indicating for Eamon to return home to proclaim his feelings to Phoebe.

"'Tisn't that simple, Finn," Eamon murmured. "She told me yesterday she'd never believe anything I told her again after our time on the steamboat. That she'd always resent me." He paused and met his brothers' startled gazes. "And hate me for marrying her out of pity."

"Feck," Ardan muttered, as he rubbed at his temple. "What did you do to the lass on the steamboat?"

"How could you have been less than a gentleman?" Kevin demanded, his anger building.

Holding up his hands to placate them, Eamon shook his head. "I was a gentleman, aye, but I realized after we'd become friends that I ... couldn't become attached to her. Refused to become attached."

"Why?" Kevin and Ardan shared bewildered looks. "You're perfect for each other."

Eamon stared into the distance, as though envisioning long past scenes. He closed his eyes. "I never wanted to bind myself to a woman who only felt resentment and duty to me, never anythin' more. I had just watched Declan have his heart torn out. I promised myself that I'd never be like him."

Ardan rose, cupping his strong hand around Eamon's neck. Peering deeply into his younger brother's eyes, he spoke as though only they were present. "I imagine you swore to yourself, sometime in the past, that you'd never allow yourself to be like Da." He paused until Eamon gave a nearly imperceptible nod. "That you'd never love someone so much that you'd lose a part of yourself if she died or left you."

Continuing to stare deeply into eyes that matched his own, Ardan spoke softly in a passion-laden voice. "Don't let the past, or the fears learned during the long years without Mum, define you now. For, if you do, you'll rob yourself of your chance for future happiness."

Eamon shrugged, his eyes silvery bright as he fought tears. "I fear I already have, Ard," he whispered out in a tear-choked voice. "I pushed her away, rather than gatherin' my courage to hold her close, an' she'll never forgive me."

Ardan shook his head. "Nay, you wee *eejit*, she'll find a way to forgive you and to rebuild her trust in you because you won't give up on her. For that's what you do for someone you love." He waited for Eamon to nod or to give some acknowledgment that he agreed, but Eamon remained silent and still. "'Tis what I did for Deirdre, an' I'd do it a hundred times over again to know I'd never lose her."

"How did you overcome your resentment?" Eamon whispered.

Ardan paused. "I knew Deirdre. I understood her, her hopes, and what most terrified her. And my presence in her life forced her to confront those fears. Just as Phoebe's presence in your life forces you to face the demons from your past. But you've yet to have the courage to explain to Phoebe why you acted as you did."

Eamon shrugged. "I tried, but she didn't want to hear."

Kevin spoke up in a soft understanding voice. "Imagine what she's feeling, Eamon. She's dependent on our family for everything right now. The man she thought would protect her and would support her attempted to turn her into a prostitute within hours of her arrival."

Eamon nodded and backed away from Ardan, sitting with a *thud* on the crate again. "She must feel deceived by everyone. Desperate. Devastated."

Finn cleared his throat. "Aye, an' from what wee Maggie told me, she'll most likely always walk with a limp." When Eamon shook his head in denial, Finn shrugged, as though chagrined to be the bearer of bad news. "Aye, her muscles were hurt or something. I didn't really understand all Maggie chattered on about."

129

Kevin smiled fondly, while thinking about his youngest sister. "She's found her passion in healing."

Holding his head in his hands, Eamon groaned. "If Bee knows this, 'tis another reason for her to believe I'm only offerin' to marry her out of pity." He looked at his brothers with desperation. "What am I to do?"

Ardan gazed at him with love and understanding. "Be brave. Tell her about everything in your past, Eamon. Everything that you'd rather not remember."

"Aye," Kevin whispered. "Everything that would help her understand why you acted as you did on the steamboat."

Eamon rubbed at his head, his mind swirling with what he knew he needed to do.

~

Seamus knocked on Phoebe's door, poking his head inside when she called out, "Enter." Chuckling, he strolled inside, carrying two mugs of tea. "You sound rather regal," he said with a teasing smile. When she flushed, he chuckled again. "How are you, lass?"

With a grimace, she pushed herself to sit up. "I feel a bit better each day, although it will be some time before I can leave your family in peace."

Studying her over the rim of his mug, his blue eyes flashed with irritation. "You are not a bother, Phoebe. Not now and not ever." When she looked down, her hands playing with the blanket, rather than meet his gaze, he sighed. "Come, lass. Why not tell me what's upset you to the point you consider yourself a bother and why you've provoked Eamon so that he's on the verge of fightin' the entire town?"

Her head jerked up, her eyes widening for a moment at his words. She then shook her head, letting out a huff of breath. "I was warned," she whispered. "Warned that the O'Rourkes don't play fair."

"Considering I'm not playin' at anythin', I don't know what you mean," Seamus snapped, immediately taking a deep breath. "I beg your pardon, lass. You've hurt my son, and I hate to imagine him in such pain." He set his mug beside the one she had yet to touch and leaned forward, resting his elbows on his knees as he stared at her with a fierce intensity. "I can't help my Declan. He's away, licking his wounds, and, I fear, chasin' after ghosts."

His gaze was distant a moment before he focused on her. "But I can aid my Eamon. And, by God, I will."

Phoebe scrunched up her face, attempting not to cry. Her voice emerged barely louder than a whisper, as she battled tears. "I'm not someone to be pitied."

With an incredulous snort, Seamus sat back in his chair. "From where I'm lookin' at you, you are." When his blunt words provoked such shock that Phoebe forgot all about crying, Seamus nodded. "Aye, you don't like frank talk, do you?"

An irate flush bloomed on her chest, rising up her neck to her cheeks as she glared at him.

"No, you're the sister who likes to maneuver and to manage the others, all with a smile and the appearance of being so accommodatin'." Seamus leaned forward again, his gaze hard and his voice low. "You have a good man, offerin' you his protection an' care. And more, if you would only open your eyes. You're a fool if you turn him down."

"Pity," she spat out. "I have his pity. And I refuse to settle for that."

With a shake of his head, Seamus motioned to her leg, wrapped in bandages under the blankets. "No, you have his true concern and his faithful regard. Which is more than can be said of your uncle." A pregnant pause ensued before he murmured, "Do you want me to introduce you to my friend, the Madam? She runs a much finer establishment than the one your uncle took you to. Her girls, the Sirens, earn a decent wage, although no one can say they don't work hard for all they earn."

Phoebe blanched. "I am not going to the Bordello or any such place."

Nodding, Seamus sat back in his chair, his anger apparently vented and now seemingly at ease, as he sipped his afternoon tea with the resident invalid, before setting down the mug again. "Then we are at an impasse," he murmured, his hands knitted together on his belly, as he stared at her, as though she were a curiosity. "What do you suggest we do, Miss Mortimer?"

Phoebe noted that he no longer referred to her in a familiar way and lifted one shoulder in a shrug. "Let me discover a way to help my sisters that doesn't involve your son."

"An' how do you imagine you'll do that?" Seamus continued to stare at her. "And what skills do you sisters have?" When she stared with surprise at Seamus, he added, "Or will you be the only one of the three to work? So you alone will support the three?" Respect flared in his eyes, as she met his challenging gaze. "Are you an heiress, but keepin' such good fortune to yourself?" At her quick shake of her head, he began to tick off ideas. "Are you hoping one of the men headin' to the mines will take you three on? Or do you think you'll manage to start a business and fend off all your uncle's schemes by your own wit and determination?"

"Just because I'm a woman doesn't mean I'm weak," Phoebe snapped, groaning as she jostled her leg.

"I've never intimated I think women are weak. My Mary, Niamh, and Maggie are the strongest people I know, an' they've lived through trials I don't care to contemplate." He let out a long sigh in an attempt to calm his strong emotions. "I do know this world isn't kind. It isn't just. And a woman alone, never mind three attractive single women, will prove too tempting to the worst sort of men. I'm afraid the sheriff is taken in by your uncle's fancy words and posturin' and would never protect you as he should, so I would forget appealing to that man for aid."

Phoebe's defiance deflated slightly, and she stared at him with a hint of desperation.

After a long pause, Seamus murmured, "I've heard my Mary and wee Maggie talkin', and it seems you're much more loyal to your sisters than they are to you." At her sharp indrawn breath, he watched her with compassion.

"They're all the family I have." Her eyes gleamed, daring him to disagree with her.

"For now," he murmured.

A tear slipped down her cheek, the silver line a herald of her inner grief. "I wanted more than a marriage of convenience, Mr. O'Rourke." She closed her eyes.

"Tell me, lass. What did you dream of when you were alone at night, wishin' for your weddin' day?"

Her eyes remained closed, and a smile almost broke free. "I imagined my groom would be waiting for me, anxious and excited, but nervous too. That I would walk toward him in a beautiful dress with a scalloped neck adorned with lace, and he couldn't take his eyes off me. That I would be so enamored of him that I wouldn't hear a word of the preacher's sermon, my whole focus on him. Our friends and family would be around us, celebrating, and we would have a wonderful party. And then we'd start our life together, in our own home." She paused before whispering, "A home filled with love, respect, and desire. So much more than regard and duty."

"You could have all that, Phoebe. You must believe in it and 'twill come true."

She opened her eyes, meeting Seamus's bittersweet gaze. "I have to accept my fate, don't I?" At his subtle nod, another tear leaked out. "Fine," she breathed. "I'll marry him. But nothing more."

"That's enough for now, lass," Seamus said as he rose. He squeezed her shoulder. "Rest. I know Eamon will visit you soon enough."

CHAPTER 9

Phoebe rested on her good side, taking pressure off her injured leg, while she stared at the wall and counted the minutes until she was compelled into a farce of a marriage. She pushed her head into the pillow, hoping it would muffle the sound of her tears as they spilled from her eyes.

Unbidden, images from her dream wedding formed in her imagination, like a mirage in the desert. Rather than a patched-together ceremony with a traveling priest, she envisioned standing in front of her parish priest, who had baptized her in Saint Louis. She would carry a bouquet of fresh flowers from her garden, her sisters beside her, with tables full of food waiting for the wedding party. Friends would smile as she walked down the aisle, wearing a beautiful wedding gown made of silk and satin, heading toward her groom, and he would stare at her in wonder, marveling that he was fortunate enough to marry her.

With a sob, she forced away that vision, knowing the following day's ceremony would be a sham. She'd lay in this bed, with Eamon standing beside her, in a patched-up nightgown, stiffly saying vows that bound them together forever, while little joy was expressed and even less elation was felt. Food might be prepared, but she'd have no stomach for eating it, and no friends would be present. Only her disapproving sisters would look on.

Fingers traced down her shuddering back. Stifling a shriek, she rolled over and then gasped out a groan of dismay as the rapid movement provoked severe pain in her leg. "What are you doing here? You shouldn't see me before the wedding!" Swiping at her sodden cheeks, she grimaced at Eamon, witnessing her sobbing.

"Oh, Phoebe," he whispered, sitting at her bedside and resting his elbows on the mattress. "Please tell me that you aren't sobbing because we are to wed."

She hiccupped out a breath, shrugging.

Blanching in the faint light cast by a lamp he'd left on the bureau, his eyes widened in horror. "If you find the idea of marrying me so repulsive, we don't have to wed." He closed his eyes, and he hunched forward in defeat. "I had hoped we could find a way forward, Bee."

"How?" she whispered. "I haven't seen you in days."

His piercing blue eyes pinned her in place, as he stared at her. "I've been here, every day. Eager to speak with you. But, every time I come to your room, you've been asleep. Or busy with Maggie. Or a sister. You never had a moment to spare for me." He yanked at his hair. "I know 'tis not proper for me to be here now, but I had hoped to speak with you before the weddin'. Alleviate some of your fears."

Tears trickled down her cheeks, but the outpouring of sobs had ceased. "How would you do that?"

"I want to explain why I acted as I did on the steamboat. I need you to—" He broke off when she shook her head and looked at him with deep disappointment. "Bee?"

"I don't want to hear your excuses. I don't want to hear all the reasons you believe I should trust you now. You and I both know why you acted like you did."

"Do we?" His brows furrowed as he stared at her. "Why?"

"You were bored, and, for a while, you found me entertaining. Then you found me more tedious than the journey."

"No—Bee, that's not true!"

She stared at him with loathing mixed with sorrow. "I heard you, Eamon. Talking with Finn. I heard you say only a fool, or a desperate man, would ever bind himself to one of the sisters."

Eamon shook his head, over and over again, as though that action would somehow keep her from believing what she'd heard. "No," he rasped. "You must have misheard. I never said that." He held up his hand as she was about to argue with him. "Finn may have very well said that, but not me. I would never have said that," he repeated. After a moment, he whispered, "I readily admit I was mean and dismissive to you for the last weeks of the journey. Let me explain."

"No, Eamon," she said in a cold voice. "I have no need of your excuses." She took a deep breath, her gaze as frigid as her voice. "But let me reassure you, I will be a good wife to you, Eamon. I will find a way to bring harmony into our home."

He nodded dumbly, his shoulders stooping forward. "A good wife, of course. Harmony. What more could I want?"

She sat in stony silence, the tracks of her tears now drying on her cheeks as she fisted her hands in agitation. "I have the right to one last night alone. I understand, after tonight, I will be at your beck and call. But tonight, at least, remains mine."

"Bee," he whispered. "Please, it won't be like that."

She stared at him with implacable stillness, until he rose

and slipped from the room, the door closing with a quiet *click*. Only after he left did she allow the tears to fall again.

~

The next morning Mary knocked on Phoebe's door, poking her head inside after she heard a weak "Enter." She offered a tentative smile as she stared at the woman lying on the bed, who expressed as much eagerness for a wedding as a surgeon about to perform an amputation. At the younger woman's gentle nod, Mary entered and closed the door. "Are you well today, Phoebe?"

With a shrug, Phoebe remained cocooned under the blankets, as though she could prevent what was to come if she refused to participate.

Mary perched on the chair beside her bed, her hands reaching forward to stroke her forehead in search of fever. When Phoebe flinched at her touch, she yanked her hand back. "Forgive me. It has become habit these past days." She sat in stilted silence for a few moments, her earnest gaze taking in the miserable young woman. "Are you in pain?"

With a shrug, Phoebe whispered, "I'm always in pain. I fear I'll never know a time without pain again."

Mary nodded, her hand slowly reaching forward to clasp Phoebe's, even though it was buried under a pile of covers. "In this life, there are all kinds of hurts, lass. Some are physical, like your leg pain, and I pray every night that your wound heals and that you'll soon have moments you forget you were ever injured in your act of bravery." She squeezed Phoebe's hand. "Other aches are much deeper, and harder to soothe, for they are wounds to our souls. The scar is not as easy to see, aye? But the pain is all the more acute for it."

She smiled softly as tears coursed down the younger

woman's cheeks. "Oh, lass, I never meant to make you cry." She swiped at her cheeks. "Eamon will be irate with me."

"He should be thankful for you," Phoebe sputtered out, mouthing her thanks as Mary handed her a handkerchief. "I've never known what it is to have a mother truly concerned about *me*."

"Ah, lass, I'm certain you are mistaken. All mothers worry about their babes. It's just that some are better at showing their concern than others." She gazed at Phoebe a long moment before whispering, "Does the mere notion of marryin' him send you into a panic?"

Phoebe shook her head.

Smiling, Marry squeezed her hand again. "Good. For I know he's out there, pacin', eager to have you as his bride."

Phoebe swiped at her cheeks. "I wish we weren't forced to marry to protect my sisters."

Mary tilted her head to one side and stared at her in wonderment. "Due to your sisters?" She fought to hide her amusement but knew she failed when Phoebe glared at her. "Your sisters have little to do with Eamon's decision, lass. 'Tis all about you."

"You're wrong, Mrs. O'Rourke, but I thank you for trying to ease my fears."

Mary sat in quiet companionship with Phoebe for a few moments. "I have no idea what occurred between you and Eamon on the steamboat. 'Tis none of my business. However, I would ask that you think about your life. Have you never done something you regretted? Have you never acted out of fear?" She paused as she saw Phoebe staring at her with a mutinous stubbornness. "I almost lost my chance for happiness again with Seamus. I refused to risk my future happiness by clinging to the pain of my past disappointments."

"How?" Phoebe whispered, the word bursting forth, as

though torn from her. "How were you brave enough to trust him?" She shrugged. "I never realized you and Mr. O'Rourke had fought."

"Oh, lass, we never fought. We had a horrible misunderstandin'. I gave birth to Maggie soon after our arrival in Montreal, nearly nineteen years ago in the middle of a typhus outbreak. One of the nuns moved me to a small shed to keep us safe from the illness. Another mistakenly informed Shay we had died. He left Montreal, believing he was a widower, while I waited for him, thinking he had deserted me and my babe." Her eyes were haunted, remembering those long-ago moments of grief, fear, and determination to survive.

"What did you do?" Phoebe asked, fascinated at Mary's story, even though she'd heard a similar version from Maggie.

"I married another man." Mary shifted uncomfortably, now in discomfort at recalling her time away from the O'Rourkes. "A mean man who relished punishing me. Thankfully he died. And I traveled here with my brother-in-law, who was just as cruel."

"And you met Mr. O'Rourke and fell into his arms again!"

Mary laughed. "Oh, dear God, no," she said. "At first, I didn't trust Seamus, and I was filled with anger. And hurt. And resentment that he seemed unscathed by our years apart, while I ..." She took a deep breath. "I suffered."

Phoebe scrunched up her brows, as she thought through what Mary said. "How did you forgive him?"

Staring over Phoebe's shoulder, as though seeing a distant scene, she smiled. "I listened to him. I heard the sincerity in his voice. I realized he had suffered just as greatly without me as I without him." She paused, recalling those moments of reconciliation with Seamus. "And I listened to my heart. I knew I wanted to be with Seamus. I'd never been happy without him. I knew I could be again, if I were brave."

Phoebe frowned. "But Mr. O'Rourke loved you, Mrs. O'Rourke. It's obvious when he stares at you." She ducked her head. "Eamon sees me as a sister."

"Does he?" Mary asked in feigned innocence. "I fear you are as blind as he's been." She paused as Phoebe considered Mary's words. "Now, Maggie, Aileen, Deirdre, an' I want to help you prepare for your weddin'. Niamh wanted to be here too, but Nora believes she should be on bedrest as she nears her time. Niamh sends her best wishes. 'Tis important to have your womenfolk around you as you prepare for such an important day." Mary paused and studied Phoebe, who remained silent. "Assumin' you will marry the lad?"

Phoebe ignored the omission of her sisters from the list of women who would help her today. "Yes, I'll marry him," Phoebe said. "I gave my word."

Rising, Mary kissed her head. "You won't regret it, lass. Soon you'll be an O'Rourke, an' I'll have another daughter. 'Twill be yet another reason to celebrate." She slipped from the room to gather the O'Rourke women, leaving Phoebe deep in thought.

When Mary returned soon afterward with Aileen, Maggie, and Deirdre on her heels, Phoebe clenched her hands together and battled tears. Each woman carried something to enrich her wedding day. Mary carried a brush, her nimble hands playing through Phoebe's gold-spun locks as she asked if Phoebe wanted her hair up or down. Maggie carried a pan filled with warm gardenia-scented water, towels draped over her shoulder to aid Phoebe with her sponge bath.

Sighing with relief as she felt pampered for one of the first times in her life, Phoebe asked Maggie, "How did you know?"

Maggie smiled at her with her impish charm. "It's your wedding day. Every woman should be spoiled a bit on her big day."

As Deirdre explained the menu for the party, Phoebe's eyes rounded and filled with tears. "Now there will be roasted venison, vegetables, mashed potatoes, fresh bread, and cake. Always cake." She laughed as Maggie sighed with delight. "I know it's a simple meal, but, with our numbers, there will be plenty, and we won't be chained to the stove."

"It's not simple at all. I can't believe you've gone to such trouble for me," Phoebe whispered, her eyes glistening with unshed tears. Mary squeezed her shoulder, her hair shining like a beacon as it hung loose.

"It was no trouble, Phoebe. You are my new sister. We celebrate each other's happiness together." Deirdre beamed. "And it always brings me joy to cook for the family."

Mary clasped Phoebe's hands, staring deeply into her eyes, before frowning at the confusion in Phoebe's gaze. "We are your family now too, Phoebe, and it brings us pleasure to help you prepare for your wedding to Eamon. For I know you will be blessed. With happiness, joy, and love." She squeezed Phoebe's hands again.

Phoebe's eyes swelled at Mary's words. "I've never felt such kinship."

"Oh, lass. Don't cry, or Eamon will scold me," Mary teased. "Besides, we've saved the best surprise for last." She turned to Aileen.

Aileen had remained silent in the background, but she now stepped forward, cradling a gown over her arm. "I wanted to make you something beautiful for your special day. I wanted it to be partly a surprise as well, so I hope this gown comes close to your dream wedding gown." She carefully unfolded the gown and held it up for Phoebe to see. The cream-colored satin gown had a scalloped neckline with touches of lace at the wrists. "Do you like it?" When Phoebe remained silent, her mouth opening and closing as she shook her head in wonder, Aileen frowned. "Do you not like it?" Aileen stared in dumbfounded silence at her mother-in-law. "But Seamus said this is what you wanted. What you dreamed of."

Openly crying now, Phoebe nodded. Reaching out a shaking hand, she traced a finger over the finely wrought gown. "How can this be for me?"

Aileen passed the gown to Mary and enfolded Phoebe in a gentle hug. "Oh, Phoebe, of course it's for you. You must have known that we never would have wished for you to be married in your night-robe." She giggled and shook her head. "We all have a bit more vanity than that."

Phoebe laughed, her spirit light and filled with hope at the kinship offered so effortlessly by these O'Rourke women. "Thank you," she whispered, looking at each woman for her priceless gifts.

After exchanging smiles, each of the O'Rourke women gently hugged the bride-to-be, all four whispering a blessing into her ear.

～

Eamon took a deep breath as he stood outside the door to Phoebe's room. He felt as though the usual wedding day ceremony had been flipped on its head, as she waited for him to approach her. Mary had stepped outside for a moment to delay Eamon a bit more, reassuring him that Phoebe was still getting ready.

When his mother returned not long afterward and

nodded that he may now enter Phoebe's room, he took one more deep breath, and Eamon crossed the doorway. Ignoring his chattering family, the sullen looks from her sisters, and the quiet presence of the priest by the head of her bed, he stared at Phoebe.

Rather than the exhausted, pale woman who had fought a terrible illness, she sat in a resplendent glory, her hair cascading over her shoulders, gleaming like the sun shone on it. Her mysterious green eyes were filled with trepidation and, he hoped, a touch of eagerness. She held a small bouquet of fresh-cut flowers, and her wedding gown had beautiful embroidery at the neck and sleeves. Kevin and Niall played a sweet tune on a tin whistle and a fiddle, a song that reminded him of home and filled him with the promise of tomorrow.

Smiling, he remained wholly focused on her as he approached her. "You are a vision." He tried to ignore her instinctual grimace, not believing him. Once he reached her bedside, he motioned for the priest to move to face the two of them. Reaching down, he clasped one of her hands, but couldn't raise it to his lips without causing her distress. Tugging the chair to the side of the bed, he sat beside her, kissing her palm as he gazed deeply into her gaze. "Hello, love," he murmured.

"Eamon," she breathed. She bolted as the priest spoke in a deep voice.

Fighting a chuckle, Eamon continued to gaze deeply into her eyes, ignoring the man's words, until it was time to exchange vows and to give her a ring. He slipped his simple gold ring on her finger, raising her hand to kiss the finger after it slid into place.

As the priest intoned, "You may kiss the bride," Eamon leaned forward, gently kissing her on her lips. Rather than deepening the kiss as he would like, he eased away to accept the congratulations from their family. For she was an O'Rourke now.

He rose, accepting his father's embrace. Soon he moved to his brothers, until he arrived at Ardan. "Ard," he whispered.

"Congratulations, Eamon," Ardan said with pride. "Endeavor to understand her needs, what her desires are, and you will be happy."

Eamon studied his eldest brother for a long moment. "I must focus on her," he murmured. At Ardan's nod, Eamon smiled. "Well, that will be no hardship, for she fascinates me."

Ardan chuckled. "You say that now. Wait until she infuriates you." He stepped aside to allow Maggie to throw herself into Eamon's arms.

"Eamon!" Maggie squealed. "I'm so excited. Finally you've married her. Now she's truly my sister." She kissed him on his cheek.

"Thanks, Mags," he said, as he watched his bride flush at something Finn said. He frowned as he saw her delight fade at her sisters' approach. "I'd think they'd be pleased for her."

Maggie shook her head, following his gaze to watch the sisters interact. "No," she murmured with a shake of her head. "There's a difficult history between them that I don't understand. I fear it only brings your bride pain."

He grunted his agreement as he saw the pleasure of the moment leech from Phoebe's expression. With a squeeze to Maggie's arm, he moved to Phoebe's side again. Pushing his way through the sisters, who had formed a small wall around their sister's bed, he barreled his way to his wife's bedside. Bending over, he kissed her cheek, murmuring, "Do you want them to leave?" At her subtle shake of her head, he rose with a sigh.

"Eamon, I had wondered if you would arrive today," Winnifred said in a sly, cutting voice. "Made for a nice change from the usual wedding tension. Generally the guests are left to ponder if the bride will make a run for it."

Stiffening at the snide comments, Eamon glared at her. "You had no reason to doubt I would arrive to marry my bride. I adore her, and I was eager to marry her." He bent over to kiss her softly again, before facing Winnifred. "Anyone who questions my sincere devotion to her is mistaken. And, I fear, not to be trusted."

Winnifred stepped away. "Forgive me for wanting to wish my sister well in her marriage. I had thought congratulations were in order."

"As long as they are sincere," Phoebe murmured, her gaze toward Winnifred filled with mistrust and hurt.

Eamon watched as Phoebe looked to Lorena, but her eldest sister remained quiet. After a moment fraught with tension, his bride's sisters sauntered away. Soon Finn was bantering with Winnifred, and Lorena had escaped the crowded room.

Eamon sat on the chair beside her, grasping her hand. "What can I do for you, Bee?" He frowned, as she pasted on an impersonal smile.

"Nothing, Eamon. Everything went as we expected. We are married. And all is well."

Swallowing what more he would have said, he accepted a glass of whiskey from Finn as Da raised a glass to toast the newlyweds. Eamon forced himself to focus on his father's blessing, rather than his growing unease.

~

Phoebe watched as Eamon moved away from her to interact with his family, and she wished for the thousandth time she could move about freely. She stared with envy at Maggie, who laughed and flitted from group to group, before she sat with a joyful sigh by Phoebe's side.

"Who is the man you just spoke with?" Phoebe asked, staring at a man who lurked in the shadows and corners of the room. He was taller than the O'Rourke men with long russet-colored hair. He seemed to only have eyes for Maggie, as his gaze tracked her every move around the room.

Maggie glanced in the direction of Phoebe's gaze and smiled, although she couldn't hide a flush. "Oh, you mean Dunmore?" She shrugged in an attempt to appear nonchalant. "He's a family friend."

Shaking her head, Phoebe murmured, "I think he's more than that." She broke off what more she would say at a commotion in the doorway. A finely dressed woman in a shimmering turquoise dress entered the room. Phoebe stared at her, attempting to remember where she had seen her before. "Who's that?"

Maggie beamed at the new arrival. "Nora. The Madam. She's a close friend of the O'Rourkes."

Phoebe watched the Madam embrace first Seamus and Mary before Eamon. Phoebe fought an irrational anger at the woman touching her husband and forced her hands to unclench. When she saw Eamon's discomfort, a portion of her ire eased.

As Nora approached her, Phoebe fidgeted and bit her lip. The woman's eyes were too knowing. Too all-seeing. Phoebe felt as though a fly stuck in a spider's web, and she had no desire to be so trapped.

"Nora!" Maggie squealed, as she jumped up and hugged the older woman. "You missed the ceremony."

Grimacing, Nora sat in the chair beside Maggie. "I'm afraid I couldn't escape my duties this morning. Although I'm delighted to arrive while you are celebrating." Her astute gaze landed on Phoebe, and she smiled with compassion. When Maggie left to aid her mother, Nora scooted over to the chair directly beside Phoebe that Maggie had vacated. "I'm happy to see you are recovering from your ordeal."

With rounded eyes, Phoebe blurted out, "You were the woman on the boardwalk. The one I had hoped would help me."

Nora nodded. "Yes. I did what I could. I spoke with the O'Rourkes."

Rolling her eyes, Phoebe said, "As if they would have done anything." She gasped as Nora gripped her hand.

"Never doubt their sincerity in aiding you, Miss Mortimer—or should I say, Mrs. O'Rourke now?" Nora said in a low, solemn voice. "Do not presume you understand what others would or would not do for you by the disappointments of your past." Her gaze flickered to a pouting Winnifred. "By the lack of charity of those who should have always supported you."

Phoebe nodded, flushing. "I managed to save myself."

"Yes, at great personal cost," Nora said. "Have pride in what you accomplished, but do not doubt that the O'Rourkes had a plan afoot to aid you." She smiled as she saw Mary and Maggie returning with slices of cake. "I see I missed Seamus's blessing. What a pity, as I always enjoy them." When she saw Phoebe turn even more into herself, Nora murmured, "Again, girl, don't doubt you deserved his blessing. If Seamus said it, he meant it."

At Maggie's shriek, anything Phoebe would have said was forgotten. Maggie was on the floor, two pieces of cake and shattered dishes around her, as Phoebe's uncle stood in the doorway. Dunmore had moved with surprising speed to aid Maggie and to prevent any further harm from befalling her, while a wall of O'Rourkes had formed near the doorway.

"You are not welcome here, Chaffee," Seamus said. He

stood tall with arms crossed over his chest as he faced his adversary.

Nora gripped Phoebe's hand, quietly soothing her, as Phoebe saw her uncle for the second time since she had arrived in Fort Benton.

"Where is she? If she's whoring for anyone, she's whoring for me!" Uriah Chaffee yelled. His jowls jiggled as he bellowed.

"How dare you?" Eamon said, as he stepped forward, almost blocking her uncle from her view. "She's my wife, and she is a respectable woman. You have no say over her life ever again."

Uriah snorted. "Until you bed her, the wedding is worth nothing more than the paper it's written on." He fisted hands at his hips. "And having your father proclaim your union is not binding."

Seamus shook his head. "No, Uriah. We had a priest, and the union is binding. Your nieces are out of your sphere of influence, for any harm to any of the Mortimer lasses is as though you've harmed an O'Rourke."

Panting and looking around at the unified front, Uriah hissed, "You can't keep me from my own flesh and blood. It's unconscionable!"

"Unconscionable?" Eamon asked. "I would have thought that was what you did. Draggin' your newly arrived niece to a saloon to turn her into a prostitute." He shook his head. "My marryin' her because I deeply care for her is the opposite of unconscionable."

"I am her guardian, and she agreed to my plans for her. She was eager when she met Mr. Bell."

"Lies!" Phoebe said in a tear-laden voice that cut through the room as though she had bellowed it. "Lies, Uncle. You were only too happy to have that man carry me off over his shoulder, kicking and screaming in protest, as you contem-

149

plated your potential earnings. And I know you envisioned doing the same with my sisters."

Uriah glared at her with malevolent hatred. "If you'd done what was expected of you, you'd never have been injured, and the O'Rourkes would never have interfered in our affairs!"

Eamon snorted, his hands on his hips. "You are a fool. We would have outbid any and all men in that saloon for Phoebe. She never would have suffered as you had planned."

Phoebe gasped as she heard of their plan, confirming what the Madam had tried to tell her just moments ago.

Uriah paled and then flushed beet red again. "I could have beggared you. I could have gained control of your store." He glared again at Phoebe, as though she were the destroyer of all his dreams. "If only you hadn't escaped!"

Smiling at his wife, Eamon returned his focus to Uriah. "How does it feel to be outsmarted by a woman?" He took a menacing step toward the man. "Today is my weddin' day. The only such day I'll ever have. You are not an invited guest. You are not a desired guest. You've already ruined two pieces of Deirdre's delicious cake. Leave while you can still walk."

"Is that a threat?" Uriah asked.

"Save it," Seamus snapped. "We know you proclaim to be a lawyer, but be forewarned. You harm one of us, and you will pay the price." He paused as he saw the man swallow as he nervously looked around the room, filled with virile men, intent on protecting those they cared about, which included his nieces.

"I have every right to be here!" Uriah proclaimed. "I should be considered family too!"

Laughing derisively, Seamus shook his head. "Not while I draw breath." He leaned toward the paunchy lawyer. "If you are the high-falootin' lawyer you claim to be," Seamus said, adding a thick note of doubt to his tone, "you know we can bar you from our home. *Out.*"

Huffing out a frustrated breath, Uriah stormed from the room. Seamus followed him to ensure he left and that Mary was well.

Nora squeezed Phoebe's hand one more time before releasing it. "Seems you'll have trouble with your relations for a while." With an apologetic smile, she murmured, "I fear it would be best if that poor man either left town or drowned in the river."

Nora rose as Eamon approached, vacating her seat for Phoebe's husband. Nora whispered something to him, before stroking a hand down his arm. "Goodbye for now, Mrs. O'Rourke," Nora said. "I wish you all happiness."

Phoebe met her gaze fleetingly. "Thank you, Nora." She bit her lip as she stared deeply into Eamon's concerned gaze. "I'm sorry."

At her whispered words, he frowned. "For what? For having a miserable excuse for an uncle?" He smiled. "I'm certain, if we still lived in Ireland, I'd have relations who'd embarrass me too." He raised her hand and kissed it. "Don't worry, love. If he doesn't understand now, he soon will that you are an O'Rourke and not to be trifled with."

CHAPTER 10

That evening, Eamon chuckled as he closed the door to the bedroom he would share with Phoebe as she continued her convalescence, any outward display of his gaiety disappearing with the *click* of the door. He rested his head against the cool wood, taking deep breaths as he struggled with an overwhelming sorrow. Rather than joy and hope and wonder, the day had been filled with stilted silences, forced laughter, and a sickening sense he had just made the greatest mistake of his life.

Although he had relished defending her from her uncle, he knew she doubted the sincerity of the emotions behind his desire to marry her. Even though she had attempted to hide her instinctual stiffening at his approach, her strained conversations and pasted-on smiles had made it abundantly clear she had little desire for his company.

Rather than move through the room, chatting with his brothers, he would have far preferred spending the day sitting by her side and visiting with her. However, her cool demeanor had made him feel unwanted. He feared he would feel this way forever.

"Ignoring me won't make me go away," her voice called out from the bed.

He stiffened before nodding and turning to face her. "I know. But then I thought that was your role. Pretending I didn't exist." His blue eyes flashed with hurt, as he beheld her dressed in a beautiful nightgown with lace at the collar and sleeves—another gift from Aileen. Rather than remark on Phoebe's beauty, which he'd quickly learned she would discredit, he moved to the bureau to undo his cuff links.

"What do you think you are doing?" she asked, her voice shrill and trembling with a panic she couldn't conceal.

"Undressing."

"Oh, no, no, no, no," Phoebe stammered out. "You are not sleeping with me. I'm still injured. What kind of man are you?"

He spun to face her, his jaw clamped so tightly shut that it ticked with his anger, while his gaze shone with hurt and disillusionment. "I'm your husband, Bee. The man who pledged to always honor and protect you today." He pointed to the space next to her bed. "Right there, to be precise." Shaking his head, he stared at her in dismay. "How can you believe I'd do anythin' to harm you?"

She had pulled the covers up to just under her chin. "I … I'm not ready."

"Knowing you, you'll never be ready," he muttered, as he yanked off one boot and then the other. After tossing his waistcoat over the back of a chair, he pulled down his suspenders and tugged his shirt free of his pants. "Don't worry," he muttered, as he toed off his socks and heard her breathing ratchet up. He feared she was on the verge of hyperventilating. "I'll sleep in my underclothes. But I am sleeping next to you. I'll be damned if I'm consigned to that uncomfortable chair for another night."

"Another night?" she whispered in confusion and then

yelped, forgetting his comment as he crawled over her like a panther.

He laughed, humor and joy lighting his expression for one of the first times that day since his da's blessing. Everything had turned sour then. "Don't make so much noise, or the family will get ideas."

"Hush," she gasped, covering his mouth with her fingers. Her eyes rounded when he tenderly kissed her fingers.

"I promise on all I hold holy, Bee, I'll never intentionally do anything to hurt you. Never again," he whispered. "Let me under the covers." He waited as he saw uncertainty battle with hope, until she eased her death grip on the blankets with the hand not touching him. "Thank you." He crawled under the covers, sighing with pleasure. "Punch me if I snore," he mumbled, as he closed his eyes.

"Snore?" she asked, leaning up on one elbow. "You snore?"

He shrugged. "Most men do." He opened one eye to stare at her indignant expression. Her wariness and anger were gone, her innate curiosity shining through. He gazed at her lustrous blond hair, gleaming green eyes, smooth creamy skin, and his breath caught. "God, you're beautiful, Bee," he whispered, frowning when he saw the openness in her gaze shutter. Perplexed, he leaned up on one elbow to stare at her as she collapsed onto her back, breaking eye contact and attempting to ignore him.

"Why, Bee? Why do you deny what you are?"

She smacked him on his arm, and he grunted from the surprise of it. "Why do you lie? I know what I am. A plain woman, not blessed with the curves, the personality, or the beauty of my sisters." She snapped her mouth shut, as though she had revealed too much.

"Plain?" he breathed, his hand reaching forward to tangle through her silky hair. "How could you ever think yourself plain?" This time, he pressed his fingers to her lips, his smile tender as he gazed deeply into her eyes. "You're beautiful. Bewitching. Captivating." He paused as he saw pain in her gaze. "For some reason, you were never shown how remarkable you are." He leaned forward, softly kissing one cheek and then the other. "But you're also much more than your beauty, Bee."

"I am?" she gasped, her breaths emerging as pants.

With humor and love shining through his voice, he ran his thumb from her temple down her cheek to her jaw and back up again. "Yes, so much more." He kissed her jaw and nibbled a path down her neck, grinning when she arched into his touch. He eased away, his hand still tracing circles on her skin as he looked deeply into her gaze again. "You're smart, kind, patient, and loyal." He paused. "And you're mine. To cherish and to adore."

She bit her lip. "Are you mine?"

He frowned at the question.

"Never mind," she blurted out. "I'm foolish." She yanked on the covers, thwacking him in the face. He toppled to his side, as he massaged his head and blinked rapidly.

"For the love of God, woman, you could have blinded me," he muttered, rubbing at his eye.

"Good night, Eamon." She had pasted on a placid expression, as she rested on her back.

Leaning over her, he blew out the candle and then settled beside her. "Good night, Bee, my wife." After many long moments, when he heard her breathing deepen and even out as she slipped into sleep, he whispered, "Aye, love, I am yours."

～

Phoebe woke, experiencing the deepest sleep she'd had since departing Saint Louis. It was as though all her concerns had decided to give her overwrought mind a night off. With a satisfied sigh, she stretched. In that moment, she realized she was not alone in her bed. Just as quickly, she remembered she had married the previous day.

Married.

She rested with her eyes closed, as she fought panic at the thought of having married Eamon O'Rourke. A man she adored but who only tolerated her. She took another deep breath and frowned at an unexpected and unfamiliar weight on her belly. She stroked a hand down, her fingers tracing over the strong hairy arm curled over her, holding her close, and she sighed.

Unwilling to break the small contact with him, she continued to think about her predicament. Although she had dreamed of marrying her entire life, she had never desired a marriage of convenience. Or a marriage to ensure her sisters were safe. Was it such a crime to wish there had been some tenderness between the bride and groom the previous day?

She continued to caress Eamon's arm as she sniffled. All throughout the long afternoon yesterday, she had hoped he would turn to her with a wink and the unfettered delight he had shown her a few times on the steamboat. That he would whisper he was glad they were more than friends. That she would have felt like something more than an obligation to him. Instead he had sat by her as though it were his duty as a husband. As though he were proving to everyone present, himself included, that he were an honorable man and able to keep his vows.

Envy had filled her, nearly sickening her, as she stared at Ardan and Kevin with their wives. With women they had married out of love. Not pity. She'd thought her heart would

157

break when she saw Seamus whisper tender words to Mary and the reflected love in her gaze. When she had watched Dunmore track Maggie's every movement with a covetous gaze. Even he was more in love with the unwed Maggie than Eamon was with her. Why was such devotion and adoration to be denied her?

Winnifred had relished in Phoebe's husband's absence from her side. Phoebe had tried to ignore that Eamon had abandoned her the minute after he kissed her, preferring to spend time with his family rather than accepting congratulations for the both of them together. Winnifred's words had been particularly sharp, piercing the fragile armor Phoebe had erected around her heart.

"Why look, Bee," Winnifred had said in a mocking voice, using Eamon's nickname for her. "He can't even tolerate standing beside you for a moment longer than necessary after the ceremony ended. And that kiss was more for a sister than for a wife."

Although Eamon had interrupted anything more Winnifred could have said, he had been increasingly uncomfortable during his father's toast. Which made sense, as it was about love and wealth and a lifetime of happiness. They couldn't even cobble together five minutes of joy. She frowned, suddenly fighting tears.

A finger caressed her cheek, and she jolted, her eyes opening to meet her husband's brooding gaze. "Was sleeping beside me that awful?" he asked, his voice a deep rumble.

She shivered at the sound and shook her head.

Soft, yet callused fingertips continued to trace over her cheeks and then to her jaw before rising to her temple. "What's the matter, love?"

"That," she croaked out. At his perplexed look, she closed her eyes in defeat. "You call me such words but don't mean them."

"Ah, Bee," he breathed. "Don't tell me what I mean." He

leaned forward, his lips following the path of his fingertips. "And don't believe you know what I feel."

She gasped as he kissed her under her ear, a surprisingly tender spot that befuddled her and made her lose her train of thought. "Eamon," she gasped, as she raised her hands to tangle in his thick black hair.

He continued to kiss his way down her neck to her collarbone before kissing his way up the other side. "Yes, my love?" he asked, his breath raspy, as his eyes gleamed with passion. He placed a finger over her lips and shook his head. "I fear you'll ask a question that will ruin the moment."

She flushed and then smiled, joy and happiness filling her expression.

He paused, stunned at the transformation. "I thought you beautiful before. Now you are a goddess," he whispered, leaning forward to kiss her deeply before she could protest. His hands roved over her, awaking nerve endings she didn't know she had.

Finally he broke away, falling to his side as he panted for breath, although he kept one arm wrapped around her waist and a leg hitched over her, resting his head beside hers. "Soon, Bee. Soon."

She ran her hands over his back and through his hair, any pain in her leg momentarily overshadowed by the passion they had shared. Never before had she felt such elation as when he touched her. She tried to convince herself that this was just as special for him too.

CHAPTER 11

Niamh Ahern poked her head into Phoebe's room. "Hello. Do you mind if I sit?" she asked with a chagrined smile. She waddled forward before Phoebe said anything. "I'm Niamh. Eamon's sister. I haven't met you already because the baby was acting up." She rubbed at her protruding belly.

"Niamh?" Phoebe whispered, saying her name haltingly. *Nee-ev*, she said silently in her mind, trying to remember a way to pronounce her name properly. "You're his older sister."

Niamh smiled and nodded. "Aye. An' I'm awaiting the arrival of my second wee beast. As far as anyone can tell me, he's late. But he's the one to make the schedule, not me." She gazed fondly at Phoebe, her hands on her belly. "My daughter, Maura, is keepin' my parents entertained."

"You are fortunate," Phoebe said, her hands playing with the blankets. She then fiddled with her hair.

"You look gorgeous, an' you know it," Niamh said with a teasing smile. "There's no need to fret about how you look with family. Family doesn't care. We know the best and the worst about you, yet love you anyway."

Gaping at her, Phoebe stared at her in stunned silence.

Niamh watched her with apprehensiveness, her ease evaporating as she saw her sister-in-law fidget. "At least that's how it always was in the O'Rourke household."

Clearing her throat, Phoebe said in a weak voice, "Not in the Mortimer home." As Niamh stared at her with a friendly openness that encouraged the sharing of secrets, Phoebe said, "Appearances were vital. What you wanted or needed was never important if it conflicted with your social obligations. Or to appear as attractive as possible."

Frowning, Niamh continued to rub her fingers over her belly. "How odd." She shrugged. "But then it could be because I was mainly raised by men. I never learned the ways of women." She glowered for a moment. "I never cared to acquire any of the skills my stepmother wished to teach me."

Phoebe relaxed at Niamh's easy conversation, and her fingers lost their death grip on the blankets. "My mother always despaired of my disinterest in how to style my hair or to bat my eyelashes at a man."

Niamh chortled with laughter. "I never knew that was possible, until I saw the Madam." She nodded, leaning forward, imparting a deep secret. "She's close friends with Mum and Da." She groaned and rose to pace a few steps. "Oh, this one had better decide to come soon. I can't handle many more days like this."

After a short circuit around the room, she sat again beside Phoebe. "Now, tell me all about the wedding. I'm devastated I wasn't there."

Phoebe paused as she considered her wedding day, and then she shrugged. "It was like any normal ceremony. The priest gave us a blessing. We celebrated with family and had cake."

Frowning, Niamh studied Phoebe. "Well, I know 'twas no normal ceremony as the groom had to walk toward you, not the other way 'round." She raised an eyebrow with a wry expression, as she waited for Phoebe to say more.

"That is true. I wished I could walk to him in my new gown." Her gaze was distant. "The ceremony was lovely. He sat beside me, held my hand, stared deeply in my eyes. Made me believe for a moment ..." She shrugged to banish her foolishness.

Niamh absently ran her hand over her abdomen, her gaze intent as she studied Phoebe. "I know what it is to have little faith in a man's promises. In his words." She reached forward to grip her sister-in-law's hand. "I know what it is to wish my life were different and to feel powerless to change how things are." She took a deep breath, debating how much more she would share. "I was married before Cormac. To his brother."

"His brother?" Phoebe gasped. "Isn't that scandalous?"

Niamh laughed and nodded. "Most likely. I've found that, if I have my family's blessing, I do not much care for the townsfolk's opinion. They'll focus on something else soon enough." She paused. "The most important thing I learned, Phoebe, is to look to what a man does, not what he says." She paused as she saw Phoebe battling tears. "What has Eamon done?"

"One moment he acts as though I'm precious to him and the next as if he wishes he were far away from me! The ceremony was lovely, but then he spent almost the entire celebration away from me, barely sparing me a glance."

Niamh frowned. "Did you smile at him or give him any indication you wanted him beside you?"

"I shouldn't have to do that! I'm his wife now."

Rising again to pace and arch her back, Niamh shook her head. "Nay, Phoebe, men are as prickly, or more, than we are.

If he's uncertain of how you feel, he'll be less inclined to spend time with you. When did he seek you out?"

Blushing, Phoebe shrugged her shoulders and tugged at the blankets. When Niamh stared at her patiently, as though she were a recalcitrant child, Phoebe sighed and finally spoke. "When I was having trouble with my sisters. We don't have the best relationship. He came over to smooth things between us. And then your father gave a blessing." She paused. "Eamon didn't return again until he had to defend me from my horrible uncle."

Unable to hide her delight at the unfolding tale, Niamh sat again and tried to lean forward, but her pregnant belly impeded such movement. "Oh, I hate that I missed such an interesting day! Did they fight your uncle?"

"No, but Eamon ensured Uncle understood I'm now an O'Rourke and that no Mortimer sister is to be harmed." She paused. "And the Madam was here. She seemed like a very nice woman."

Niamh burst out laughing. "Oh, what a day. No wonder you can't make heads nor tails of what occurred." She patted Phoebe's hand. "And Nora is. She's quite remarkable." After taking a deep breath and shifting in her chair, Niamh said, "How I love Da's blessings. What did he say?"

Phoebe closed her eyes, remembering the solemn moment and the discomfort Eamon had attempted to hide immediately after his father had intoned his benediction. "He said, 'May happiness and joy fill your days, unimpeded by sorrow. May your hands be forever employed, and may hunger and want never visit your home. May your lives know an ever-greater love, with despair ever absent. I wish you every blessing, Eamon and Phoebe.'" With a sigh, Phoebe opened her eyes, fighting tears.

"Oh, Da," Niamh whispered, extracting a handkerchief to wipe at her nose. "He's always had a way with words." She giggled. "And your attempt to mimic his accent wasn't half bad."

Phoebe laughed. "Oh, I know it was awful. But it sounds better the way he said it."

"In any accent, the blessing was beautiful. And heartfelt." Niamh considered her sister-in-law. "Why should it make you uncomfortable?"

"Your family marries for love, Niamh. Mine marries out of desperation, if we marry at all." She ducked her head, as though she had said too much.

"Well, you are married now. And I'll continue to hope his blessing proves true for you. I have a sense you've had little good fortune in your life as of yet. I think Eamon could be just what you need." She winked at her. "And you're exactly what Eamon needs." When Phoebe rolled her eyes at her in exasperation, Niamh said, "Eamon defending you from your sisters and your uncle shows his care of you, Phoebe. Surely you see that?" Niamh frowned as she studied Phoebe as though she were someone she failed to understand.

Picking at a loose thread, Phoebe muttered, "I hate that he feels this need to protect me. I can protect myself! And I hate that he only married me out of pity."

Niamh laughed. Ignoring Phoebe's glare, she swiped at her eyes. "Oh, I haven't had such a laugh in days. Thank you for distracting me from the upcoming birth and Cormac's absence." With exasperation, she gently chided, "How can you seem so smart but truly be so foolish? Eamon would never marry out of pity." She swiped at her cheeks. "Oh, how I wish I could have seen the two of you together."

Phoebe huffed out an aggrieved breath.

"As for protectin' yourself, we all know how well you can do that," Niamh said with a soft note of reproach in her voice. "Allowin' a man to care for you, to shelter you, doesn't mean you're weak, Phoebe. It shows you trust him and have faith in him. I've found 'tis somethin' a man needs."

Sitting in contemplative silence, Phoebe whispered, "How do you show your husband you trust him?"

A pleased smile spread, as she had a far-off look in her eyes when considering her husband. "Oh, we have a different sort of relationship. I'd known him for years before we married, although I had to overcome my fear that he was like his brother. Irrational though it was, it was still a fear I had." She sighed. "I show him by seeing him and not Connor. I show him by believing he'll never hurt me the way Connor did. I show him by turning to him for help, even if I could do the task on my own. Just because I could do it on my own doesn't mean I have to." She shared a long look with Phoebe. "The hardest thing you'll ever do is love, Phoebe. For, if you truly love, you're laid defenseless if he hurts you. If he doesn't feel the same. If he mocks you."

Niamh leaned forward to grip Phoebe's hand. "Believe you are worthy of his love. Believe you deserve more than a chaste kiss on your forehead at night." When Phoebe blushed, Niamh smiled. "Passion between a wife and her husband is to be celebrated, for 'tis too often a rare gift." She rose with a groan. "I must let you rest. Welcome to the family, Phoebe."

❧

"Winnifred, this is not a sound idea," Lorena whispered, as she walked beside her sister in what she hoped was a calm manner. For years, she had successfully hid her deepest emotions and had mastered the art of displaying only the emotions accepted by society. Never did she show the rage or the soul-crushing despair hidden deep inside. She had agreed to bury her deepest emotions to be a part of the family again after her disappointment. However, after watching the O'Rourkes and the way they confronted the pain from their past, she had begun to wonder if denying all she had lived through was truly wise.

"Quit being such a ninny. You know that's why Mama always favored me. I was like her. Brave. Bold. Daring." Winnifred walked with a sassy sway to her hips, reveling in the attention garnered as she lowered her lashes in a flirtatious manner. Her smile of satisfaction spread at a low whistle. "Oh, we've spent too long cooped up in that house."

Lorena felt a bubble of resentment toward her youngest sister. Although Mama had instructed Lorena to care for Winnie and to learn from Winnie's example, Lorena fought doubts that her mama had been wrong. "You know Mr. O'Rourke doesn't want us walking around town unchaperoned. It isn't safe, Winnie."

Winnie halted, her eyes snapping with irritation as a black tress curled around one cheek. "I'm sick and tired of having to live by his dictates. Not even Mama was so strict."

Lorena nodded. "Mother had a different notion of how we were to act." Although her words seemed to mollify Winnifred, her youngest sister failed to hear the irony in her voice. "Winnie," she whispered as she grabbed her sister's arm, pulling her up short. She stared at the man who approached them with disdain. "Uncle."

"Oh, what a fine day it is to see my nieces free of the yoke of those troublesome O'Rourkes." He rocked onto his heels, his voice loud enough that it carried to the curious bystanders. "I couldn't believe they had made you two precious young women work for them. Like you were little more than servant girls to earn your keep." He sighed in a dramatic fashion at the injustice thrust upon them.

Lorena studied her uncle and shook her head. "They had

a different sort of occupation in mind for us than you, Uncle."

He choked at her words, as though coughing up a bone. After a moment, he recovered and shook his head. "Oh, how you misunderstand me, my darling nieces. All I've ever yearned to do is care for you."

Lorena looked to Winnifred, her frown intensifying as she sensed Winnifred being taken in by the lies he spouted. "Is that before or after we earn our daily wage as a whore for you?"

"Lo!" Winnie gasped. "Don't be rude to our uncle. He's our only living relative."

Uriah Chaffee gripped the lapels of his black jacket and smiled at the youngest Mortimer sister. "Finally one of you has seen sense," he said with an avaricious gleam to his gaze. "I've always known my dear sister couldn't have raised three half-wits."

"No, just one," Lorena muttered. She heard a snort behind her and looked over her shoulder to see Finn O'Rourke leaning against a post, watching the unfolding scene. His presence eased some of her tension, and she faced her uncle again.

Winnifred either didn't hear her or ignored her as she took a step toward their uncle, dragging Lorena with her, as Lorena had looped her arm through Winnifred's. "Uncle, I fear we would be disappointments to you, as far as your idea for an auction would go." She waited a long moment as he stared at her in disbelief.

"Are you telling me that you're … that you've had …" he sputtered and shook his head. "Damnation," he muttered. "I should have suspected as much with Marilda as your mother."

"Mother was a good woman," Lorena snapped.

"As good as the Madam," Uriah said with a glower. "So

neither of you will do for a virgin auction." He boldly looked them up and down. "Never worry. I'll find some other use for you. For now, don't allow yourselves to become entangled, especially not with an O'Rourke!" He spun on his heel, muttering under his breath about women always ruining all of his best-laid plans.

"Winnie, how could you?" Lorena whispered.

"I thought he should know. That way, he can focus on giving us our inheritance without expecting anything from us." Winnifred shrugged, believing her rationale were sound.

"*Eejit*," Finn hissed from behind them. "You've give him more ammunition. Any regard he would have had for you is gone." He looked at each sister. "Now that he knows you aren't ... chaste"—he glowered at Winnifred, as she tilted her head up in defiance—"he'll have even less concern for you."

Winnifred freed her arm from Lorena's and stood with her hands on her hips. "Who are you to sneak up behind us and listen in on our private conversations?"

"You can hardly consider a conversation *private* when on a boardwalk, Winn." He looked around at the number of men loitering about. "And you should take pride in the fact you've proclaimed you're eager for another bedmate to the whole town." He spun on his heels and stormed away.

"I did no such thing," Winnifred hissed with a stomp of her foot. She looked to Lorena who shook her head with regret.

"Come, Winnie. Let's return to the house. We only have one day off a week, and it's proven to be too much of an adventure for me." Lorena walked the short distance to the O'Rourke house, sighing with relief when they entered the home she had begun to consider her sanctuary.

CHAPTER 12

"How's married life, Phoebe?" Winnifred asked a week after the wedding. Against Maggie's objections, Phoebe had insisted she wanted to have time alone with her sisters. Now Winnifred sat beside Phoebe's bed, her hair in a perfect coiffure and wearing one of the pretty silk dresses she had brought from Saint Louis. Today, a soft breeze blew in through the open window, cooling the room on a hot day in late June. "Do you like your husband's attentions?" She gazed intently at her middle sister.

Phoebe tried not to squirm under the scrutiny but knew she had failed when Winnifred preened with triumph that her barb had hit its mark. Phoebe hated that she felt dowdy in one of the three cotton dresses she had worn since arriving at the O'Rourke house. Today's was a faded blue with tattered cuffs. She fought envy when looking at her unharmed perfectly beautiful sisters. "Of course I do."

Winnifred rolled her eyes as she smirked at her sister. "I've heard he won't touch you. Not truly. That he's only biding his time until you have your own home, and he can be his own man. That the thought of having to bed you makes him ill."

Clearing her throat and attempting to find any scrap of bravado, Phoebe chuckled. "No gentleman would ever talk about what occurs between husband and wife. He's very respectful, Winnie."

Lorena frowned, her book forgotten, as she watched the exchange between her two sisters. "Winnie, that's enough," she whispered in protest at her sister's cruel words.

"Tell me that after he starts to visit the Bordello regularly," Winnie snapped, ignoring Lorena's warning, her cheeks heated, and anger filling her gaze. "He'll discover what pleasure truly is and won't ever seek out your company again."

"He won't. He wouldn't," Phoebe stammered, unable to hide her shock or distress. "He's respectful and caring."

Laughing as though she had just gained the upper hand, Winnifred shook her head. "No, dear sister, he's considerate. He only married you to ensure we were safe from uncle. Did you truly believe he cared for *you?*" She rolled her eyes, as though her sister were the naivest of women. "Now that we are safe, and now that you won't be harmed by uncle again, he's free to do what he wants." She nodded, as Phoebe paled.

"If that's so, then I'm free to ensure you never disparage my wife again," Eamon said in a deceptively friendly voice as he leaned against the doorjamb, his arms crossed over his chest. He wore an impeccable gray suit with a waistcoat that matched his eyes. His blue eyes were glacially cold as he looked at Winnifred and then Lorena. "That you never again spew your poisonous words at her."

Winnifred paled, as she gaped at Eamon. "I never meant ..."

Nodding, Eamon pushed away from the door and approached her. "Of course you did, Winnie. On the steamboat, I thought you were amusing, the way you always argued with Finn. But now I realize you are filled with a venomous discontent. And you want everyone near you to be as miserable as you are." He shook his head. "I won't let you harm my wife, or our relationship, ever again."

"I speak the truth," she proclaimed, her chin tilted up.

His gaze raked over her with disdain. "You wouldn't know the truth if it bit you. Phoebe is the best sister you could ever dream of having. She's loyal and kind. But you intentionally hurt her because you've filled your mind with fantasies of betrayal and nothing will free you of them. From now on, you are barred from Phoebe's room. And when we move to our new home, you are forbidden from visiting." His gaze flit to Lorena, so as to include her in his pronouncement. "As are you, until you can find the nerve to stand up against the bully in your family."

"Forever?" Phoebe whispered.

Eamon cast a worried glance in his wife's direction before focusing on Winnifred again, largely ignoring Lorena, as though understanding Winnifred was the instigator of his wife's distress. "Until Winnifred has a change of heart and can be civil and honest and can prove she truly cares for you. Until then, she is barred. *Forever.*"

"You have no right!" Winnie screeched.

Eamon smiled, standing tall and calm, as Winnie became hysterical. "I have every right. I'm Phoebe's husband. And I promised to protect her." He paused. "Out."

Winnifred tossed her head up, storming from the room, Lorena on her heels, the door slamming shut behind them.

Phoebe sat in stunned silence, staring at her husband as he paced the room like a caged animal. "You didn't have to involve yourself," she said. Whatever more she might have said sputtered to a halt when he spun to glare at her. She noted the ire in his gaze, before ducking her head in shame. "I'm sorry you felt the need to intervene."

Eamon sat on the chair beside the bed and stared at her with abject frustration. "Bee, how could you expect me to stand by and to listen to her treat you horribly and to disparage me and how I feel about you at the same time and to say nothing? I couldn't. I refuse to."

"They're just words," she whispered.

"Aye, an' as powerful as any blow," he murmured. "I won't tolerate anyone harming you, love."

Bending her head forward, she refused to meet his entreating gaze. "I knew what she said was true, Eamon."

When he swore and reached for her, she raised startled eyes to meet his furious gaze. Now he appeared angrier with her than he'd ever been with Winnifred. "What part of that vicious nonsense was true, Bee?" When she stared at him in open-mouthed wonder, he whispered, "That I would tire of you and seek out comfort at the Bordello? That I had been forced to marry you solely to save your sisters? That I don't care for you?"

Phoebe shrugged, mesmerized by what she saw in his gaze. "I don't know what to believe. I thought I knew, but then everything changed on the steamboat."

"Bee, if you'd just let me explain—" He swore under his breath at the knock on the door, glaring at Maggie as she poked her head in. "What is it, Mags?"

"Don't growl at your sister," Phoebe commanded. "It's not her fault we're at odds." Phoebe looked to Maggie, who watched them with frank amusement. "Maggie?"

"It's time for Phoebe's walk. She needs to keep moving, if she's to regain strength and her independence."

Eamon jumped up, waiting to help her from the bed. "Of course."

Phoebe motioned for him to leave, and he shook his head.

"Eamon, Maggie and I are fine." When a deep hurt entered his gaze, Phoebe reached forward to grab his arm but missed him as he moved too fast from the bed. "Eamon!" she screeched as she started to tumble from the bed.

One minute, she was falling, and, the next, she was cradled in his arms. The memory of falling—of not knowing if she would land or if she would die when she did land—coursed through her memory, and a shaking overwhelmed her. Her teeth chattered, and she clung to Eamon as he sat on the floor with her in his lap. "Hold me," she pleaded, soaking his shirt. "Don't let me go."

"*Shh*, love," he murmured in her ear. "You're well. You're fine. You're here in my arms, and I'll never let anyone harm you again." He continued to speak soft words of comfort and love in her ear, as he rocked from side to side.

After long minutes, Phoebe calmed, hiccupping out shaky breaths. "Forgive me," she said, as she wriggled to be let up.

"Stay," Eamon said. "Please. Let me hold you a little while longer. For me." When she had settled, he whispered, "What happened, Bee? What did I do wrong?"

"Nothing," she said, as a tear coursed down her cheek. "Nothing." She looked to Maggie and flushed, sighing with relief when Maggie slipped from the room to leave them alone. "I never realized I could hurt you," she whispered. When he made a noise expressing his confusion, she said in a soft voice, "I never thought you cared enough that something I did would hurt you."

Cupping her face and turning her head so she looked at him, he looked deeply into her eyes. "Heed me, Bee," he said in a low, passionate voice. "I care. And I'm tired of being doubted."

Another tear trickled down one cheek as she nodded. "I saw the pain in your eyes, and I realized I wanted to walk with you. To hear you banter with Maggie as I leaned against

175

you for support." She leaned against him, as she stiffened from her memory. "But you moved too quickly, and I knew I would fall. And then the memory of falling from the saloon rushed back."

Eamon stared at her with horror. "From the day you were injured."

Nodding, she pressed her face against his chest. "I thought I'd die. Or become crippled. Or never stop falling. I still have nightmares where I wake up falling."

He ran his strong hands over her back, pulling her even closer. "I thought you'd dream about your painful injury."

"It was injured in the fall. It's all tied together."

"Feck," he whispered. "I'm so sorry, Phoebe. I'd make it better for you, if I could."

She wrapped her arms around his back and sighed deeply before whispering, "Don't you see? You already do."

His arms tightened at her words, causing her to squeak as he pushed the air from her. "I do?"

"I've never had someone hold me through one of my terrors," she whispered.

Eamon helped her up and eased her onto the bed. He kicked off his boots and crawled in, drawing her in to rest beside him. "Come, love. Let me hold you a little longer."

～

Phoebe woke to the calming sensation of feeling cherished. She rested in her husband's arms, her head on his strong chest, while his hands slowly stroked her back. He kissed her head, murmuring soft words and sounds of comfort as he held her. With a sigh, she wished she could remain asleep forever, just like this.

"Are you awake, lass?" he murmured with another kiss to her head.

"Yes," she whispered, her voice filled with regret as she moved to ease off him. When his arms tightened around her, she settled again on his chest. At his soft "Stay," a tear leaked out.

"Let me hold you." Fingers traced patterns on her back. "Soothing you soothes me, my love."

"I'm fine," she protested, although her voice emerged slurred, as she battled slipping into sleep again.

"You are now," he agreed. "However, I hate envisioning what you suffered." When she shivered, he said, "Share the memory with me."

Tilting her head up to meet his gaze, she frowned in confusion. "Why? What purpose does that serve?"

Callused fingers traced over her silky cheek, while he stared intently into her eyes. "It helps me to understand. And it takes away the power of the memory over you."

Sighing, Phoebe rested her head on his chest again, her fingers rising to play over his shoulder. "I was taught to be dutiful. To respect my elders. When my uncle insisted on showing us around the town, I thought to appease him." She paused. "Lorena and Winnie refused, in part because I think they knew I would agree." With a sigh, her fingers dug into his shoulder. "I can't blame them. I can't be angry with them."

"But you are," he murmured, as he kissed her head again.

"I wonder, over and over, how it might have been different if we'd stayed together."

Eamon made a sound of disagreement. "You do realize Mr. Bell alone could have harmed all three of you and made it harder to ensure your safety? It was easier to bring your sisters here because they were at the hotel, not locked upstairs at the Daybreak."

"I know," she said in a voice filled with shame. "I knew something was wrong by the way Uncle encouraged men to leer at me." She shivered. "I should have done something. But

177

I didn't know what. And I never would have imagined he had planned something so terrible. I'm his niece!" Gasping, she whispered, "And then he forced me into the saloon."

When her voice broke off, one of his hands rose to clasp the one gripping his shoulder. He linked their hands to weld their strength together. "What happened after that?"

"All I remember is panic. And praying someone would help me. Would show me mercy. Instead they seemed amused. And eager." She shivered, pressing into his strong hold. "And then a giant of a man stepped out of the shadows and threw me over his shoulders, promising that I'd be ready for tonight's entertainment." She took a stuttering breath. "I realized that *I* was the night's entertainment."

She raised her head and looked deeply into her husband's tormented gaze. "I ... That's not who I am." She paused, as though expecting him to disagree. When he remained quiet, she lowered her gaze. "He tossed me into a windowless room and locked me inside."

He ran a hand down her head, his voice filled with pride. "And you had the strength and the determination to break through a wall and to jump to freedom." His thumb traced over her cheek. "Never doubt how remarkable you are, Bee."

"I'm not remarkable," she protested. "I was desperate." She shivered. "And terrified. I thought I'd die. From the fall. And, if not from that, I knew they'd find me, and the beating I'd receive would be worse than anything I could envision."

Eamon's jaw tightened at the mention of her being harmed. "No one will ever mistreat you, Bee. You'll never know how thankful I am that you chose the O'Rourke home as your place of refuge." He kissed her forehead and swiped away a few tears. When he noted she continued to appear ashamed, he shook his head. "I wish you could see what I see, Bee. Too many would have accepted their fate. You fought back." He leaned forward, kissing her softly. "Take pride in who you are, love. For I know I do."

She rested her head against his chest, crying softly, as she attempted to banish those fearful moments. "Thank you," she whispered.

"Always, Bee. Always."

CHAPTER 13

A few days later, Phoebe walked around the first floor of the O'Rourke house, holding on to the wall or pieces of furniture for balance. Although the stitches had been removed with surprising ease and little pain, her strength had not returned as quickly. Sweating, she leaned against a wall, closing her eyes in defeat, as she had only made two circles around the lower living space today, rather than the three yesterday, before having to stop.

With a frustrated huff, she hit the wall with her open palm, then pushed away, intent on walking faster and with less of a limp. She moved quickly, and her foot caught on the edge of the rug. With a yelp of distress, she tumbled to the ground, landing with a groan of agony.

"Phoebe!" Maggie gasped, as she emerged from the kitchen, swiping her hands on a cloth. "Are you all right?"

Rolling onto her uninjured side, Phoebe rested with an arm slung over her face, as tears leaked out. "I'm fine. Don't worry about me."

"Don't be a ninny," Maggie scolded. "Of course I'll worry about you. You're my sister now." When Phoebe gazed at her in abject amazement, Maggie smiled. "Besides, I like you too." With a mischievous wink, she knelt beside Phoebe and pulled at her skirts. "Let me have a look at your leg and ensure you didn't break open the scar."

Phoebe pushed at her skirts and dug her heels into the rug, until she had scooted herself away from Maggie and sat, leaning against the sofa. "It's not proper to look at my leg in the open." A scarlet flush covered her cheeks.

"No one's here except Mum," Maggie said with calm understanding. After a long moment, where Phoebe's frantic breathing calmed, Maggie loosened Phoebe's hands and eased up her skirt. She gave a satisfied nod and smiled. "You didn't do any damage, although you might have a new bruise." She rose and held out her hand. "Come. I knew I should walk with you."

"I'm not a child." Phoebe immediately ducked her head at the petulance of her words.

"No, but I imagine we've made you feel like one. All coddled and making decisions for you." She paused, her hazel eyes shining with concern. "You do understand it's because we care for you and don't want any more harm to befall you?" She pulled Phoebe into a hug and then looped her arm through Phoebe's, as they walked slowly to the kitchen.

"Mum," Maggie called out, "do you have any tea for Phoebe? Walking is thirsty work." She winked again at Phoebe, as she motioned for Phoebe to sit, before Maggie bustled around the kitchen.

Phoebe sat with a relieved sigh, rubbing at her injured thigh, as she watched the two women work with envy. She wanted to have such ease of movement again but dreaded she never would. A deep fear settled inside that Eamon had saddled himself to a cripple, and he would come to regret his rash decision.

A cup of tea was set in front of her, prepared just the

way she liked it, with a splash of milk and a tiny bit of sugar. Somehow Mary never forgot how someone liked to drink their tea. After a comforting squeeze to her shoulder, Mary returned to the stove to work on the evening meal, leaving Phoebe to join in the conversation or to sit in silence.

Rather than enter the speculation about where Dunmore and Cormac were, and whether Cormac would be in town when Niamh had her baby, Phoebe sat sipping her tea in a daze. The fear of never walking unaided had taken root inside Phoebe, and she didn't know how to quell it. Eamon had shown her a tremendous kindness since their marriage, but she knew better than to confuse kindness with affection. Or love. Rubbing at her head as a headache brewed, she finally noticed the kitchen was unusually quiet, when Maggie and Mary always chattered away while they worked together. She raised her head to find them both watching her with concern.

"I'm fine," she said in a quavering breath, her eyes closing for a moment in defeat at her inability to speak without betraying her inner turmoil.

Mary watched her with an assessing gaze, before joining her at the table with an appreciative sigh, a mug of tea between her palms. *"Fine,"* she murmured. "I've never been keen on that word. I feel it fails to fully express any true feeling." She took a sip of her tea as she stared at her newest daughter-in-law, a note of challenge in her beautiful hazel eyes. "How are you really?"

"Terrified," Phoebe blurted out, before she bit her lip and dipped her head.

"Of Eamon?" Mary asked, her concern deepening in her gaze.

"No, never of him," Phoebe said, closing her eyes in defeat. "Partially," she admitted on a nearly inaudible breath.

Maggie gasped but quieted after a "Hush" came from Mary.

Mary sat in quiet companionship with Phoebe at the table, sipping tea as the sounds from town entered through the open window on the warm early summer day. Carts rolled past, horses neighing and their hooves clomping, while drivers called out greetings and warnings to those they passed. Chickens clucked as they roosted in the chicken coop, while a dog barked in the distance. Soothing everyday sounds of a thriving town.

"I hate that I have a limp," Phoebe whispered, her hand dropping to her leg again as though of its own volition.

Mary nodded, sending another quelling glance in Maggie's direction. "Are you angry?"

"Angry?" Phoebe shook her head. "I'm grateful I have two legs. That I can still walk. But I'm vain."

Maggie sputtered out a laugh. "You're the least vain of the Mortimer sisters."

That earned a rueful smile. "That isn't saying much. I've always known I was the plainest of the sisters. There was never much reason for me to primp and to fuss in front of a mirror."

"*Plainest?*" Mary asked with a confused tilt of her head. "Who filled your head with such nonsense?" Sensing the deeply rooted hurt within Phoebe, Mary spoke in a soft motherly tone. "You're beautiful, lass. You've hair that shines like gold in the sun and beautiful green eyes that remind me of Ireland."

"There's no need to lie. I know what I am."

Maggie snorted and sat with a huff. "No, you don't. For too long, you've believed the lies you were fed. Just like I did." She cast a worried glance in her mum's direction before continuing to speak. "I believed I had to be quiet, to not have opinions, to never laugh louder than a whisper. For if I did,

I'd be allowing my *pagan roots* to shine through." She beamed at Phoebe. "I've come to realize I like who I am."

"But that's because you're an O'Rourke," Phoebe protested.

"So are you," Mary said, a determined gleam in her eyes.

"I didn't know I was one until a year ago," Maggie said with a shrug. "Acceptance and trust can heal so many hurts, Phoebe. But you have to open yourself up to such gifts."

Biting her lip, Phoebe whispered, "I'm not sure I'm strong enough." She frowned as the two O'Rourke women burst into peals of laughter. "I didn't say anything funny."

"Oh, lass, of course you did," Mary said, wiping at her eyes. "You're so much stronger than you give yourself credit for." She reached forward, gripping her hand. "Why are you afraid of Eamon? What has he done?"

"Nothing," Phoebe whispered, in an instant battling tears. She sniffled and firmed her shoulders. "He shouldn't be forced to live with a cripple."

"*Cripple?*" Maggie asked with a shake of her head. "You are far from crippled."

"I can't walk without a limp. I don't have the strength to do anything!" She pointed into the living room. "You saw what happened when I tried to walk farther today."

"You won't heal overnight, Phoebe." Shrugging, Maggie stared at her, nonplussed. "You fell. You'll fall again. It's what we do when we are trying to push ourselves to improve, Phoebe." Her eyes filled with remorse. "I fear I failed you. I did the best I could, but I should never have presumed I could heal you."

"No!" Phoebe gasped, gripping Maggie's hand to prevent her from rising and leaving the kitchen. Phoebe knew she could never race after her. "No, Maggie. From the little I've heard during whispered conversations at the dinner table, I'm most fortunate you attended me and not the doctor. I know you did everything possible to help me. I'm feeling sorry for myself."

Mary laid her palm over the two younger women's clasped hands. "Nonsense. Maggie did her best, and you will recover as best you can. If you have a limp, 'twill never detract from who you are, Phoebe." She paused a moment, squeezing the hands under hers, her focus on her son's wife. "'Tis normal to mourn what has been lost or what has changed. It means you are sensible, and I like to believe my son married a sensible woman." She waited for Phoebe to speak, but, when Phoebe remained silent, Mary sighed.

"You must trust Eamon," Maggie murmured.

As the back door opened, Phoebe jerked her hand away from the two women and sat with a prim posture. She half smiled at Eamon, one hand rising to fiddle with her teacup.

"Are you well, Phoebe?" he asked, as he poured himself a cup and stared at her. He waved a hand around his head. "Your hair's a bit wild."

Gasping, Phoebe patted at her head, discovering her braid had loosened, and strands hung loose down her back. Mary and Maggie chuckled as they slipped from the kitchen. "I'm fine. I had a … tumble while walking around."

"Tumble?" Eamon asked, sitting across from her. "Are you well? Did you hurt yourself?"

"I might have a bruise, but my scar is fine." Keeping her gaze averted, she whispered, "You shouldn't trouble yourself."

Her husband gently took hold of her chin, tilting it up so she would meet his gaze, now filled with concern. "And who should I concern myself with? Winnifred? Lorena?" His eyes flashed his displeasure. "I worry about my wife."

Her eyes filled with tears. "I don't want you to feel a duty …" Her voice broke.

Sliding his hands around her face to cup her cheeks, he

stared deeply into her luminous green eyes. "Of course I feel a duty. To protect, to honor, and to cherish you. How could I not? You are precious, Phoebe. To me."

A tear dripped down her cheek. "I fear I'll never be what you want."

His bright smile caused her breath to catch. "How can you not realize you've always been exactly what I desired?"

～

"Am I interrupting?" a soft voice called out, early the next morning.

Phoebe looked to the door to see Aileen, Kevin's wife, staring at her. Although, at first appearance, she seemed rather plain and plump, her smile and quiet confidence enhanced her subtle beauty and natural charm. "No." Phoebe set aside the book she was reading and squirmed around in the bed in an attempt to find a more comfortable position. Her leg ached, but she knew she was hours away from drinking any more tea to soothe the discomfort. Maggie was strict on the dosing of her teas. "Thank you again for the beautiful gowns you made me. You went to such trouble for me." Her voice held a note of uncertainty, as she stared at the young woman with gleaming chestnut hair tied back in a soft knot.

"You are my sister," she said with a broad smile. "It's never trouble to aid a family member." She set a basket beside her in the empty chair. "I had thought you might be bored and desired company. If you don't, I'll sew in the kitchen with Maggie and Mary."

Phoebe stared at her basket and the woman offering her friendship, the silence lengthening between them. Finally she said in a hesitant voice, "I'd like the company. But I fear I have little by way of conversation. I haven't been outside this house in far too long."

Aileen laughed and pulled out what looked to be a chemise to hand sew. "But you just arrived from Saint Louis. You've been out of the Territory more recently than I have." She smiled engagingly, her brown eyes lit with delight. "I'm certain you have news I'd find interesting."

Phoebe gaped at her and shrugged. "I fear you'll find me a disappointment."

Aileen shook her head. "Never." She smiled as she overheard Maggie and Mary singing together. "How are you settling in to being an O'Rourke?"

Startled, Phoebe shrugged. "Fine. Why wouldn't I?"

Aileen bit the needle with one side of her mouth and tried to smile with the other half. "Oh, I know how welcoming they can be. But they are also a little intimidating and overwhelming. There are so many of them!" She chuckled. "I find having my own home with Kevin helps. We are here for meals, but we have our own refuge. It's the perfect balance."

"Are you an orphan?" Phoebe asked, flushing as Aileen stared at her. "I beg your pardon. I shouldn't be so impertinent. It's just that I've never seen any of your family here."

Aileen grimaced. "Well, part of that reason is that my aunt, Mrs. Davies, who traveled to Fort Benton with me, is not welcome here. She is an intimate friend of your uncle." When Phoebe blanched, Aileen nodded. "Yes, not the most charitable of women. My mother died when I was quite young, and my aunt raised me. My father has an inveterate need to wander. I met him last summer for the first time since I was a girl, and he attended my wedding. After a few weeks here, he set out on another adventure." She focused on her sewing for a moment before meeting Phoebe's gaze. "I pray every night he'll decide to winter here."

"Oh, Aileen," Phoebe breathed, reaching her hand out to clasp one of the other woman's. "I hope he returns soon."

Aileen nodded. "I receive a letter here and there. And Cormac will give me an update, if he sees or hears something about him as he travels about the Territory. But it's not the same." She grimaced, embarrassed by her show of emotions. "I should be used to his absences by now."

"Perhaps. But now you've seen him again. And seen his regard for you." A wistful sigh escaped. "That must be lovely."

Aileen squeezed Phoebe's hand, before returning to her sewing. "It is." She frowned. "I'm sorry about your uncle. I can only imagine what a shock it was to arrive and to be confronted with the type of man he is."

Phoebe shivered. "He's the opposite of my other uncle. Uncle Harvey was generous and kind and supportive. He was protective. The exact opposite of Uncle Uriah."

Aileen smiled. "Well, now that you're an O'Rourke, you'll never lack for family. They'll be as loyal to you as they are to each other."

"I had never really expected such a possibility," she breathed. At Aileen's nod, Phoebe rested against her mound of pillows, considering all Aileen said. For the first time, Phoebe allowed herself to envision that she could have the family she'd always dreamed of. If only she could learn to trust in Eamon.

CHAPTER 14

As was now his custom, Eamon took breaks from the warehouse to poke his head into the room he now considered his and Phoebe's, smiling when he saw her sitting in a comfortable chair he had moved into the room. The window was opened, and a breeze fluttered the curtain. She looked up from her book, and he hoped he detected a flash of pleasure in her composed gaze. "Hello, love," he murmured as he entered, kissing her softly on her forehead. "How are you today?"

"Frustrated and bored," she blurted out, before regretting her blunt words. "I shouldn't complain. I know how fortunate I am."

He pulled out the wooden chair he had sat on for nights on end, waiting patiently for her to say something else. When she stared at her book cover, her fingers tracing over the title, he murmured, "But ..."

"Everyone scurried the moment Aileen arrived with the news Niamh was having her baby," she said in a rush. "I offered to help, but your mum and Maggie insisted I remain here." She looked around the room, as though it were a prison. "I would have been in the way."

"Oh, darling," Eamon murmured, as he scooted closer to pull her in his arms. "They never meant to hurt you." He kissed her forehead again, as he smoothed back her hair that had slipped free from its loose braid. "They were trying to follow what I'd asked them to do."

"I don't understand," she whispered.

"I didn't want you to leave the house without me." He shrugged. "It's silly, I know, but I wanted you here, protected in the house." He looked around and smiled with embarrassment. "Although I should have realized an empty house is no true protection."

She fell forward against his chest, sighing with pleasure when his arms tightened around her. "I must be on my own some of the time, Eamon, even though we are married."

Running his knuckles down her cheeks, he gave her a chagrined look. "Until we are properly married, Bee, I won't run the risk of your uncle believing he can push for an annulment." His eyes flashed with anger and fear. "I won't risk him putting you in danger again. Ask anything of me but that."

She stared in wonder at the impassioned plea in his gaze. After a long moment, she nodded. "Will you do something with me?" At his soft smile, she ran a finger over his chest. "Will you help me make supper?"

"Supper?" he sputtered out on a huff of air. "Forgive me," he muttered. "I had thought, with the empty house, and the likelihood they'll be gone for hours ..." His gaze flitted to the bed and then back again, a wry smile forming.

"Eamon! It's the middle of the day!"

He chuckled and pulled her against him. "Aye, 'tis," he murmured. "Someday you won't protest about the time of day." He kissed her forehead and rose, holding his hand out

192

to her. "Come. Let's raid my mum's pantry and see what we can make." With a sardonic smile, he murmured, "I hope you can cook better than I can, or the family's in trouble."

Laughing, as she giggled and called him incorrigible, he eased her to standing, sighing with pleasure when she leaned against him as she regained her balance. All felt right with the world when she was in his arms. After she pushed away from him, he winged out his arm, and she slipped her hand through it, as she walked with him into the kitchen.

After poking around in the icebox and the pantry, they decided to make a stew. "Not very original," Eamon muttered with a chagrined shrug.

"If they want original, they can visit Deirdre," Phoebe muttered. "She's the chef in the family." Gasping, she quickly said, "Besides your mum and Maggie."

"And Niamh," Eamon said, as he chopped vegetables. "Niamh's an excellent cook, but she'll be too busy with her babe to cook for a while." He sighed. "Have you heard about your sisters at the café?"

Phoebe sat with a huff of relief and shook her head. "No. They sit far away from me at supper and never speak with me. They are taking your edict seriously." She smiled at him, as he set a chopping board, knife, and vegetables before her and then set up the same for himself at the table across from her.

Eamon smiled wickedly. "Ardan told me that they've had a hard time adjusting to working. Especially Winnifred." At Phoebe's wry smile, he chuckled. "Seems they always want to take a five-minute break or offer their opinions on Deirdre's cooking."

"Oh, that would be awful," Phoebe breathed, wide-eyed, as Eamon stared quizzically. "Neither of them have a good sense of taste. Everything they cook is too sweet or too salty."

He shared a conspiratorial grin with her and nodded. "It

seems Deirdre has discovered just that and is refraining from asking for their opinions."

Giggling, Phoebe gazed deeply into his beautiful eyes. "I know how much they will resent working there." Phoebe focused on peeling a carrot, her mouth scrunched up as she concentrated.

"Why?" Eamon asked. "Everyone should work to help out the family. 'Tis what we do."

"I've come to realize that's true for you, but our mother raised us to believe we should be waited on."

He gave a grunt of disagreement. "You mean, that *they* should be waited on. You're used to working." When she shrugged, he reached out to still her hands' erratic movements. "Calm yourself, love, or you'll harm yourself and need Maggie's tending again." He smiled tenderly as she blushed. "You've always allowed them to treat you differently, haven't you?"

Setting aside the knife, she firmed her jaw as it quivered. "You don't understand, Eamon."

A scraping sound filled the room as he pushed aside the cutting board in front of him and reached across the table to clasp her hands. "Aye, you're right. I don't. Help me to?"

Gazing deeply into his curious, loving gaze, she whispered, "Our house was filled with shame. I did what I could to alleviate it."

"Shame?" He shrugged in confusion. "I don't understand."

Phoebe bit her lip and whispered, "I never thought I'd tell you this, until we were fully married. Until I knew you couldn't leave me."

Eamon leaned across the table, one of his strong, callused hands rising to caress her silky cheek. "Even after we make love, Bee, I can leave. In myriad ways. Nothing can make me stay." When he saw the panic in her gaze, he continued to stroke his fingers over her skin. "No law, no preacher's incantation, nothing will make a man stay who doesn't want to."

"What are you saying?" Her green eyes were luminous and were filled with trepidation.

"I'm here because I want to be, love. There's nowhere else I'd want to be. No one else I'd rather be talking with."

"Why?" she whispered.

"Because of you," he murmured. "Remember that as you worry about talking about shame. Nothing you say would ever make me"—he broke off, choking on a word—"esteem you any less."

She looked deeply into his eyes, the vegetables and the stew forgotten, as she attempted to fathom the depth of his emotions. Taking a deep breath, she marshaled all her courage and whispered, "My mama was gorgeous. One of those women the poets imagined as they wrote their sonnets and odes. She was said to have been the beauty of Saint Louis."

When Eamon squeezed her hand, she relaxed marginally and lost herself in storytelling. "She learned from an early age that all she was valued for was her beauty. And she despaired of anything that she considered a flaw." Phoebe fingered her freckles on her nose. "These were seen as the Devil's mark. And I was overly serious and never mastered the art of flirtation with ease, as Winnie did. Nor did I have my sisters' curves."

"You're gorgeous," Eamon breathed, holding a finger to her lips and shaking his head. "Don't argue with your husband."

She bent her head and smiled, kissing his finger. "I won't argue with a man who's clearly so wise."

"And you claim you can't flirt," he teased, lowering his finger. "I still don't understand your talk of shame, Bee."

"I know you're astute, and I know you've wondered why

the three sisters don't look more alike." She brushed at imaginary crumbs on the tabletop before meeting his gaze. "We have different fathers. The one trait we share from our mama is her eyes."

"And her smile," he murmured.

"Yes," she whispered. "When Winnie isn't conniving and Lorena hiding, when we are truly happy, we have the same smile."

"Again, I don't understand the shame."

Phoebe reached forward, clasping his hand, taking strength from his presence. "Our mama was a beauty, but she also feared poverty. We were never meant to have servants or to live in a fancy house, but that was my mama's goal. She thought it her right. She did not believe she could be so attractive and suffer the life of a maid." She cleared her throat. "Thus, she found men to protect her, although each of our fathers left when he found out she was with child."

Eamon nodded, murmuring, "How did you survive after Winnie's dad left? That must have been years ago."

Phoebe squirmed in her seat and sighed. "Mama had successive friends who cared for her and her household. We were never to be around when they called, especially as we got older."

He smiled tenderly at her. "I imagine she feared the competition. And I hope she did not desire such a life for you and your sisters."

"She wasn't maternal, like your mother." She cleared her throat. "Uncle Harvey was generous, when he could be, although he passed away a few years ago."

Eamon nodded, sitting in contemplative silence for many moments. "You're concerned I'll think less of you because your mum was like Nora. Like the Madam?" At her defeated nod, he stroked a hand over her head. "Do you wish you could have a life like hers?"

"Like hers?" Phoebe breathed in horror.

"Free to do what you want. Free to find a man who suits your fancy at any given time."

"No, no, no, no," she stammered, flushing, while he watched her with loving amusement. "I've never wanted her life."

"Then why do your sisters resent you so much?" he asked.

She shrugged. "It's like all families. There are misunderstandings and resentments."

"Perhaps, but we usually fight them out and are over them within a few days. The only time a disagreement has lasted is this one with Declan." He rubbed at his forehead. "I wish I were certain I did the correct thing."

Arching over the table, Phoebe stretched so she could caress his forehead free of worry lines and then to run her fingers over his face. "You know you did, Eamon. From what Maggie told me one day, while I was convalescing, you did all you could for your brother. No one could ask you to have done anything more."

"Ardan would have found a way to talk him 'round, so that Declan would return home. Ardan never would have left Declan in Saint Louis, alone and suffering, for another year." He paused as he saw her staring at him with deep emotion and devotion in her gaze. "What?"

"You are as good a man, as honorable a man, as your big brother. I wish you could see that." She paused and swallowed before whispering, "I wish you could see what I see."

"What do you see?" he asked in a voice barely louder than a breeze.

As the back door slammed shut, she jumped, releasing her hold on Eamon's hand. Dropping her gaze to her forgotten vegetables, she picked up her knife in an attempt to focus on chopping again. However, her hand shook, and she had trouble concentrating.

197

Eamon turned to glare at the interloper. "Finn," he muttered.

"Lovebirds," Finn said with a sly smile. "I'm sorry to interrupt your interlude."

Phoebe focused on Finn and frowned. "Do you have news of Niamh and her babe?"

Sighing, Finn collapsed onto the bench beside Eamon. "No. Only that 'these things take time' and that 'men should learn patience for once.'" He rolled his eyes, as Eamon snorted. "The first was a quote from Mum, the second, Maggie."

Phoebe giggled and shared an amused look with her husband. "From what I've heard, they're correct. Where's your father? He could soothe them."

Eamon stared at her in confusion, before looking at his younger brother.

Shrugging, Finn grabbed a piece of carrot. "He's playing with Maura. I'm sure he'll arrive here soon with her. Niamh doesn't want her daughter to hear her screaming, especially when she's swearing at Cormac and Connor."

"Why both of them?" Eamon asked, as he played with one of Phoebe's hands. His fingers tickled her palm, and he was momentarily distracted by the fetching color that rose on her cheeks.

"Connor, for putting her into this state, and Cormac, for being away from home," Finn said, as he rose with a wink. "I'll be at the store with Niall and Luc." He departed as abruptly as he had arrived.

Phoebe traced her thumb over Eamon's fingers, tugging gently at her hand. "I'll need both hands if I'm to help with supper."

He stared at her intently for a long moment before releasing her hand. "One day, I pray that's you," he whispered.

"What?" she breathed.

"I pray, one day soon, that I'm the madman pacing the porch, as I wait for news of the birth of my—our—babe. I never realized how much I wanted that until now."

"Eamon," she breathed.

"Come. Let's finish this stew, for I know they'll descend on us like a pack of hungry wolves."

That evening after supper, Eamon and Phoebe retired to their room so an exhausted Phoebe could rest after the day's exertions. Eamon held her in his arms as she slipped into sleep before easing away from cuddling her. He pulled on his pants and tugged on a shirt before walking into the kitchen in bare feet. "Da," he whispered, as he saw his father wandering around the kitchen, humming to himself. "I thought I heard someone pacing."

"Eamon, lad," Seamus murmured. "I didn't mean to wake anyone." He motioned to the table, and they sat, an unopened bottle of whiskey in front of them.

"You didn't. I couldn't sleep." Eamon thrummed his fingers on the tabletop. "I'm worried about Niamh. 'Tis takin' too long, aye?"

"Nay," Da murmured. "It could take up to a day or longer if she's unlucky. Seein' as she's having her second babe, I pray 'twill be easier for her."

Eamon nodded, his brows furrowed as he stared at the whiskey bottle. "Am I a fool, Da?"

Seamus grinned and nodded. "Oh, most likely. All men are, especially when we are in love."

Matching his father's grin, his countenance brightened for a moment before he sobered. "I fear she'll never care for me as I do her." He ducked his head after his quiet confession. "I don't know what to do to inspire her love."

"Ah, lad, you already are a fool." When Eamon flushed, he gripped his shoulder and squeezed it. "For you cannot see what is plain to us all." He paused as he waited for Eamon to fully focus on him. "Your wife cares for you, as much or more than you do her, but she's terrified of feelin' so much."

Eamon gave a huff of disbelief.

"And 'tis it any wonder? She's suffered terribly, from the sounds of it."

A resounding silence filled the room, with only the distant sounds of the town entering the cracked open window. "I know you were harmed by Colleen. I'm sorry, lad."

Eamon gaped at his da, unable to deny his words. "'Twas a difficult time for all."

Seamus made a sound of regret in his voice. "Don't, lad. Don't diminish the damage done by my marriage to her. Not to you." He closed his eyes, as though facing his son's sorrow was too much to bear.

"Da, I don't blame you. I never have." He stared at the icebox, but his gaze was focused on distant scenes. Of listening to his da and Colleen fight. Of jumping in front of Finn to take his brother's punishments when Finn sought love. "She didn't have the capacity for love that we needed."

"No," Seamus breathed, "nor did I. Not for her." He took a deep breath and met Eamon's gaze. "Forgive me, Eamon, for ever marrying a woman who would hurt the family. Hurt you."

"'Tis all right, Da. We're all together again. Mum and Maggie are returned to us."

"Aye, an' you'll find your happiness with Phoebe. I know it."

"I know you want to reassure me, Da, but I fear you are

wrong," Eamon whispered. "I almost blurted out that I loved her today, and I thought she would faint from disappointment."

"Perhaps 'twas shock," Seamus murmured. "Your wife has known too much disillusionment in life to believe in mere words."

Eamon tapped his hand on the tabletop, his eyes flashing with indignation. "What more am I to do, Da? I sat by her bedside every night for over a week, praying to God and bargaining with the Devil to keep her healthy. To keep her with me. I married her to keep her safe and because I can't imagine a life without her by my side. I protected her from her hurtful sisters. I ..." His voice broke off, as he fought tears of frustration and impotence.

"You're doing what you must to show her your steadfastness." Seamus sighed. "But I think your wee wife needs a push too. Encourage her to want your embrace. To miss your kisses. To want more than a brotherly cuddle in bed." He looked mildly chagrined at the last bit of advice but shrugged, as though it couldn't be helped. "She must know you want her as a wife, not as a cook or friend."

"But I do want a friend," Eamon murmured.

"Aye, but 'tisn't all you want, and she needs to understand that," Seamus said with a wry smile. He looked to the door, as it burst open, and Mary barreled inside. "Love, *a ghrá*, is all well?" He rose, his chair nearly toppling backward with his haste.

"Aye," she said, as she beamed at him, panting. She radiated joy and excitement with a hint of exhaustion. "Niamh is well. The babe is well. A fine big boy."

"A boy," Seamus breathed. "My first grandson." He opened his arms wide, pulling Mary close as he held her, kissing her head. "Oh, to be so blessed."

Eamon eased from the room, leaving his parents to

quietly celebrate the arrival of Niamh's baby, as Eamon returned to Phoebe. To dream of a day when he was so fortunate.

～

L ater that evening, Mary rested in bed, fighting sleep, as she waited for Seamus to return. His desire to see Niamh and to meet his grandson had prevented him from resting, and he'd whispered he would return after a quick visit. Sighing with gratitude, Mary said a quiet prayer of thanksgiving that such a man was her husband.

Rather than her abusive, abrasive second husband, Francois Bergeron, who had taken pleasure in destroying her spirit and in tormenting her children, Seamus was the opposite in every possible way. He relished being a father and rejoiced in every new family member. *Although the Mortimer girls are proving a challenge,* she thought with a wry chuckle. She hoped they would find their way, although Mary was losing her patience with Winnifred.

Curling onto her side, a smile bloomed as the door creaked open. "*A chuisle,*" she murmured, her eyes glowing with delight as Seamus gazed at her with absolute devotion as she called him "my heartbeat" in Gaelic. "You've returned to me."

He chuckled as he stripped. "Aye, love, I'll always return to you." He groaned with pleasure to pull her into his arms as he crawled into bed, her head resting on his shoulder. "Heaven," he breathed.

She ran her hands over his chest, kissing him every few moments, frowning when she sensed a deep tension thrumming through him. "What's the matter, love?" She pushed up, her auburn and gray hair falling over one shoulder. "Is Niamh ill? The babe?"

"*Shh, a ghrá*, they're well. They're fine. Maggie will spend the night there, as will Aileen. Kevin insists on sleepin' on one of the chairs, so, if there's trouble, he'll run for us." He kissed her head, his strong hands running over her back. Little by little, he relaxed in her arms.

"What is it, love?" She pushed up so that her forearms rested on his chest, her fingers stroking his trimmed beard.

One of his fingers traced over her delicate jaw, before caressing the elegant line of her throat. "Never doubt how much I love you. Or adore you," he whispered, a soft plea in his voice. At the flash of fear in her gaze, he pressed two callused fingers to her lips. "I spoke with Eamon tonight. About Colleen." He closed his eyes a moment. "I hate how my decisions harmed all the lads. Niamh too."

Mary heaved out a breath, wrapping her arms around him, as she pressed herself fully against him. "Oh, Seamus, dear God," she gasped. "Never scare me like that again." When he cupped her head and tilted it so she met his confused gaze, she bit her lip. "I feared you'd met another. That you ... didn't want me—"

He rolled her under him so quickly that she barely had the opportunity to gasp out "*Oof.*" He panted, pressing his lips to her cheek, as a shudder ran through him. Inching away from her, he rasped, "Not want you, lass? That I'd met another?" He shook his head over and over again, his startling blue eyes filled with a fierce determination, as his hands held her almost to the point of pain. "Never. Never," he vowed again, dipping forward to capture her lips in a searing kiss. "Dear God, what must I do to rid you of this fear?"

A tear trickled out, and he chased it with his lips, and she shivered at the soft caress of his mouth. She took deep heaving breaths to stifle her sobs, but a keening wail managed to burst forth. "Nothing. I'm foolish."

"No," he said, as he held her and refused to allow her to

move away from him. To hide from him. "What have I done to give you such doubt?"

"It sounded like you were saying goodbye to me," she whispered. Her eyes closed, shielding her from his penetrating gaze.

"Please, love, don't hide what I've done to hurt you." His voice broke. "I can't bear the fact I've hurt you." He paused, before breathing, "Again."

"Shay," she cried, her eyes opening to expose the anguish in her gaze.

"Tell me what I did," he pleaded, his head lowering with his failure. "Tell me what I said to hurt you so badly."

Mary took a trembling breath, her fingers playing through his silken locks. Finally she whispered, "Those were the words you whispered to me before I had our baby. Before I had Maggie. The last night we were together in Montreal." She paused, as they shared a tortured look. "They brought me back to the time I lost you. To my deepest fear."

He gaped at her, dumbfounded. "I do love you. I adore you, *a ghrá mo chroí*." He spoke the Gaelic words, "love of my heart," like a vow.

"I know," she whispered, her cheeks now soaked. "And I you, Shay. Some memories are hard to overcome. Some fears impossible to ignore."

"I will be here tomorrow … and the day after … and the day after that," he promised. "I will not lose you again."

"Hold me. Help me to believe," she cried, wrapping her arms tightly around him.

He held her, finding comfort in comforting her. With a shaky sigh, he felt the tension about his regrets from his second marriage ease as his whole focus was on his first love. His Mary.

CHAPTER 15

Phoebe sat in the living room of the O'Rourke house, quietly fanning herself as the day warmed. Even though she knew she should be thankful her new family was so protective of her, their insistence she not leave the home for a walk made her feel hemmed in. Although her uncle would never be a man she would esteem or would have faith in, she believed that the O'Rourkes would keep her safe.

With a jolt of disbelief, she sat back against the sofa. *Trust.* She trusted the large, at times overbearing, family. For, no matter what, they had shown devotion and dedication to each other. A steadfastness she had only dreamed of.

Letting out a huff of frustration, she heaved herself to her feet and walked to the kitchen. As she approached the back door, Maggie jumped in front of her. "No, Phoebe. 'Tis better if you don't go outside just yet."

Frowning at Maggie, a woman who was becoming closer to her than either of her sisters, she said in a low voice, laced with hurt, "Why are you keeping me a prisoner? Why can't I walk in the small yard or sit on the steps and watch the chickens? I want to be outside for just a few minutes."

The back door opened, and Eamon entered.

"Eamon," Maggie said, "please tell me that it's time."

Eamon gave a small nod, and Maggie sighed with relief.

"Time for what?" Phoebe asked in confusion. "I don't like surprises."

"Well, I'm afraid you'll have to accept this one," he said with a wink. He had a fine sheen of sawdust on his clothes and hair. "Come." He waited for her to grip her cane and walked with her in slow, measured steps out of the house, ignoring her persistent limp.

"Oh, how lovely," she breathed when she was outside, the soft breeze billowing over her. She stilled and closed her eyes, raising her face to the sun. A contented smile spread, her worry easing. After a moment, she jolted and covered her face with her free hand. "Oh, no! They'll worsen."

"What will?" he asked with a perplexed frown.

"My freckles."

"You daft woman, who cares if you are happy? Enjoy the sun. You've been deprived of being outside for too long as it is. And part of that is my fault." He raised one of her hands to kiss it. "I fear I didn't tell you the full truth. Although I did want to protect you from your uncle, I also wanted to give you a completed wedding present."

"A wedding present?" she asked with a shake of her head. She slipped her free hand through his arm, walking with him a short distance from the large O'Rourke home.

"Aye," he said with pride. "Our home." He paused at a small cabin with a covered front porch and two rocking chairs.

"Ours?" she breathed. "When? How?"

"My brothers and I have been working on it during every free minute. Which we haven't had enough of lately." He bit his lip as he looked at her. "Do you want to see the inside?"

"Yes!" She followed him up the steps, pausing at the threshold.

He swooped her into his arms, laughing as she shrieked with surprise, and carried her inside to a large room still dirty with sawdust everywhere. He gently set her down and kissed her deeply. When he broke the kiss, he stroked a thumb over her cheek, murmuring in a low voice, "Finally we have our own home to share." He swung his free arm wide, waiting for her response, his blue eyes shining with a hint of trepidation.

No furniture or curtains were present, although a potbellied stove stood on bricks along one wall. "You just built this?" she asked, wonder in her voice.

"'Twas nothing," he said. "The shell of the building was here. My brothers an' I finished it. Filled in the gaps in the walls. Rebuilt the floors. Made sure the roof won't leak come winter." He shrugged as though none of that were difficult work.

"Oh, Eamon," she breathed, before throwing herself into his arms, earning an "*Oof*" from him. "Thank you!"

"I know it looks a mess, but—"

She covered his mouth with hers, and, when she broke away, her green eyes were lit with an incandescent joy. "No, it's wonderful. It's ours." A tear tracked down her cheek. "I can see how it will be. With curtains over the windows and a bed in one corner. A small table with a pot of flowers." She sighed with pleasure. "Our home."

"Aye," he whispered, pulling her close. "Our home."

～

One week later, Phoebe worked diligently in the cabin to clean it and to make it feel like a home. A cloth was spread out on the table, as she labored over the curtains for their windows, gasping as she pricked her finger. She'd never liked sewing. She resented the fact she would need to sew more as a married woman, mending ripped hems and replacing buttons.

At a knock, she gladly set aside her project, limping to the door. "Maggie!"

The younger woman grabbed her in a quick hug before looking into the small cabin. "Oh, you've made progress." Her blue eyes shone with teasing. "Although you'd be further along if you allowed me to help you."

Phoebe sighed and rubbed at her blond hair. "I fear you are correct. I wanted to do something on my own." Her shoulders drooped, as though admitting she'd failed.

"Nonsense," Maggie proclaimed. "We're family, and I like to think we're friends. We help each other." She paused when she heard Phoebe's stomach growl. "Never tell me that you haven't eaten since breakfast." At Phoebe's embarrassed flush, Maggie towed her out the door.

"Wait! My cane," Phoebe protested with a laugh. Rather than head in the direction of the large O'Rourke family home, Maggie led her in the direction of the saloons. "I … I shouldn't walk in this direction."

"It's all right, Phoebe," Maggie soothed, her arm linked with her sister-in-law's. "You're not alone. Besides, Deirdre makes some of the best food you could ever eat, and I know she longs for company." Her eyes sparkled with mischief. "Besides, I thought you'd want to see how your sisters are doing."

Ducking her head, Phoebe bit her lip, so as not to laugh and to agree with Maggie's pronouncement. Ever since Seamus had declared that the two uninjured Mortimer sisters needed to work to earn their keep, Phoebe had been intensely curious about how Lorena and Winnifred were coping working at Deirdre's café.

Chuckling at Phoebe's silence and her display of loyalty, Maggie murmured in a conspiratorial manner, "I heard Ardan tell Kevin that Winnifred is driving poor Deirdre to distraction. Always complaining that no woman should have to work so hard."

"Oh my," Phoebe muttered. "I fear we've all been ... coddled."

Squeezing her arm, Maggie shook her head. "Not you, Phoebe. For some reason, you're not much like your sisters. Especially Winnifred," she said, with a disgust-laced voice. She marched up the back steps to the café and trooped inside, pulling a recalcitrant Phoebe along with her.

Phoebe stood stock-still upon entering, her gaze roving over the room. Bowls were set out on the butcher-block table, while stew bubbled in a pot on the stove, and bread cooled on a rack. Phoebe inhaled the intoxicating scents, realizing she had been wrong—she'd believed nothing could smell better than the O'Rourke kitchen. However, Deirdre's kitchen was heaven.

After taking another breath, she focused on Ardan's wife, Deirdre—a beautiful woman with red-gold hair, who stood with her hands on her hips as she glared at Winnifred. They stood near the pantry to the side of the room. For her part, Winnie stood with a mutinous expression on her face as she returned the glare.

"How could you have ruined the butter?" Deirdre demanded, ignoring Phoebe and Maggie. "'Tis a simple-enough process."

"Don't act all high-and-mighty when I'm the one with a sore arm and calluses on my hands, due to the manual labor you expect me to perform every day!" Winnifred snapped. She stomped her foot on the ground with a huff.

Lorena worked at the sink, washing a mound of ever-growing dishes, ignoring her sister's outburst. Phoebe edged closer to Winnifred as Deirdre pulled off the lid, before jumping back a step at the rancid smell.

"Mother of God, that reeks," Maggie gasped. "What did you do?"

"I put the cream in there to churn," Winnifred said with a defiant shrug of her shoulders.

Sighing, Deirdre rubbed at her forehead. "Did you wash it out with scalding water before each use, as instructed?" At Winnifred's baleful stare, Deirdre nodded. "Fine. Take it to the creek and clean it out."

"I'll go with you," Maggie said, with an encouraging smile to Deirdre. "That way you won't be alone, Winnie. But you have to carry it and to clean it yourself." Ignoring Winnifred's affronted gasp, Maggie spoke to Deirdre. "Can you fix Phoebe something to eat? She's been working hard at her home and forgot to eat lunch."

Deirdre nodded, her expression brightening only at the sight of Winnifred trudging out of her kitchen. "Please, have a seat," she murmured, as she spooned a healthy portion of venison stew and set a thick slab of oatmeal bread beside her bowl. "Eat up. If you're still hungry, I made cookies."

"Oh, you're too generous," Phoebe protested, her eyes closing with delight at the delicious aromas wafting around her.

"You're family, Phoebe." Deirdre glanced at Lorena, working diligently in the corner. "Does she ever talk?" she asked in a low voice.

"Rarely," Phoebe murmured. "Before the War, she was vivacious and opinioned, like Winnifred. But not mean, like Winnie." She hung her head, as though she'd been disloyal. When she saw no judgment in Deirdre's gaze, she said, "Something happened. I know she lost the man she loved. But I have the sense something more occurred."

"You don't know what it was?" Deirdre asked, as she mixed together the batter for a cake for the evening rush.

Shaking her head, Phoebe shrugged. "It was never to be discussed. A veil of silence descended, and no more was to be said about Lorena's disappointment."

Deirdre cast a worried glance in the eldest Mortimer's direction. "Well, it appears to have been traumatic." She paused in her fluid motions about the kitchen to focus on Phoebe. "Although she appears to be Winnifred's puppet, I've detected no true malice from Lorena. I sense it's more a way to deflect notice from her as she continues to mourn whatever she lost." She noted Phoebe's intent stare. "She reminds me of myself, before I met Ardan."

"Ah, love," Ardan murmured, as he entered the kitchen. "Before you had the good fortune to be swept off your feet by a man like me?" he teased, as he rubbed his strong hands over her shoulders. He winked at Phoebe, as Deirdre groaned with pleasure as his fingers worked to ease knots of tension.

"Aye," she sighed. "Before I realized that a life alone was no life at all."

Phoebe watched the O'Rourke couple, a fierce yearning filling her for her relationship with Eamon to evolve into so much more than it was.

～

A few weeks later in mid-July, Phoebe scrubbed and polished the floors, stove, and table in what would be her new home with Eamon. After weeks of working, the sawdust and grime had been washed away, the curtains were hung, and the bed had been made. She looked around the one room of her new home, and she smiled with satisfaction.

Standing at the door, a large bed with a pile of pillows and a homemade quilt sat against the left wall. The stove and cooking area were to the right of the doorway, with a small table to one side of the door. At the foot of the bed sat two rocking chairs, waiting for Phoebe and Eamon to relax and to share stories at night. They were a matched pair to the two rocking chairs on the front porch, for cool evenings outside.

Phoebe stretched her arms overhead, gasping as she lost her balance from trying to balance on her injured leg. She yelped as strong arms wrapped around her middle, pulling her against a solid chest. "Eamon," she breathed.

"I've got you," he murmured, kissing her head as he stabilized her. "You've done too much today, and you should rest."

Feeling like a petulant child, she wished she could throw a fit. That she could stomp her foot or could yell her frustration at her weakness and her need for help. Instead she took a deep breath and swallowed, hiding her annoyance. "Thank you for ensuring I didn't fall," she said, wriggling to free herself from his embrace.

"Hold still," he breathed into her ear. "Let me cradle you a little longer."

Her eyes closed at his soft voice, teasing at a memory from when she was sick. "You sound much like your father," she said, as she relaxed against him, sighing with pleasure as he kissed the side of her neck. "I never realized that until today."

"Da has a much stronger accent than I do," Eamon said. "I've only picked up a few words here and there that make me sound like I'm an Irishman."

She chuckled, her hands playing over his strong forearms. "No one would ever doubt your heritage, Eamon." She gasped as the palm of one hand stroked up over her belly to her breast and then back down again. "I'm a mess. I need a bath."

"You're beautiful as you are, but, if you want a bath, you'll have one." He kissed her one last time on the side of her neck and then carefully released her, ensuring she had regained her balance before stepping away from her.

Phoebe raised a hand to her head, smiling with embarrassment as she realized her shakiness had nothing to do with her injured leg but with her husband's embrace. Drawing in a deep breath, she silently berated herself to pull herself together and to stop acting like an infatuated schoolgirl.

She turned to find Eamon pouring a pan of steaming water, always waiting atop the potbellied stove, into the large wooden tub set near the kitchen stove. He added cooler water and then tested it.

With a smile, he held out his hand to her. "Come, love. The water's perfect for a bath. 'Twill ease the soreness of your muscles."

She balked, backing up until she met the wall. "I couldn't possibly undress in front of you, Eamon. You'll need to wait on the front step." Her hand clutched at the collar of her high-necked light-green calico dress.

"Bee?" he asked, with a shake of his head. "We're married. 'Tis fine for a husband to see his wife unclothed." He fisted his hands, holding them on his hips to prevent himself from reaching out to touch her.

"No, it isn't. It should never be proper," she gasped.

With an exasperated snort, Eamon muttered, "Who do you think helped you into and out of the ice baths when your fever raged? You weren't wearing anything then."

Paling, Phoebe pressed into the wall as though she were on the verge of fainting. "I presumed your mother and Maggie attended me. I know your father sat beside me at night. His soft words soothed me."

Shaking his head to clear it of confusion from the nonsensical words she had just spoken, he approached her.

"What are you talkin' about, Bee?" With careful, slow steps, he approached her. "*I* lifted you into and out of the bath. *I* sat beside you every night, calming you as you fought fever dreams. *I*—" His voice broke off, and he closed his eyes in defeat at the horror in her gaze.

"You?" she gasped. "All the time, it was you?" Her eyes widened with wonder, as she continued to stare at him. His head was bowed, and he stood in defeat in front of her. "You didn't forsake me?"

His head jerked up, his blue eyes shining with a fierce devotion. "Never, Bee. Never. From the moment Da told me that your uncle was a scoundrel, I was intent on finding a way to aid you." He took a step closer, his hand trembling as it rose to brush at her golden hair. "Nay, from before then. I knew on the steamboat that I'd find my way back to you after a little time. I was a fool to ever let you go. I had hoped to have more time with you in Fort Benton, as I accepted what I felt for you. As I hoped to earn your trust."

Her chin trembled, and her eyes filled while she battled tears. "I … I thought I was too much of a bother …" She broke off with a gasp, as he leaned forward, kissing her. His hands cupped her face, his fingers twining in her hair, as he held her close to deepen the kiss.

Moaning in distress as he backed away, Phoebe clutched his shoulders, tugging him close again.

"Never a bother, my beloved," he breathed. "Never." He kissed her softly again, before gazing deeply into her eyes with unguarded tenderness. "Come. Your bath water is cooling."

She ducked her head.

"Be brave, Bee," he urged. When she continued to stare at her feet, he murmured, "I'll lay on the bed and stare at the ceiling while you bathe. If you need me, you can call out for help. But we can still chat." He paused. "Or do you prefer to be completely alone?"

She raised her gaze to study him, shaking her head. "No, I have no desire to be completely alone." She looked around their small home with a rueful smile. "I know I will love our home, but I find I am missing the chaos of your family's home."

He grinned at her. "As am I. But we can join in the bedlam at any time. Remember that." He kissed her on her forehead and then moved to the bed, kicking off his boots before crawling onto it, resting with his hands on his chest and his eyes closed. "Get in, love, before it feels like you're having another ice bath."

She giggled and slipped off her clothes, keeping her back turned to him the entire time. Thankful for the curtains, which now made their home feel like a private oasis, she slipped into the bath with a contented sigh. "Ah, heaven," she whispered. Rather than chatter away, she rested in silence, soaking up the warmth of the bathwater, but also the peace of being in her husband's company with no words needed between them.

After many minutes, she forced herself to open her eyes, and she reached for the nearby soap. Rather than a harsh lye soap, this was a gentle soap that smelled of vanilla. She sniffed appreciatively. "Thank you, Eamon," she murmured. She cast a glance in his direction and saw his smile. She bit her lip before blurting out, "I know I never let you explain why you acted as you did on the steamboat. I'd like to understand that now."

He leaned up on his elbows, looking into her eyes. "I want you to understand." He smiled as he beheld her in her bath. "But I'd prefer talking with you when you are dressed and not such a temptation."

Flushing, she whispered, "How can you find me fetching while I'm in my bath?"

He groaned, flopping onto his back so he stared at the ceiling. "Don't be a tease, Bee."

Phoebe washed hastily, sloshing water over the sides of the tub before she rose. Grabbing the large bath sheet Eamon had set beside the tub, she wrapped it around herself, limping to the bed to perch on the edge of it as she faced him. "I'm not a tease. Winnie and Lorena were the flirts in the family."

Eamon rolled onto his side, his arm bent at the elbow, as he propped himself up while he took in the beauty of his wife. "Well, from where I lay, you're a temptation that is hard to deny, Bee." He paused. "And I never wanted your sisters. It's always been you."

Hope flared in her gaze as she stared at him, one hand wrapped tightly around the bath sheet knotted in the crease between her breasts, the other reaching out to stroke his leg. She needed to touch him in some way. "Help me to under-stand why you were so cruel to me." Her eyes were filled with pleading.

"Bee," Eamon breathed, as his hand caught hers, his fingers caressing and playing with her delicate fingers. "I was afraid. You've heard the story about how my mother and Maggie were separated from us for nearly eighteen years." He closed his eyes, reliving that pain. "I've had little faith in forever. Or the promise of constancy."

He paused, speaking in a low voice. "My da married again. A woman who was miserly with her love. She resented Da's inability to love her as he had loved Mum. She hated his children with Mary because he was devoted to us and adored us. We were a constant reminder of what Colleen would never have."

"What did she do to you, Eamon?" she whispered, her hand stroking over his leg.

"She'd find an excuse to punish one of us. Her favorite was Finn. He was so young, and she'd convinced him that he'd earned every blow." He shook his head. "How can a child be punished for crying because he missed his mum?" His eyes glowed with impotent rage. "I took as much of his punishment as I could, and we never told Da."

"Oh, Eamon," she breathed.

"I learned that love only brings pain, Bee," he whispered. "And, when I met you, it terrified me." He swallowed as he stared at her. "I'm sorry I hurt you."

Phoebe nodded and scooted up the bed, closer to him, as her attention was wholly riveted by his words and the sharing of his childhood pain. "Colleen is dead, and your mother has been back for a year now. Surely you trust Mary will not leave again."

Staring deeply into her gaze, Eamon shrugged. "On the steamboat, I wondered if she would be here when we arrived. I wondered if her return had been a dream. If she had come back to torment us, to taunt us, with what we could have had." He paused, studied his hands. "Mum isn't cruel, and I should have known better."

"You were afraid," she whispered in understanding.

"Aye," he said in a barely audible voice. "Terrified. And I hurt you. I'm so sorry, Bee. If I had been brave, I could have prevented you from being harmed. All of this is my fault." His hand stroked her injured thigh.

"Hush," she said, as she leaned forward, pressing fingers to his soft lips. By now, she had forgotten all about her bath sheet, falling loosely around her. "I've had too much time to think these past weeks, and I believe nothing would have been different. Even if you were courting me when the steamboat docked, I would have insisted on going to a hotel with my sisters. I would have seen my uncle, and nothing would have been different."

He kissed her fingers. "I hate that you were hurt." When he saw her nod at his words, he murmured, "But you understand your injury has not changed my regard for you? My desire for you?"

She looked down, gasping to find the bath sheet gaping open. Tugging at it, she tried to pull it closed. However, as she had scooted toward him, it had tangled on the bed behind her, and her attempt to wrap it tighter around her only stripped her more fully of any coverings.

Eamon opened his arms. "Come here, love."

With a groan, she fell forward, pressing into his embrace. She shrieked as he rolled them over once, effectively wrapping her up in the comforter that had been on the bed.

"Better?"

"So much better," she said into his neck, her arms wrapped around him. "I feel like I'm in a cocoon."

His hand stroked up and down her back. "Sleep," he urged as he held her close. "Rest in my arms."

She nestled her head under his neck, sighing with pleasure as she tumbled into sleep on his chest.

Eamon woke from a light doze with Phoebe wrapped tightly in his arms. He sighed with relief to feel her snuggled up against him, breathing deeply as she slept in his embrace. Running his palms lightly over the silky skin of her back, he relished this chance to hold her. To cherish her.

For too long, he had felt they were out of step with each other. Today, as he had revealed his fears, he felt a flicker of hope for what they could have, if they were both brave and if both shared the truths they kept hidden in their hearts. After weeks watching his parents and his married brothers, Eamon knew he wanted a marriage similar to theirs. One filled with love, respect, admiration, affection, and trust.

When she struggled in his embrace, not fully awake, he murmured, "*Shh*, love, you're safe. You're well. No one will hurt you. I promise."

"Eamon," she breathed, her eyes closed, and her voice sleep-slurred. "I wish this were more than a dream."

"Wake up, love, and you'll see that it is. Wake up, beloved." He ran his hands over her cheeks, brushing her hair back as she pushed herself up, staring at him in confusion. "Hello, Bee."

"Eamon," she gasped. "What are you doing here?" She dropped down onto him again with another gasp, causing him to grunt as she knocked the air out of him. "Why don't I have clothes on?"

He kissed her head, his hands soothing her as he sensed her panic. "You took a bath, and then we chatted. Your towel fell off, and we wrapped up in the blanket." He smiled as she calmed at his rational explanation.

"You mean, we didn't ..." She tilted her head up to look into his eyes, flushing when she saw the amused patience in his gaze.

"No, love, we did nothing more than have a wee cuddle." His hands continued to rove over her soft skin. "If you haven't noticed, *I'm* fully dressed."

She gave a small shriek, pushing away from him while attempting to clutch the blanket to her. In her haste to get away, she stripped herself bare, before falling to the floor with a resounding *thud*. "Ouch!"

"Bee!" Eamon cried as he scooted to the side of the bed to look at her, huddling with her knees drawn up, her blond hair a riotous mass around her head. "Did you hurt your leg?"

"My leg is fine," she snapped. "My pride is damaged." She glared up at him. "I'm sure this is a common occurrence for you." When he stared at her with befuddlement, her glower intensified. "Waking up with a naked woman in your arms. Charming her with your soothing, melodic voice. Easing her of her sense of propriety."

Eamon gaped at her for a long moment, his cheeks flushing beet red with aggravation from her words. "You know nothing." His voice emerged as a low hiss, before he flung himself back onto the bed, ignoring her on the floor.

"Are you offended I'm not eager for your attentions?" she asked in a mocking voice.

He let out a long sigh before muttering, "Don't spout your sisters' nonsense, Bee. It doesn't suit you. And it does not honor what we have." He took a few deep breaths, willing his anger to calm. "You are wrong." He spoke in a deliberate, low voice. "You're the first woman I've ever had in my bed. The first naked woman I've ever held in my arms." He waited, unable to hide a triumphant gleam in his gaze when she poked her head over the top of the mattress to look at him. "I won't lie to you, Bee. I've kissed other women. But I've never slept with another. I've never made love to another."

"Why?" she whispered. "Surely you had the opportunity."

He rolled onto his side and stared at her, as though studying her and seeing her for the first time. His gaze never left hers. "You have a horrible opinion of men. I suppose that's fair, for I've had barely a better one of women all these years." His lips turned up in an imitation of a smile as they stared at each other. "When I was a mere lad, I thought I'd enjoy women, take what was offered, but never allow myself to be bound to one. Never give a woman the chance to hurt me as I saw Da ache after he lost Mum. As I saw Da suffer during his miserable second marriage."

"Eamon," she whispered, her hand reaching forward to

stroke his arm. "You could have gone to a place like the Bordello."

He huffed out a laugh. "You've met Da. He'd thrash us if he knew we visited such places. He's tried to instill in us that a man should respect, and hopefully revere, the woman he is with. And that frequenting a place like the Bordello makes a mockery of what should be sacred."

"How does he explain his marriage to his second wife?"

Eamon shrugged. "He was a widower, terribly lonely, with six children to raise. I think he lied to himself, convincing himself he could care for another woman as he did, as he does, for Mum. Yet he and Colleen were miserable."

"I thought he had a relationship with the Madam."

Eamon nodded. "Aye, he's good friends with her, although never anythin' more. He found he missed having a wise woman's insights. Da doesn't lie, and he swore he never had an affair with the Madam." He smiled wryly at Phoebe. "I doubt my mum would have befriended the Madam if he had."

Phoebe bit her lip, as she stared at him a long moment, assessing if she could trust what he said. Finally she said in a low, hesitant voice, "You've never woken with a woman in your arms before?" When he shook his head, a subtle tension eased from her shoulders. "You've never seen a naked woman before me?" He jerked his head no again. "You truly want me?" Her voice broke on *me*.

He angled his body so he could stroke the tips of his fingers over her cheek. "What more do I have to do to prove it to you, Bee? I was a fool on the steamboat, and I'm sorry." His brilliant blue eyes glowed with remorse. "But, ever since we arrived here, I've done everything I can to show you my constancy."

She swallowed. After a long moment, she breathed, "Yes."

"What do you need from me, Bee?"

A tear trickled down her cheek, and she whispered, "Nothing." She arched up onto the bed, her nakedness ignored as he pulled away to scoot farther away from her. "No, Eamon, that's not what I mean." She crawled onto the bed, pulling the tangled blanket around her. Kneeling by his side, she reached forward to cradle his face in her palm. "It's me, Eamon. I have to find the strength to believe that I am truly what you want."

Eamon opened his arms, holding her close as she tumbled forward. "You are, my Bee. You are." He felt her shiver, and he wrapped the blanket tighter around her. "Come. Get under the blankets. The nights are still cold here."

She arched up, kissing him and silencing what more he would say. "No," she gasped, as they broke the kiss. "I want you to love me. Show me what we can have, Eamon."

Toppling her to her back, he leaned over her, his gaze filled with concern. "I don't want you to feel that I rushed you. I'd never want you to regret what we do together. Or to resent me."

She smiled tenderly at him. "I could never resent you. Not now that I understand." She stared deeply into his gaze, her breath catching. "Don't you want me?"

"Don't I want you?" he repeated, his eyes widening in surprise. He trailed a finger from her temple to her jaw and back up again, his gaze roving over her beautiful face before meeting hers. "I've wanted you since the moment I saw you trip up the walkway to the steamboat in Saint Louis. Finn had to hold me back from vaulting forward and helping you because you didn't need my aid." He paused. "Every conversation, every look, every moment in your company has only made me want you more."

He leaned forward, kissing her softly. "But I need you to promise me something, Bee." He took a steadying breath and met her gaze, his eagerness and trepidation equally visible in his gaze. She frowned, cupping his face. "Our first time might not be what you dreamed it would be. Have faith that it will only get better between us."

A dazzling smile burst forth, and she wrapped her arms around his neck, pulling him toward her. "Don't be afraid, Eamon. Let's be brave together."

The following morning, Phoebe awoke, groaning as she stretched. Muscles she didn't realize she had were sore. She poked her head over the mound of blankets, frowning to find the cabin empty. With an aggrieved huff, she fell back against the pillows, pulling the blankets around her. How could Eamon have left her on their first morning, now that they were truly husband and wife?

She closed her eyes as she battled lifelong insecurities. Images and sensations from the previous night came to her, and she shivered from the pleasure she had felt in her husband's arms. She smiled as she remembered laughing and giggling with him. Never would she have thought to have found such joy in her marriage bed.

Her hands beat on the covers in agitation to be alone in their bed. She'd dreamed of waking up with his arms wrapped around her. Why would he leave?

Hearing boot steps on the front porch, her eyes widened, and she pulled the covers to her chin. What if it wasn't Eamon who entered? Peeking over the covers, panting with anxiety, she watched the door creak open. When Eamon slid inside, she collapsed backward. "Oh, thank heavens."

"Bee! You're awake," Eamon said. Something clattered on the tabletop, and he murmured a few words to someone on the porch steps, and then the door was shut and bolted.

Leaning on her elbows, she glared at him. "Where were you? Why did I wake up alone?" She sniffed, her stomach grumbling.

Chuckling, Eamon smiled. "I brought us sustenance, dear wife. I woke up ravenous, for you and for food." He winked at her, his smile broadening at her fetching flush. "I didn't have the sense to bring over supplies yesterday, and Kevin and Aileen eat at the big house most days, so I thought we could do the same."

"What will your mother think? A wife who can't even care for her own husband." Phoebe held a hand to her head.

Eamon opened a trunk and pulled out a robe for her, urging her to rise and to slip into it. When she stood in front of him, he stole a kiss. "My love, she'll never care about that. She only cares if her sons are happy. And she can see we are. Desperately so."

Her luminous green eyes met his, and she traced her fingers through his stubble. "You are?"

He nodded, his eyes lit with a fierce rapture. "How can you doubt after the night we spent together?" He kissed her softly, backing away before he deepened the kiss. "I hoped to find passion, Bee, and we did. But I never thought to find joy and humor. I never knew we'd laugh and talk so much." He shook his head, as though words failed him.

"I never knew I could share so much of myself without fear," she whispered, her gaze filled with vulnerable hope.

"Yes, my darling. And I trust you would keep my fears, and me, safe." He pulled her close. After a moment, he groaned. "Come. I promised myself I would ensure you ate before I coaxed you back into bed."

She giggled, her hands running through his silky black hair. "Some promises can be broken." She nipped his lower lip. "Come back to bed, husband," she entreated, tugging on his hand to follow her. "I've never cared whether a meal was cold."

"Oh, you are a temptress," he murmured, as he worked to kick off his boots.

She smiled at him, her eyes glowing with the promise of further shared passion. "Only for you, my Eamon. Only ever for you."

CHAPTER 16

Answering the knock on her front door a few days later, Phoebe smiled with relief to see a grinning Maggie and a serene Mary. Phoebe had an irrational fear of seeing her sisters, as she knew Winnifred would say something sly and cutting. Phoebe had no desire for anyone to tarnish the joy she had found with Eamon. "Hello," she said, unable to hide a blush, as this was the first she'd seen her husband's family since she had moved to her cabin. Eamon had brought food home every day as they had a short honeymoon.

"Oh, thank heaven," Maggie said, as she launched herself forward, hugging Phoebe and nearly tumbling the two of them to the ground with her exuberance. "I feared you'd still be abed. Or not dressed." She rolled her eyes. "Eamon was cross that we wanted to visit you today."

Flushing at her husband's name, Phoebe attempted to appear nonchalant at the mention, although she couldn't hide her pleasure at hearing it spoken.

"Newlyweds," Maggie muttered with a roll of her eyes and a snort of disgust.

"One day you'll find yourself in a similar situation, and you'll have no desire to be interrupted," Mary said with a soft stroke down her daughter's back. "I'll have to encourage Phoebe to be more charitable and to refrain from heckling you."

"Mum," Maggie murmured, flushing bright red. "You know I won't marry for years and years."

"Oh, I doubt that," Mary said, before wisely turning the conversation away from Maggie. "I hope you're not disappointed 'tis the two of us visiting rather than your sisters."

"No! Of course not," Phoebe stammered out. "I imagine they're busy at the café, helping Deirdre."

Maggie snorted. "Lorena is a true help, as she washes dishes and doesn't complain too much. Winnifred's chattering is enough to drive anyone to murder." She shook her head. "Now that she doesn't churn butter, Deirdre has her chopping vegetables, sweeping floors, and doing anything else needed." With a roll of her eyes, she said, "She carries on as though Deirdre were on the verge of murdering her through too much work."

"Maggie," Mary admonished, as she saw Phoebe flushing with embarrassment. "We're here because we hoped you would join us as we visit Niamh and her wee babe."

Phoebe nodded. "Oh, I'd love to." She glanced inside her cabin and then looked at her in-laws with embarrassment as she saw the baskets at their feet. "I wish I had something to bring her."

"Niamh will enjoy the company," Maggie said. "Besides, we have enough food for a week, and she won't eat half of it because Cormac's not home."

"He's still not home?" Phoebe asked, as she grabbed her cane and shut the door. They walked at a leisurely pace the short distance to Niamh and Cormac's home, allowing

Phoebe to enjoy her time outside and to prevent her from overtaxing her weakened leg.

"Nay," Mary said in a mournful voice. "Hopefully within a day or two. I know Niamh is fretting, but there's nothin' to be done. He must work when there is work."

Phoebe's eyes lit with delight. "Can you imagine his joy to return home to realize he has a beautiful son?"

Maggie giggled and looped her arm through Phoebe's free one. "You've never met the wee beast, as Niamh calls him. You don't know if he's beautiful or not."

Shrugging, Phoebe said, "All babies are. And, with Niamh as his mother, there's no way he could be anything but handsome."

Mary nodded, approval and affection shining in her gaze for Phoebe. "Aye, an' his father is an attractive man, although you've never properly met him. He departed right after your injury, and you were out of your mind with pain the night he was at the house when you were hurt."

Phoebe smiled. "It will be nice to meet him."

"And Dunmore. You never properly met him at your wedding," Maggie said. "He's another family friend. Although he's busy now, driving his stagecoach."

Phoebe bit back a smile as she looked at Mary. Eamon had told her about Dunmore's interest in Maggie, and Phoebe had witnessed Dunmore watch Maggie with a covetous gaze after the wedding ceremony. However, Maggie persisted in her claim that they were only good friends. Phoebe knew time would tell what their relationship would become.

She fell back a step as Mary and Maggie led the way into Niamh's comfortable home. Although it had originally been a one-room cabin, like the one she shared with Eamon, the O'Rourke men had expanded it to have two small rooms off the back, so that Maura had her own space, and Cormac and Niamh had a proper bedroom.

The three women tiptoed inside, in case the baby was sleeping, but Mary called out a hello when she found Niamh in the rocking chair, breastfeeding her son. Phoebe looked around the large comfortable room with a sofa and chairs scattered around.

"Where's Maura?" Maggie asked, as she moved to the kitchen area to place food in the icebox.

"With Da. He stopped by a while ago to take her on a ramble. Wants to wear her out so she'll sleep through the night." She kissed her mum's cheek and then held out a hand to Phoebe. "'Tis grand to see you, Phoebe. You're finally out of that bed."

Flushing, Phoebe nodded. "Yes, and you have a beautiful son."

Niamh nodded, lifting him up to rest on her shoulder as she patted on his back. "Aye, he's a fine lad, although he waited long enough to finally join us. Now he's eager to meet his da." She kissed her son's head, tucking him under her chin after he gave a satisfactory burp. The baby had arrived a few weeks later than they had thought he would, but he seemed healthy and well.

Phoebe stroked a gentle hand over his back, as she sat with a relieved sigh on a chair near Niamh. "What's his name?"

Niamh smiled. "I don't know. I haven't named him." She smiled at Phoebe's shocked expression. "I want to wait for Cormac. Doesn't seem right namin' him when the man's away."

"No, it doesn't," Mary said, "although I'll never understand why you hadn't decided before he left on his journey."

Niamh kissed her son's downy soft head again, speaking in a soft murmur, "I didn't want to tempt fate, Mum."

Mary smiled at Maggie, who worked to brew a pot of tea, while Mary settled in the living room area with her daughter and the woman she was coming to consider her daughter. "Now, love, you know your disappointments have come to an end. You've a fine husband, a beautiful daughter, and a gorgeous baby boy."

Niamh smiled, delight in her gaze. "Aye," she whispered. "The past can be hard to forget, Mum."

Phoebe squirmed as she felt she were intruding on a private scene, meant for only those two women. However, Mary motioned for her to remain sitting, when Phoebe rose. "I hate intruding."

"You're not," Mary said. "We are a family who talks about our past. The good and the bad. The joys and the pains. You'll accustom yourself to it."

Phoebe sat in a daze at Mary's words. "I fear that is a foreign concept to me. That's not how I was raised."

Mary gripped her hand a moment. "You'll adapt." She beamed at Niamh as she handled the precious bundle to her. "Oh, aren't you a fine strong lad?" Mary murmured, as she rocked him in her arms. "Has Nora been by?"

"Aye," Niamh said with a yawn. "Twice. I'm doing well an' not bleedin' much, so she's not concerned. She's glad I've a reason to get up and out of bed every day. Says the worst thing a woman can do is lay about doin' nothin' during her forty days."

Maggie stood still, listening with rapt interest. "Why is that?"

Niamh shrugged. "I have no idea, but I know I feel better if I do something more than lay in bed, so I find I must agree with her. Besides, wee Maura keeps me busy."

Phoebe stared at the women in awe. "Why would Nora visit?"

Mary ran a soothing hand over the back of her slumbering grandson. "Oh, did we not tell you that Nora aided Niamh in the birth of the wee prince?" She kissed his head when he gave a stuttering sigh. "Nora has quite a bit of experience with that sort of thing."

"Working in a brothel?" Phoebe gasped.

Niamh laughed, as Maggie shrugged. "You never know what you'll learn or where you'll learn it, Phoebe. And knowledge is knowledge, especially when you live in the back end of nowhere."

"You do know she is a good friend to our family?" Mary asked, with a severe stare at Phoebe. At Phoebe's nod and apparent acceptance of that comment, Mary relaxed. "All that matters is that Niamh and the lad are well."

~

Cormac slipped into the home he shared with Niamh, tiptoeing inside as he had kicked off his boots on the front porch. He knew how exhausted Niamh was as the pregnancy progressed, and he had no desire to wake her as she slept. A slight breeze wafted in through the open living room window, and he poked his head into Maura's room, smiling as he saw her curled on her side with a doll tucked along her front.

He pulled out his shirt from his pants, yanking down his suspenders, as he anticipated holding Niamh in his arms again. The long days on the trail would be forgotten the moment he could breathe in her scent and could kiss her. All would be right with his world the moment he could feel the baby move. He took a step into their room, coming to an abrupt halt as he saw her laying on her stomach. "Oh, God," he moaned. "No."

Rushing to the side of the bed, he stroked hands down her back, before rubbing at her shoulders, his fingers tangling in her long auburn hair. "Niamh," he breathed. "Forgive me." His whispered words woke her, and she mumbled as she rolled to her side.

"You should ask for my forgiveness," she muttered, as she opened one eye to stare at him and smile. "Hello, love. *A shíorghrá,*" she murmured.

"Niamh," Cormac rasped, as he fell to his knees by the bed. "The baby. I'm so sorry." Tears leaked onto his cheeks.

Niamh sat straight up, almost bashing him in the head. She glanced away from him a moment and then relaxed. "What's the matter, Cormac?" She rubbed her fingers through his beard, rubbing away his tears, and then played with strands of his long hair.

He motioned to her. "You're not pregnant. The baby. You lost the baby?" he whispered in a tormented voice. He paused as she smiled brilliantly and sat up on her knees to wrap her arms around his neck.

"No, my love," she whispered. "I had our baby, and he's a fine, impatient lad. Asleep in his crib." She motioned in the direction she had glanced a moment before. "He'll awake soon, demanding to be fed and to be changed."

Cormac's breath emerged in a *whoosh* as his worry eased. Wrapping his arms around Niamh, he pulled her close. "Forgive me, my love. My beautiful, brave, darling wife." He peppered kisses over her face. "Forgive me for not being here. I should never have agreed to drive to Helena."

She kissed him, losing herself in their embrace. "Don't be daft," she breathed. "'Tis the busy time of year, and I know you must work." Cupping his cheeks, she murmured, "I wanted you beside me, holding my hand. I wanted to hear your voice, encouraging me and reassuring me, as I thought I'd never survive the pain."

She sighed as he kissed her forehead. "But I understand, Cormac. You must earn for us now, so we have money to survive the winter. 'Tis the way of our life." She smiled at him. "You'll have plenty of time to change nappies and hold our boy in the off season."

His blue eyes shone with regret. "I want that time now. I hate missing a second with you and the children."

Niamh ran her hands through his hair, her hazel eyes filled with wonder and a deep fatigue. "Do you know, Cormac, what it means to me to have you return to me? To have you *want* to return to me?" She turned her face into his palm, as he thumbed away a tear. "To know your love, not your disdain?"

"Always, my Niamh, always," he vowed. His glance flitted to the cradle. "Tell me about my son."

Niamh laughed softly and fell forward into his embrace. "He's a good sleeper, who wakes only to eat." She smiled lovingly in the direction of the crib. "He has blue eyes and downy black hair." She bit her lip. "I waited for you to name him."

Cormac rose to peer into the crib. "He's beautiful, Niamh." Reaching out a shaking hand, he traced his fingers over the baby's smooth cheek, his breath catching as his babe's mouth turned up into a smile at the soft caress.

Niamh had crawled over to watch, a devoted, loving smile bursting forth. "He's always cheerful. He only cries if his nappy is wet or if he's hungry."

"What a good lad," Cormac murmured, stroking a hand over his head one more time before turning to Niamh. "What a lucky lad to have such a mum." He caressed her head and shoulders. "I'm so sorry I wasn't here, love."

"You're here now," Niamh murmured, pulling at him. "Hold me. Tell me about your adventure. Too soon I'll have to rise with the wee demon."

Cormac laid beside her, pulling her into his arms with an appreciative sigh. "Heaven. All is right in my world when you are in my arms." He kissed her head, his gaze returning to the crib in the corner of the room. "What should we name him, darling?"

She shrugged. "I always think of Irish names, but I want to know what you would like."

He caressed her shoulders. "Almost any name would be fine with me."

She kissed his jaw and whispered, "Da suggested a few names. Rian or Cillian."

"Why did he like them?" he asked, as he pressed kisses to her cheek and brows.

"Rian means little king," she said with a sigh. "I think he simply likes the name Cillian."

Cormac leaned away, smiling at her. "Either would be a perfect name for our boy." He gazed into her shining eyes. "Which do you like better?"

"I think Cillian. He will already be treated like a little king as the first grandson. He doesn't need a name to match." They laughed together.

"Thank you, Niamh," he breathed. "Thank you for this life. Driving my oxen home today, knowing I had you and Maura to return to …" His hands shook as they stroked through her long hair. "I never realized how different everything would feel to know I had a wife and child to come home to." He kissed her. "And now, children."

She beamed at him. "I never realized how I would feel, knowing it was you returning to me." She kissed his lips and cuddled against his chest. "I love our life, and I can't wait to watch our children grow."

Cormac murmured his agreement, holding her close. as he waited for Cillian to wake to hold him in his arms for the first time.

CHAPTER 17

In early August, Phoebe wandered from the small cabin she shared with Eamon, wanting a few moments alone. Although she loved her new family, at times she yearned for a little quiet. Although she now had space that was solely for her and Eamon, someone in the family invariably dropped by for a visit, which left her little time for her silent introspection. She found she was in desperate need of it.

Now, over a month after her marriage to Eamon, she felt like she was finally becoming part of his family. Although they had always been friendly, ever since she and Eamon had moved to their cabin, their welcome had become less guarded. She understood Seamus and Mary would be protective of their son, wanting him to find a happiness akin to theirs. However, Phoebe knew Eamon would never love her as Seamus loved Mary.

Phoebe paused as she approached a small stream that entered the Missouri a short distance away. Here, it meandered and tumbled over rocks, with willows along the banks. Birds called to each other, before swooping out in an attempt to scoop up an unsuspecting insect. The sounds of the town faded away, as she let out a pent-up breath, fully relaxing.

Love. Eamon used that word to refer to her, but he had never said he loved her. The omission was intentional. It had to be. For, if he loved her, why wouldn't he say so when they shared passion? Why wouldn't he whisper it in her ear before they fell asleep?

"He doesn't love you," she whispered to herself. "He won't lie and say what he doesn't mean." She bowed her head, as though the admission of such a truth was more than she could bear.

Footsteps sounded behind her, and she turned to see who would interrupt her quiet interlude. Blanching, she breathed, "Uncle."

"'Bout time I got you alone," he muttered. "Those O'Rourkes have kept you under lock and key." He stared her up and down and frowned. "Damn, you're no good to me now."

She stood tall, her hand gripping her cane. "I was no good to you before, Uncle. I never would have agreed to your plot."

He rocked back on his heels as his eyes gleamed with jovial malice. "You must understand, dear niece. What you desired had no part to play in your future. All that mattered was what I deemed necessary." He glowered at her. "All that changed when those confounded O'Rourkes interfered." He waved one pudgy hand in her direction. "Now they've ruined you and any potential profit I could have made."

"You do understand you are a vile, disgusting man."

He shrugged, the motion causing the middle button on his scarlet waistcoat to pop open. His black suit was slightly faded, as though it had been washed a little too vigorously. For her uncle, she suspected today's outfit was tame for his standards. "What you think of me doesn't really matter. I wish you'd taken any other boat. It's my misfortune you took the one steamboat this year that carried the O'Rourke brats home." He sighed. "How fortune can continue to spite me so …"

"Whereas I will be forever grateful they were on my steamboat." She held her head high to walk past him, although she had to lean on her cane, as her leg ached after the walk to the stream and standing in place for so long. She gasped when he grabbed her arm in a punishing grip.

"You might have escaped me for now, but I will find a way to make you pay for thwarting me."

Phoebe wrenched her arm free, bashing her cane against his shin to force him to release her and to back up a step. "Never touch me again. Never speak to me again. You are not my uncle. You are not my family. I am a married woman, and I look to my husband for guidance. Never you." She leaned heavily on her cane as she limped away.

"A virile, healthy man like that O'Rourke boy will never be satisfied with a cripple. Mark my words, you'll come begging to me for help. And I'll show you no mercy!"

Phoebe made her slow, painful way to her cabin, refusing to burst into tears until she had closed and latched the door behind her. She curled onto the bed, soaking her pillow with her tears. Ignoring the knock and Maggie's voice calling to her, Phoebe laid in quiet misery, her uncle's words replaying in her mind.

～

E amon looked toward the back of the store to see Maggie hovering near the rear entrance. She never visited the store, as he knew she hated the attention the men gave her. Eamon also wondered if it was because she feared the return of her step uncle, Jacques Bergeron, although Jacques would know better than to ever set foot in their establishment. "Mags," he murmured, glancing to ensure that Finn and Niall were fine without him. He'd come to realize his presence wasn't necessary, as Niall had filled in so ably during his absence.

"Eamon, I'm worried," Maggie burst out. She gripped his arm, as he frowned at her. "I visited Phoebe twice today, and both times she didn't answer the door. The second time, I'm certain I heard her inside crying."

"Crying?" Eamon whispered. "What could have happened?"

Finn approached, clapping him on his shoulder. "Is everything all right?" His astute gaze took in Maggie's worried appearance.

"I have to check on Phoebe," Eamon said. "I know I'm not here enough. I'm sorry."

Finn shook his head. "Niall and I are fine. I know you'll work hard for me when it's my turn to be a newlywed." He winked at his brother. "Go. Ensure your wife is well."

Eamon smiled at his brother and best friend, before rushing from the rear entrance of the store. He paused long enough for Maggie to catch up with him. "I'll escort you home first, Maggie." When she shook her head, he stared at her in confusion.

"No, if she's hurt, I should be there. If it's nothing I can help with, I'll leave." She squeezed his arm. "I promise."

Eamon tugged her along, walking at such a fast pace that Maggie nearly jogged beside him. He vaulted onto the sturdy porch and pushed against the door. With an "*Oof,*" he slammed into it, finding it locked. He slammed his hands on the door, calling out in a voice loud enough to carry inside, but hopefully not so loud to announce to the entire town that his wife had locked him out. "Phoebe?"

He leaned forward, squinting, as though that would aid him in hearing better. At the sound of a sniffle, he pounded on the door again. "Bee, open the door, or I'll break it down."

He heard a faint moan and then a *thud*. Backing up to ram the door, he caught himself just in time as the door eased open. "Bee," he breathed, his voice catching at the sight of her tear-ravaged eyes and reddened nose. "Nothing could be that bad."

Before she was shut out, Maggie stepped forward. "Do you need me?" After Phoebe shook her head, Maggie backed away. "Comfort her, Eamon," Maggie murmured, before slipping down the steps in the direction of home.

Eamon absently nodded, his gaze wholly focused on his wife. "Bee, my love, what happened?" He urged her inside, shutting the door behind them and latching it again. He grasped her arm, stilling when he saw her wince at his soft touch. "Bee?" His breath ratcheted up. "Who dared hurt you?"

"I'm sorry, Eamon," she whispered. "I wanted a little time alone." She looked around their cabin. "Your family—our family—is friendly and welcoming, but I rarely have time just for me."

"All you'd have to do is tell them," he whispered.

"I didn't know how," she said, as she ducked her head. "I'm not used to anyone heeding what I want or need."

He tipped her head up with gentle pressure under chin. "We might seem overbearing, but we O'Rourkes understand the need for a little time by ourselves, love. If you ask for it, they will try to give it to you."

She nodded and stepped into his arms, sighing with relief as he enfolded her in a gentle embrace. "It will be hard for me to believe that, but I will try." She tightened her arms around his waist. "I went on a walk."

"A walk?" He cupped her face, his gaze filled with distress.

"I know it was foolish, Eamon," she cried, tears coursing down her cheeks. "But I wanted to feel normal. Like any

241

normal woman who didn't have a cruel uncle eager to turn her life into a living hell. I wanted to feel the sun on my face, walk in the tall grass, listen to the birds sing."

He smiled at her, his hands caressing her head. "And did you?"

She met his smile, her eyes glowing for a moment. "Yes. For a short time. It was wondrous."

"Tell me about it," he urged. "Tell me about your wonderful outing, before it was spoiled."

She closed her eyes, a smile lifting her lips, as she spoke in a soft, eager voice. "The wind played with my skirts, and I remember laughing at the feel of it, cooling me off and playing with my hat and skirt at the same time. The walk to the small creek was longer than I thought it would be, or I'm weaker than I hoped I'd be after so long."

She sighed, as though what she envisioned delighted her. "The creek still had plenty of water, and it tumbled over the rocks, creating a soothing sound. The birds chirped and sang and swooped overhead, unfettered and free. The grass swayed in the breeze, and I forgot about the town and all the rowdy men. For a moment, I was filled with peace."

He made a soft murmur, kissing her forehead.

"And then he came," she said, stiffening in Eamon's arms. She opened her eyes, regret and fear in her gaze. "My uncle. He took one look at me and said I was no longer of any use to him." She frowned. "I was relieved but also offended. I don't understand what he meant."

Eamon ran a finger over her cheek. "You have the look of a well-loved woman, my darling. He realized you were no longer the innocent you were when you arrived. He also must know I'd kill him if he harmed you again." He frowned as he recalled her flinch at his touch on her arm. "Did he?"

She nodded. "Yes. He gripped my arm, although I might have made it worse when I wrenched it away from him."

"Don't exonerate him, Bee. He has no right to touch you. Ever." His blue eyes glowed with his sincerity and passion. "Whoever is allowed close to you is always your decision. Whoever touches you is always your decision. I'm sorry he provoked such sorrow in you again."

She smiled, her pride evident in her tone. "I hit him with my cane. Thwacked him in his shin, so he backed up a step and yelped."

He chuckled, his hands softly brushing over her hair and shoulders. "Good. 'Twill teach him to think twice before he approaches you again."

She pressed closer, wrapping her arms around him again. "Why did you come home? I didn't think I'd see you until tonight."

"Maggie was worried," he whispered. "I know this will make you believe we're overprotective, but she meant well."

"I'd never be upset with her because she's concerned about me," she said. "I'm not used to warranting such consideration."

"You're my wife. You will always be worthy of our care, love." He held her close, soothing her and himself. However, he couldn't banish the sensation that something more had upset her. Nor could he dispel the disappointment that she had failed to share it with him.

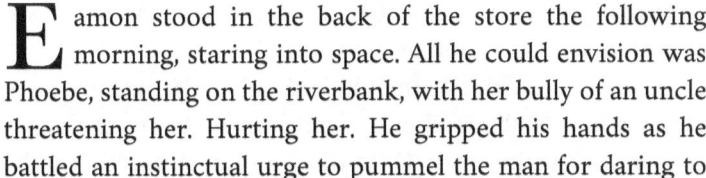

E amon stood in the back of the store the following morning, staring into space. All he could envision was Phoebe, standing on the riverbank, with her bully of an uncle threatening her. Hurting her. He gripped his hands as he battled an instinctual urge to pummel the man for daring to intimidate his wife.

Finn poked his head into the back and frowned. "What's

the matter now?" he asked. "I thought you were better, since things with Phoebe had improved."

"How long until we open the store?" Eamon asked in a low voice.

"You know we open when we want. None of the men here are what you'd call early risers. Besides, we don't have much left to sell." He paused, his black hair longer than ever, his blue eyes filled with concern. "She has you tied in knots, Eamon."

Heaving out a sigh, Eamon turned to face his brother and best friend. "Aye, but that's what happens when you're in love." He rubbed at his hair, freshly cut from a recent trip to the barber's. "I'm fighting my natural inclination to kill her uncle."

Finn rolled his eyes and perched on the edge of a table in the back room that Da used as a desk, when he wasn't at his office at the warehouse. "What's the man done this time?"

Eamon took a deep breath in an attempt to calm his roiling emotions. "The problem is, I'm not certain. I have the sense Bee didn't tell me everything. From what I do know, he scared her and left a bruise on her arm." He saw the flare of disgust in Finn's eyes and nodded.

"Da doesn't want us to physically harm the man, but Chaffee should know he has no right to torment any of the Mortimer women." Finn rubbed at his head, pushing a strand of ebony hair behind one ear.

"Aye, but how do I do that without actually beating the man to a pulp? The sight of him fills me with rage." Eamon closed his eyes and took deep breaths.

Rising, Finn tapped him on his shoulder. "Come. Let's see if Kevin and Niall are about. Should be fun to see the man's reaction at having four O'Rourkes approaching him as he eats his breakfast at the café."

Eamon smiled. "Ardan will be there too."

"Aye, so five of us. Come." He nodded his head in the direction of the back door.

After enlisting Niall, Kevin, and Lucien's help, the small band of O'Rourke brothers ambled toward the café. Although still early, the August day held the promise of the heat to come. A flock of pelicans swooped low over the river, while moving with a graceful synchronicity.

Eamon entered the café first, noting that Uriah sat at a table near the rear of the café with a half empty plate in front of him. Today Chaffee wore a black suit with a burnt-orange waistcoat.

"Boy, I tell you. The food isn't nearly as good as before," Uriah bellyached, as he shoveled in another mouthful. After swallowing, he spoke in a carrying voice. "I swear, you're trying to swindle your customers into paying more than they should for half-rate food."

Eamon pulled out the chair to sit across from Uriah, smiling with unveiled menace as the man gaped at him open-mouthed. "I suppose you're hoping, if you complain enough, Ardan will feed you for free, so you don't scare away the other customers."

"Now, see here," Uriah snapped, his cheeks flaming red. "I have every right to express my dissatisfaction."

"Aye, but not while you're also stuffing your face. If you didn't like it, you wouldn't eat it." Eamon glared at him. "Everything's a contest to you, isn't it?" He tilted his head to the side, as though attempting to understand the unfathomable. "Outsmarting our da. Earning a free meal. Abusing your nieces."

Uriah set his elbows on the table, his breath heaving from him as he glared at Eamon. "You believe you are a champion to those girls, but they'll prove you a fool. For only a fool cares to protect women who have proven themselves to be unworthy of anyone's regard."

"How do you make that out?" Finn asked. He smiled as Uriah blanched, as the man finally noted the large number of O'Rourkes lingering nearby. "Do you believe because they've known disappointment and aren't … chaste that they are undeserving of our regard?"

Uriah raised a pudgy finger to pick at a piece of food caught in a tooth. "You'll never convince me that any of the O'Rourke brothers, paragons of virtue and respectability, would choose a woman who's thrown away her innocence."

Eamon leaned forward, lowering his voice to a menacing growl. He failed to notice that all of the customers leaned in his direction, intent on listening in on the conversation. "Heed me well, Chaffee. The Mortimer sisters are now members of our family. Which means, if you harm one of them, you harm an O'Rourke." He paused. "If I ever hear of you speaking to my wife again, never mind touching her, you will regret it."

"How dare you threaten me! I'm a lawyer," Uriah sputtered. "I am owed your deference and respect."

"Respect is earned," Ardan said in his deep voice, standing directly behind Eamon. "Respect is not bestowed due to some flimsy piece of paper." He crossed his arms over his chest.

"I have every right to speak to whomever I choose, especially my niece."

Eamon shook his head. "If you truly are a lawyer, you'd understand that, when she married me, the wishes of her husband come first. And my wish is that she never suffers your presence again. For you only bring her pain and heartache."

Uriah snorted and sat back in his chair. "As if you can prevent me from approaching my own flesh and blood."

"One day, Uriah," Eamon growled. "One day, you will find yourself sorely in need of aid, and no one will come running to render it. We will discover the truth behind you, and you will be shown for what you truly are."

Uriah rolled his eyes. "I have nothing to fear, boy."

Ardan chuckled. "I fear you do, Chaffee. You should fear hunger. Contrary to what you might believe, neither my wife nor I need your business to continue to thrive. And I'm sick and tired of your baseless complaints. I'm tired of you makin' my wife cry. From now on, find another place to eat. You're not welcome here."

Uriah's eyes rounded. "You can't do that! This is the only café in town," he sputtered, as he looked from one to the other. "I'll sue you."

"Please do. You'll have to go to Virginia City or Helena to speak to a judge. We wouldn't mind the peaceful interlude," Finn muttered.

"Leave us be, Chaffee," Eamon said, "or you will sorely regret it." He rose, leaving the stunned man behind, following his brothers into the kitchen. The homey space was redolent with the scent of cooling bread and cakes, while the savory scents of bacon hinted at the recent breakfast rush. Lorena washed dishes, while Winnifred dried them. Eamon frowned as he saw his sister-in-law, Deirdre, sitting on a stool, her head bowed in defeat.

"Deirdre?" he asked, watching as Ardan approached her to murmur soft words in her ear. She leaned against her husband, seeking the solace he offered. Eamon battled jealousy as he yearned for just such a relationship.

She sniffled, her smile filled with embarrassment. "I'm fine." She looked up, blushing to see her kitchen filled with O'Rourke brothers. "I never expected so many of you to visit today."

"We had business that couldn't wait," Finn said, his gaze darting to Winnifred.

"What could you possibly have had to do in our café?" Deirdre asked, her head now resting on Ardan's shoulder.

"Ensuring Chaffee understood he is to stay away from the Mortimer sisters," Eamon said in a clipped tone.

"And to never come here to eat again," Ardan added. He smiled as Deirdre heaved out a sigh of relief.

A dish clattered to the floor, shattering into pieces. "You've banned him from eating here?" Winnifred asked, her eyes wide with shock, as she glared at every O'Rourke. "How could you?"

"How could we not, Winn?" Finn asked, his head cocked to one side, as he studied her reaction. "He's a bully, and he's a menace. He has no right to make Deirdre cry."

"It's not his fault she's so thin-skinned."

Ardan rose to stand at his full height, his blue eyes glimmering with ire. "Watch it, little girl. No matter what Da said, you're playing with fire. If you ever insult my wife again, I will not defend you."

Winnifred shrugged, as though that were no great loss, although Lorena paled as though understanding the inherent threat behind such a promise. "If you truly accepted the Mortimer sisters, you'd accept Uncle Chaffee as part of the family too."

Eamon shook his head as though he were hard of hearing, while Ardan gaped at her, and Finn huffed out a shocked puff of air. "Are you demented?" Finn finally asked. He shared a long look with Ardan. "Listen well, Winn. Either you choose the O'Rourkes as your family or you choose Chaffee. You can't have both."

Deirdre spoke up in her soft, husky voice. "Choose well, Winnifred, for you never know how much you desire someone's esteem until you've lost it."

CHAPTER 18

Phoebe gathered her courage a few days later and walked past the back side of the café, down a side alley, and to the river. Walking through the high grass, she approached the roiling river, marveling at its constant motion as it gurgled and moved ever toward the distant sea. It seemed to have dropped since their arrival, and now that it was August, steamboats docked farther down the river. Wagons arrived, carrying vast amounts of cargo, while stagecoaches ferried the multitude of passengers to Fort Benton, eager to travel deeper into the burgeoning territory.

Her blue calico dress blew around her legs in the slight breeze, and she held her face up to the sun for a moment, relishing being outside. For too long, she had been cooped up, recovering from her injury. And, if what Maggie said was true, she needed to enjoy the fleeting summer sun while she could.

"I'm surprised he let you out of his sight."

Phoebe spun to face her youngest sister's mocking smile. "Hello, Winnie. Eamon doesn't control me. He worries about me."

"Is that so?" Winnifred asked, as she sauntered toward her sister in a beautiful rose-colored dress. "Have you always been so gullible?"

Phoebe stiffened before flushing. "I know you are wiser to the ways of men, but that doesn't mean you understand my husband better than I do."

Coming to a halt beside Phoebe, the younger woman glared at the river. "I hate that horrid river. I wish we'd never been raised near it. That we'd lived in some landlocked place." She seemed to catch herself, as though she had revealed too much, and she faced her sister with a devious glint in her eyes. "How are things between you and Eamon?"

"Fine," Phoebe said, fighting a deepening blush. "He's a wonderful man and very considerate."

"Consideration doesn't keep a woman happy. Consideration doesn't keep a marriage from failing."

Phoebe spun to face her sister, glaring at her, as she crossed her arms over her belly—as though to protect herself from her sister's words. "What are you saying, Winnie?"

Pasting on an expression of innocence, she held a hand to her chest, affronted at Phoebe's challenging tone. "I resent that you believe I'm intentionally trying to hurt you, Phoebe. The fact is that I do have more experience with men. I do understand them better. And I fear what your husband is doing to you." She paused and murmured, "Or what he will do."

"What do you mean?"

"Can you imagine how he must feel, Phoebe?" When her older sister stared at her in abject befuddlement, she continued, "Forced to marry a woman? Not having any choice in the matter?" She sighed in consolation. "As we know, if there's one thing a man wants, it's a choice."

Phoebe paled at her sister's words but refrained from saying anything.

Winnifred barreled on. "And then, as the days and weeks pile into months and years, the resentment grows, until he can no longer imagine a life with a woman he never wanted but was compelled to marry. Why should he feel any responsibility toward her? Why should he stay?" She sighed again, at the misery that would soon befall her sister. "I can't imagine being as brave as you, Phoebe. Knowing what is coming, and yet still being as loving and giving to your husband."

Phoebe stood as though someone had just gutted her. Quivering, pale, and breathless. Her gaze was lost, unfocused, and she began to shake her head from side to side, in an attempt to dispel what Winnifred said. She went limply into Winnifred's hug, as though a rag doll.

"You are so courageous, Phoebe. How I admire you." Winnifred ran a hand down Phoebe's back before walking away.

For long moments, Phoebe stared in the direction of the river and the distant bank with unseeing eyes. Instead she saw Eamon. Smiling at her. Teasing her. Encouraging her. Loving her. Tears coursed down her cheeks to realize it was all a charade. How appropriate a word Winnifred had used to describe her. *Gullible.*

For she knew, time would prove his inconstancy, and he would leave to find a woman he chose. A woman he loved.

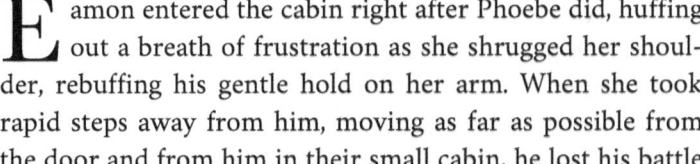

Eamon entered the cabin right after Phoebe did, huffing out a breath of frustration as she shrugged her shoulder, rebuffing his gentle hold on her arm. When she took rapid steps away from him, moving as far as possible from the door and from him in their small cabin, he lost his battle with his temper. "Bee, what in God's name is the matter?"

She sat and held a blanket up to her chest, shielding herself from him. Glaring at him, she said, "I realized I've been a fool."

He shook his head in befuddlement. "You're the least foolish person I know. What do you mean?" When she continued to glare at him, he squinted his eyes as he studied her. "Who filled your head with nonsense?"

"No one," she snapped. With a flush, she ducked her gaze and muttered, "I merely saw sense."

He took a slow step in her direction, having no desire to increase her ire or to scare her. "And who helped you see sense?" When she clamped her jaw shut, he whispered, "Was it Winnifred?" He nodded when she gazed at him in aston- ishment at his deduction skills. "Aye, she seemed a bit too pleased with herself tonight at supper. Even Maggie remarked on it."

Phoebe watched his approach and stood with alacrity, dumping the blanket on the floor as she faced him with her fists clenched and eyes blazing. "I don't care what you say, Eamon. She's my sister. She's known me the longest."

Tilting his head to the side, Eamon observed her with blatant disappointment. "No, she's manipulated you the longest. She's deceived you the longest. Don't misconstrue whatever she said today for her carin' for you. You know better than that, Bee."

"How dare you?" she seethed, hitting him on his chest. "How dare you presume to … to …" She broke off, flushing as he stared at her with compassion in his gaze. However, she saw something else. "Don't you dare pity me!"

"I don't pity you," he breathed and then yelped as she swatted him on his chest, backing up a step. "Bee?"

"I wanted a marriage where I chose to marry my husband. I wanted a marriage where I knew there was affection and caring and respect." She sniffled as she valiantly fought tears

252

of despair as she stared at him, watching her in horrified wonder. "I never wanted ..." Her voice broke off on a sob.

"This?" he rasped. "You never wanted what we have? Because you didn't choose it? Because we didn't have the fairy tale? Because you insist on clinging to anguish?"

Paling as she stared at him, she gasped, "That's not fair!"

His jaw ticked, and his cheeks were mottled with his anger. "Neither is this, Bee. Believing anything Winnifred says over what you know to be true. Over what I've shown you to be true." He paused, his blue eyes filled with disillusionment. "I thought you were better than that. I can see I was wrong."

He stormed from their home, uncertain where he would go. He knew he couldn't return to his parents' house, for he didn't want their pity masqueraded as concern. He swore under his breath. Married a short time and already miserable. He should have kept to his vow with Finn. Better an uncle and a bachelor forever than to suffer this heartache.

In the distance, he saw the gentle lamp's glow in the upstairs rooms in Ardan and Deirdre's home. Although Eamon didn't want his entire family's input, he yearned for someone from his family to give him guidance. Feeling like a fool, he knocked on the back door to the café, belatedly worrying he was interrupting a romantic interlude between his brother and his wife. However, he soon heard Ardan calling out, and Eamon relaxed at the sound of his brother's voice. Ardan had always found a way to soothe him.

"Eamon?" Ardan asked, as he thrust open the door. "You look like hell." He yanked him in for a bone-crushing hug, and Eamon clung to him, as though he were a lifeline. "*Shh*, lad, all will be well."

Shaking and unexpectedly bereft, Eamon followed Ardan's lead, traipsing behind him through the clean café kitchen and up the stairs to the living quarters over the café.

The living room had a comfortable sofa, two chairs, and side tables. Curtains covered the window, and lamps on the tables cast a warming glow over the room. A bouquet of wild-flowers sat on the low table in front of the sofa, and a book-case was half filled with tomes in one corner of the room.

"Deir, Eamon's come to call." His voice held a quiet warning to not ask too many questions. "Alone."

"Eamon," Deirdre murmured, running her hand down his arm, as she stared deeply into his shattered gaze. "I hope you will forgive me. I'm tired after a long day of cooking." She turned to kiss Ardan on his cheek, before slipping into their bedroom and closing the door to the room she shared with Ardan.

"I never meant to interrupt your evening," Eamon protested.

Ardan slung an arm over his younger brother's shoulder, pulling him close, as he urged him to a comfortable chair. "Deir understands, Eamon." He paused as he watched his brother rock back and forth in a dazed stupor. "Help me to."

"Bee resents me," Eamon whispered. "Resents she never had a choice. Hates she felt forced into marriage." When Ardan remained silent, Eamon looked up at him from his lowered gaze, afraid to see Ardan's agreement in his gaze. Instead Ardan appeared perplexed and unconvinced.

"How did she come to that belief?" Ardan leaned forward, resting his elbows on his knees, staring intently at his brother. "For she seemed delighted with you at the most recent family dinners."

"Until tonight," Eamon murmured, running his hand though his thick black hair. He rose, pacing the living space. "Tonight, it was like I was a leper."

"Aye," Ardan said in a gentle voice. "She didn't want you near her."

Eamon sighed, rubbing at his forehead, as he recalled her

jerking away from his soft touch when he passed the basket of bread from her. Or flinching when he rested his hand on her shoulder. Rather than lean into him as she always did, she had stiffened and arched away.

Ardan waited until Eamon collapsed in his chair again, his gaze bereft. "I wonder if she spoke the truth tonight, lad."

Rubbing at his eyes, Eamon said, "She seemed to believe it, Ard."

"Aye, but I wonder if 'tis because she thought it was *your* truth, and she dreaded the day you'd proclaim her worst fear." He paused. "Do you remember the fights Da and Colleen would have? How she always said things that weren't true, putting words in his mouth, as though trying to take away the power of what he might say?"

Eamon nodded. "Aye. She'd always pronounce that Da was about to leave her. Or that he thought another more beautiful. Or that he wished he'd never married her." He shrugged. "Perhaps those thoughts were true, but Da isn't daft enough to ever consider saying such words to a woman, least of all his wife."

Ardan chuckled. "No man should be that much of an *eejit*." He sobered. "But 'twas as though Colleen wanted to take away the power of the potential pain. And, by doing so, she ruined the promise of the present."

Eamon sat in stunned silence as he stared at his eldest brother. "Do you believe Bee was doing that?"

Shrugging, Ardan sighed. "I couldn't say. You know her better than I do. But it sounds like she was speaking from fear." He shared a long look with his brother. "I imagine someone who knew her well could provoke her worst fears."

Eamon nodded, his eyes glistening with near hatred. "Winnifred."

Ardan smiled sadly. "Not every family is loving, like ours. It seems your Phoebe has had a hard time with her sisters."

He paused. "Although I'm uncertain if Lorena is anything like Winnifred."

"Is there something more I could have done to show her how much I cherish her?" Eamon ran a hand through his hair again. "I fear Bee believes I cannot protect her because Bell still runs his saloon. I never challenged him. We didn't run him out of town."

Ardan snickered. "And tell me how we would have done that? The man's a giant of a beast, and his clientele is the most disreputable in Fort Benton." He made a face as he looked at his brother. "An' you know that's saying something."

Ardan shook his head. "No. I know Da is eager to find a way to punish Bell for how he treated Phoebe and the Madam, but Da's patient. And so must we be. Lull the man into complacency, and then we can find a way to hurt Bell, as he hurt us."

Eamon groaned and rested against the back of his chair and sat in silence for a long time. Ardan settled into his chair, content to wait. "You've always been the patient one," Eamon murmured. "When we were children and acting out. When we were angry because we didn't understand why Mum was gone. When we fought over food or a girl's affection." Eamon stared at Ardan with immense gratitude shining in his eyes. "You never yelled at us. You never wanted Finn and me to be anything other than we were."

"Why would I?" Ardan asked, a quizzical furrow of his brows. "You're perfect as you are, Eamon. With all your flaws and faults. They're what make you unique and ... *you*. I wouldn't want you to be other than who you are." He paused. "Nor does your wife."

Eamon clenched his jaw as he tapped his palms on his knees. "How do I overcome her fears?" His shoulders slouched as he bent forward. "I've been constant. I've shown her who I am."

Sighing, Ardan sat back in his chair with his feet stretched out in front of him. "I don't know, Eamon. I suspect she'll have to find her courage. No one can do that for her."

CHAPTER 19

The following afternoon, Phoebe sat on her front porch, the soft breeze blowing around her. She had foregone a hat, as it would have blown off, and, besides, she was in the shade. Her gaze darted from the direction of the big house to the backs of the businesses in town, searching for any sign of her husband. She had not seen him since he had stormed out of their house the previous night, and she feared where he had gone. For what he had done.

She set down her sewing, as she made a garbled mess that would need to be torn out and resewn. Unshed tears blinded her, and she could not form a straight line. A pervasive sadness filled her, and she worried she would never overcome her sorrow. Unlike other days, she could not cling to anger or any other emotion. Today her companion was sadness, and she feared she had no one to blame but herself for its presence.

When she blinked, her vision cleared, and her sister Lorena approached, wearing a demure fern-green dress that highlighted her striking coloring. Rather than tied back in a severe bun, her red hair was in a loose knot at the back of her nape, adding a softness to her and making her seem more approachable and friendly. She neared Phoebe's porch, standing a few feet away. "How are you, sister?"

"Fine," Phoebe croaked out.

Twisting her hands in front of her, Lorena fidgeted her weight from foot to foot. "Might I sit with you on the porch? I'm uncertain if that would go against your husband's edict, but I would like to speak with you."

She stared at her eldest sister for a long moment, as Lorena had desired little to do with her for years. Ever since Lorena's "disappointment," as their mother had called it. Although Phoebe never knew what that entailed. After a prolonged silence, Phoebe nodded. "I'd enjoy the company."

"You have a lovely home, Phoebe," Lorena said with an approving nod, as she sat in the large chair that was Eamon's. It seemed she would be eaten up by it. "Your husband provides well for you."

"I know I should want for nothing more."

Lorena stared at her with concern, her green eyes glowing with shame. "I fear I've not accepted the role that was my due as the eldest. I've forced you into being the responsible, dutiful sister, while I moped and dreamed."

"Lo?" Phoebe whispered.

Lorena let out a deep breath, as she stared at the backside of the burgeoning town. Men scurried from place to place, either to earn a wage or to bet what they'd earned. Dogs lolled in the shade, their gazes trained on the back doors, ever hopeful for a wayward scrap. "Do you know how much of a torment it is to me to live with the O'Rourkes?" Her eyes glowed with her passionate sincerity. "Every day I'm faced with my inadequacies. I'm forced to acknowledge how much I failed you and Winnifred." Lorena closed her eyes. "And I'm sorry."

"Lo," Phoebe breathed again in a shocked voice, her hand

fluttering around like a drunken butterfly, uncertain if she should touch her sister or not. She finally settled it again on her lap, afraid her sister would reject her offer of comfort.

"I've seen what a family should be. What an elder sibling should act like." Lorena shook her head, as she stared at the distant town buildings rather than at her sister. "Every day I'm confronted by all that I'm not."

"Stop it, Lo," Phoebe said, finally reaching forward to grip her sister's hand. "You've suffered. I know you have."

Lorena nodded. "Yes, and I've clung to the pain like it was a security blanket. I chose suffering over love. I chose the surety of my past disappointments over any promised dreams. I've been a coward, Phoebe." She took a deep breath. "And it breaks my heart to see you follow my example."

Dropping her hand, Phoebe sat ramrod straight as she glared at her sister. "How dare you imply I'm a coward?" She flushed with her anger. "Who are you to give me advice?"

Nodding sadly, Lorena's smile was filled with melancholy. "I relinquished my role so long ago, I don't know how you'd ever consider any advice I have to give. But I still have advice." She stared at Phoebe for a long moment, their matching green gazes clashing. "And I know it's far more worthy than anything Winnifred could have told you."

Blanching, Phoebe ducked her head. "Winnie told me the truth."

"No," Lorena snapped. "Winnie told you what she wanted you to accept as your truth so that you remain as miserable as she and I are. So that we remain the Miserable Mortimers. She clings to that name for us. It brings her comfort to know that none of us are any happier than she is."

Phoebe shrugged. "She said nothing but the truth yesterday."

"I imagine she told you that it must be so horrible to be married to a man who had no choice but to marry you. And

261

how awful it must be to face a lifetime married to a man who would always resent you. Why should such a man ever truly care for you?" She spoke as Winnifred would, friendly but cutting. When Phoebe paled, Lorena nodded. "Can't you hear the lies?" Lorena paused and took a deep breath. "The same lies I've come to understand Mama wove?"

Phoebe nodded.

"Mama's dead, and I've come to realize how much she manipulated us. Me," she swallowed. "How much she used my hurts and fears to ensure I did her bidding." She met Phoebe's shocked gaze, as no one ever spoke out against their mother. "Winnifred is too much like Mama."

"How can you say that?" Phoebe whispered.

"How can't you see that Winnie spun your fears and put them onto your husband so they were more believable to you, just like Mama would have?"

Shaking her head, Phoebe furrowed her brows, her eyes filled with doubt and pain.

Lorena cupped her sister's face, her fingers smoothing the lines marring her brows. "She knows what you most dread, Phoebe. How could she not? She's your sister. And rather than shelter those fears, she twisted them around and used them to hurt you and to put a wedge between you and your husband."

A tear coursed down Phoebe's cheek. "I know what she said was true."

At her sister's wailed words, Lorena made a soothing sound. "No, you don't. You're terrified of what you believe might be true. And you're risking your future by throwing accusatory words at him." She paused. "How would you feel if he said such things to you after you'd shown your steadfastness for weeks?"

When Phoebe went silent, tears coursing down her cheeks, Lorena continued. "He sat beside your bedside, night

262

after night, begging anyone and everyone for you to improve. He stood up to Uncle, daring him to harm you or us ever again. He was eager to marry you, Phoebe." She nodded when Phoebe stared at her in wonder. "Your husband confronted uncle with an army of O'Rourkes at his back, warning him to never speak to you again after he bruised your arm. And Ardan banned him from the café!" She nodded as Phoebe gaped at her dazedly.

"You know Mama. You know how many men she had around. As the eldest, I saw them more than you or Winnie. Never did I see a man show devotion and a dedication to her as I've seen Eamon show you."

"He'll leave," Phoebe whispered. "They always do."

Lorena sighed and ran a hand over the loose wisps of hair at her forehead. "Yes, he'll leave." At Phoebe's sharp inhale of breath, she met her sister's terrified gaze. "He'll leave when he can no longer envision living in a home where he is not trusted or esteemed. You'll push him away. And then you'll have to live with that agony for the rest of your life."

"Lo, what should I do? How can I find the courage?"

"Oh, Phoebe, you don't need to find the courage. You just need to believe in yourself." She pulled Phoebe close, and they rocked side to side for a long while as Phoebe cried. When Phoebe eased away, Lorena whispered, "Thank you."

"For what?" Phoebe asked, as she swiped at her cheeks.

"For letting me be your big sister. I've realized I want to be more than a woman who mourns forever. I want to be more." She shrugged.

"You will be, Lo," Phoebe said with a smile. "You'll always be my big sister. Thank you." They sat in companionable silence, before chatting about the large O'Rourke family and the few townsfolk they knew.

❧

Phoebe sat in dazed silence after Lorena's departure. Her head spun as she considered all that Lorena had said and had inferred. Suddenly she felt like she had a big sister again, a foreign sensation since she had been a girl.

With a start, she sensed she wasn't alone. She looked up to meet the Madam's inquisitive gaze. "Madam," she whispered. "I ... I'm afraid I wasn't expecting you."

Madam Nora laughed. "Few expect me to arrive on their doorstep." She pointed to the rocking chair beside Phoebe. "May I sit?" At Phoebe's nod, the Madam settled her eggplant-colored skirts. "Ah, what a lovely place to spend a quiet afternoon in contemplation."

Phoebe's gaze darted to the Madam to determine if the older woman mocked her. When she noted Madam Nora had closed her eyes and seemed at peace, Phoebe relaxed, pushing her chair into a soft rocking motion.

"Have you begun to forgive your eldest sister?" Nora murmured.

Phoebe froze, gawking at Nora. "Yes. Although I know it will take time. I have too many years of memories to overcome."

"Memories," Nora murmured, settling her head against the back of Eamon's tall chair and dwarfed by it. "They are both a hindrance and a blessing. Don't allow your coloring of what you *think* you recall to prevent you from having the relationship you desire. Not everything is as we remember, just as not everything will be as we wish."

Phoebe furrowed her brows, as she thought through the Madam's cryptic words.

"Don't think so hard, child. You'll give yourself a permanent frown." Her smile bloomed. "Wrinkles come soon enough without hastening their arrival."

Giggling, Phoebe shook her head as Nora appeared

young and vivacious, although she was near forty. "Why concern yourself about Lorena?"

Nora glanced out at the backside of the burgeoning town. Although men's voices could be heard, the perception was that they were farther away from the chaos than merely a few blocks. "I've known many Lorenas in my life." She shared a long look with Phoebe. "And too many Winnifreds to count." With a sigh, she shook her head with regret. "I wish I could say life is kind to women like Winnifred."

"I imagine we're a boring trio," Phoebe said, attempting to battle her resentment at Madam Nora considering the Mortimer sisters as *typical* women.

Nora chuckled. "On the contrary. You, dear Phoebe, are unique. You refused to accept your fate. You fought back and surprised your uncle. He's not used to women who aren't docile." Madam Nora smiled. "I've enjoyed watching his disappointment."

Shaking her head in confusion, Phoebe asked, "What do you mean?"

"You were to bring him riches, darling girl. And you defied him. Now Bell is demanding compensation, and Uriah's finding it far more difficult that he thought to free himself from the woman who latched on to him, a Mrs. Davies, and he's on the verge of financial ruin. All in all, I'd consider that a successful summer season."

"All the Mortimer sisters were to bring him wealth, not just me," Phoebe protested, cringing at the guilt in her voice.

"Oh, dear, you are naive." Nora laughed. "And you must learn to take pride in what currently shames you." She let out a deep breath and spoke in short staccato words, as though explaining a difficult concept to a person hard of hearing. "You were the only untried sister, or didn't you know that?" She raised an eyebrow as she watched shock course over Phoebe's expression. "If Chaffee and Bell had attempted a virgin auction with you and your sisters—and had been paid dearly for the honor—they would have been murdered for deceiving two of the three bidders." Shrugging, Nora murmured, "Although that might not have been such a horrible outcome for the town."

Rubbing at her head, Phoebe whispered, "How did I have no idea? They always acted terrified to take after Mama."

Nora sighed. "I don't know about Winnifred, but Lorena has the appearance of a woman who lost all she held dear. And has had to find a way to keep living." She paused. "Does that describe your mother?"

"No, Mama liked men, but she never really cared for them." She paused. "They were a necessity for her to continue to live the life she desired."

"Well, from my short interactions with your sisters, that only describes one of them." She held Phoebe's gaze a long moment. "And I hope you are intelligent enough to discount whatever sisterly advice she would deign to give you."

Flushing, Phoebe ducked her head. "I fear I've been foolish."

Nora patted her hand. "We all are, dear, when we are terrified to love." Her brown eyes sparkled with understanding and fondness as she beheld Phoebe. "What is important is that you apologize to the man you love. He's spent enough time sleeping at his brother's."

Phoebe groaned, covering her face with her palms. "Does everyone know I'm such a failure as a wife?"

"The O'Rourkes are the most talked-about family in town, and you're an O'Rourke now. Everyone is fascinated by you." She shrugged. "During downtime at my … establishment, the men talk about all of you. They seemed particularly disappointed that you decided to wed Eamon."

Phoebe shivered. "I never would have worked with you."

Nora tipped her head back, a full-bellied laugh bursting

forth. "Oh, heavens, no," she gasped. "Seamus would never forgive me, and I value his friendship more than any amount I would have earned from you." She shook her head. "No, a few wish they could have married you."

Phoebe shook her head. "They're mistaken. I'm a cripple."

"Cripple?" Nora asked with a tilt of her head, as though she were unfamiliar with the word. "How could you ever consider yourself in such a way?" After a moment, she flushed red with indignation. "Another lie from a well-meaning family member, I imagine."

"I will always walk with a limp." Her eyes gleamed with the sorrow of that truth.

Nora nodded. "Yes, you will, although it might lessen with time." She paused. "I imagine you'd esteem Eamon less if he had a limp."

"Of course not," Phoebe snapped. "That's not ..." She broke off, as she stared at the Madam in wonder.

"No, that's not love," Nora said in a soft voice. She leaned forward, her brown eyes gleaming with a fervent honesty. "Heed my words, young Phoebe. Doubting your husband's love and steadfastness will drive a wedge between the two of you that will never heal. Trust in him, as he trusts in you. Believe in him, as he believes in you. That is the very essence of love."

Nora rose, squeezed Phoebe's shoulder, and departed, leaving Phoebe deep in thought.

~

E amon halted abruptly when he entered the big kitchen of the family home and found Winnifred sitting alone at the table. "Where is everyone?"

Shrugging, she continued to work on her needlepoint,

her black hair tied back in a loose braid. "With Niamh and her children. They'll be home soon to work on supper."

Eamon poured himself a glass of water from the pitcher by the sink and leaned against the counter rather than sit near her. "Why aren't you at the café, helping Deirdre and Ardan?"

With a huff of exasperation, Winnifred glared at him. "You may have married my sister, but that doesn't give you the right to believe you can control my life as well." When he stared at her balefully, she snapped, "Deirdre doesn't want me there anymore. Finds my presence a distraction."

"A distraction or a menace?" he murmured, a malevolent gleam in his gaze.

"You have no right to speak to me in such a manner. If you knew how I'd suffered—"

"I could care less about how you've suffered," he roared. "You've clung to imaginary hurts and used them as a bludgeon against everyone who might care for you." He pushed away from the counter, breathing hard as he glared at her with his eyes flashing with anger. "Now, you've harmed my marriage. You've caused Phoebe to doubt. And, for that alone, I will never forgive you."

Winnifred gave an indifferent shrug of one shoulder, her head following the movement of her shoulder. "If she has such little faith in you, then that is your problem."

"You're a witch," he rasped, as he forced himself to pause a step away from her. "I've never been so tempted to harm a woman in my life." With a deep breath, he backed away from her and spun to face the kitchen sink, staring out the window over the sink. "I will find a way, Winnifred. I will earn Phoebe's trust and prove false every doubt you've sewn in her mind. And, when we are reconciled, there will never be a place for you in our lives."

CHAPTER 20

P hoebe paced the small cabin, battling a desire to march to the store to talk with Eamon. She knew he needed to work. Needed to earn the salary his father paid him. As it was, he had spent too much time away from his job tending to her this summer. She rubbed at her temple, hoping none of the O'Rourkes would come to resent her. Eamon hadn't spent the past two nights at home, and she worried he would never return to her.

She took a deep breath and stilled her incessant pacing. Forcing herself to truly think about the O'Rourkes, she acknowledged they were kind, resourceful, and loving. Unlike her family, they did not withhold their affection or love due to petty squabbles or cling to their hurts and allow them to fester. Unlike Winnifred, they would never intentionally hurt her.

She forced herself to confront the anger, pain, and sense of unworthiness she felt after speaking with Winnifred. These were emotions she'd experienced her entire life with her youngest sister, enhanced during recent years by Winnifred's disappointments and her need to find someone to blame. With a startling insight, Phoebe realized her sister's vision did not have to be hers. Winnifred's opinion of herself did not have to shape how Phoebe saw herself. She swiped at a tear, as a sense of freedom warred with a tremendous loss.

Exhaling deeply, she marshaled her strength, hoping she had the courage to tell Eamon everything. Her fears. Her doubts. And pray he would accept her as she truly was, as he had done since the moment she had been injured. She turned, ready to confront her fears as she watched him enter their cabin. She studied him with wide eyes, a blush on her cheeks and trepidation in her posture.

"Eamon." Her attempt at a smile failed, and she saw him freeze in unbuttoning his shirtsleeves as was his custom each evening upon returning home. He always rolled them up, undid his collar, and relaxed with her, as they talked about their day, before venturing to the big house for dinner.

His alert gaze roved over her, and he took the few steps separating them. "What is it? What's upset you?" He froze, remembering their argument, and the moments leading up to it, where she'd had no desire for him to touch her.

She took a deep stuttering breath, taking strength from his instinctual behavior to protect her. "I'm trying to be brave, but I might falter." She reached forward, spanning the distance between them, to grip his hand. She took a hesitant breath, raised his hand, and kissed his knuckles. "I love the rituals we are establishing. You, returning after a day of work and becoming comfortable. Settling in our rocking chairs to talk about the day. My hand in yours."

"You are pleased I came home tonight?" When she stared at him in wonder, he whispered, "I couldn't handle another night alone in Ardan's spare bedroom." His gaze expressed the torment he'd felt at being away from her.

"I missed you too," she whispered.

He nodded, watching her with an alert caution. "What is

it, Bee?" he murmured, when she attempted to speak but appeared overcome by deep emotion. "Are you ill?"

"No," she rasped, reaching forward to hold onto his arm. "I've realized I've allowed others to influence me, and I'm trying to be brave and to take away their power over me."

"Ah, love," he breathed, as he pulled her close, his arms banding around her, as he inhaled her subtle scent. "You are brave. You always have been."

She kissed his neck and breathed deeply of his faded cologne mixed with sweat and dust. "How can I miss you so much, and you've only been away for a few days? How does Niamh handle having Cormac away for so long?"

He chuckled, his hold on her tightening. "We're newly-weds. The fascination will end, love." He eased away, so he could trace a finger over her jaw. "Although I hope it doesn't. I hope we're like Ard and Dee." He kissed her softly. "Or Kevin and Aileen." Looking deeply into her eyes, he refrained from kissing her again. "And Niamh accepts that Cormac must work while there's work to be had." He paused as he stared deeply into her eyes. "What upset you, love? What caused you to push me away?"

"*Love*," she whispered. "You call me that all the time. Why?"

He froze, the gentle cajoling erased from his expression, as he stared at her warily. "Don't you know?" he asked, as he took a step back. When she continued to stare at him expectantly, he swiped at his mouth and turned away. "*Brave*," he muttered to himself. "'Tis my turn for courage." He spun to face her, his mouth in a resolute line, as he gazed at her with a profound earnestness. "I love you. I've loved you since the steamboat."

She stared at him, her mouth falling open in wonder and awe, before she took a halting step to breach the distance that separated them. "I hoped you did. Everything you did

271

made me think you might. But I ... I couldn't assume anything until I heard the words from you." She blushed as a smile burst forth. "I finally believe I'm worthy of your love, Eamon."

"Oh, my love, you are," he rasped, as he yanked her into his arms. "You've always been worthy."

She felt him shudder as he held her close. She ducked her head, preventing him from kissing her, hearing his confused, "Bee?" as he pecked the top of her head. "No, Eamon, not until I've told you everything." She kept her arms wrapped around him, even though his tight hold on her loosened. "First," she whispered, "I love you. So much. I've lived with such fear that you could never care for me as I care for you."

"Lies," he rasped.

She nodded. "I know. I realized that yesterday, after talking with Lorena. She helped me to see that Winnifred was not concerned for me. I finally understood that Winnifred's venomous words were her truth. Not mine. And never yours." She cupped his cheek, her gaze softening as he turned his face into her palm. "I finally understood that I'd allowed other's words to control and to influence me for too long. That I'd allowed them to color my understanding of what I knew to be true."

His adoration-filled smile caused her breath to catch. "And what do you know to be true?" He kissed one eyebrow.

"I know that you will not abandon me. I know that your love will prove true." She took a deep breath, as she continued to gaze deeply into his eyes. "I know that I'll love you forever."

"You will? Forever?" he whispered, his eyes shimmering. When she nodded, her eyes glowing with her deepest emotions, he groaned, leaning forward to capture her mouth in a passionate kiss. He deepened the kiss, backing her toward their bed. "I know you need to tell me so much more," he murmured, as his hands worked at the buttons to her dress. "But I need you, my beloved."

"Yes," she gasped, as she arched into a kiss along her neck. "I need you too." She giggled as they collapsed onto the bed, her hands stroking his thick ebony hair, joy suffusing every part of her.

He leaned onto his elbows, grinning down at her. "I never thought to know such laughter and joy. I thought the happiness my parents have, or my brothers have, was never meant to be mine."

She shook her head, urging his head down to kiss her. "No, love. It was always meant to be ours."

E amon played with the long strands of her golden hair that cascaded down her back, his soft touch to her hair and skin earning a purr of delight from her. "We'll miss dinner," he murmured.

She rubbed her cheek against his chest, earning a soft groan of pleasure, raising her head enough so she could meet his delighted, passion-filled gaze. "We'll survive a night of hunger."

He chuckled. "You know my mum will send one of the lads over with plates of food to leave at our doorstep. We won't be hungry." He kissed her nose. "I don't want you to be embarrassed."

She shook her head. "That they know how much I adore my husband and want time with him? That would never mortify me." She pushed up to rest on her elbows so she could reach out and trace a hand through his disheveled hair and scrape her fingers through the whiskers on his cheeks. "I love seeing you so relaxed and content."

He shook his head. "I'm not content, Bee. I'm overjoyed.

Enraptured." He paused. "Worried." When she frowned at his last word, he ran soothing hands over her back. "Share with me what upset you a few days ago. I'd know every worry you have and happily carry that burden."

"Oh, Eamon," she breathed, as she pushed up to kiss him. It was a fleeting kiss, not meant to rekindle their passion. "I talked with Winnie. And I still had my uncle's words in my head to overcome."

He nodded, silently asking her to share her troubles with him.

"Winnie claimed that, although I might have your interest right now, I would never be successful in keeping it. That you would be fickle, as all men are. And that a man forced to marry me would never want to be with me forever. That today's happiness would only make tomorrow's sorrow that more acute." She bit her lip, hesitating. "Her words, combined with my uncle calling me a cripple, sent me in a spiral of self-doubt and loathing."

Eamon sat up, his blue eyes blazing with anger. "Cripple?" he hissed. "How dare anyone call you that?" He shook his head, as he saw fear and doubt in her gaze that she valiantly tried to conceal. "You were horribly injured, Bee. You walk with a limp. But you are not and never will be crippled."

"I can't do what your mum and Maggie do," she said, as tears dripped down her cheeks. "Oh, I thought I'd banished these fears!" she cried, as she lowered her head in an attempt to hide behind her hand. As her shoulders shook, she fell to her side, her arms wrapped around her middle.

Eamon levered himself up on one elbow, his hands stroking over her, soothing her as he waited for her to calm. Finally he said, "Tell me what you believe you cannot do."

In a weak, defeated voice, she said, "I cannot cook like your mum and sisters. I cannot sew like them. I will not have the strength to run after a child and care for him or her as your sister does. In every regard as a wife, I am less than what you need."

He raised an eyebrow at her self-assessment. "Less than what I need?" He made a face, evaluating all she had said to determine if any of it had any merit. He held up his hand that had come to rest on her hip, raising fingers as he ticked off items she had mentioned. "I've eaten your food, and 'tis delicious. I've seen you sew, and 'tis acceptable." He kissed her as she sputtered at him. "I know you'll continue to regain your strength, and you'll care for our babe, as each need arises." He shook his head, when she started to speak and interrupt him.

"You're under the impression, my love, that you must be as adept or as proficient as every other member of my family at their particular skill. That, if you aren't, it's because of your hurt leg. You seem to have forgotten that my mum and Maggie rarely sew, except for Maggie sewing up injuries. Maggie would prefer to never cook or sew but does both out of necessity. And Aileen hates to cook. No one thinks them lacking or crippled because they do what they excel at." He stared at her with an abiding tenderness. "Find what you love, and we will support you."

She stared at him in awe. "I love to tat lace, but I was always told it was a waste of time."

He beamed at her. "I'm certain Da would love to sell it in our store. And, if it doesn't sell here, we'll ship it on to Helena and Virginia City. There are more women there, and I'm certain they miss the small touches that are reminiscent of home." He raised her hand, tracing his chest, to kiss her fingers. "And you could tat at the kitchen table, while chatting with my mum and Maggie as they cooked."

"Why don't you believe I'm crippled?" she asked in a low voice. "I'll never dance smoothly. I'll never walk without a hitch in my gait. I'll never run after our child without falling on my face."

He rested his hand over her heart. "None of that matters, Bee. What matters is who you are. To me." He saw the question in her gaze. "You're my love. The woman I trust above all others. My heart sings at the sight of you."

"Oh, Eamon," she whispered, as her eyes filled. "I thought your father was the poet."

He grinned at her. "Aye, Da's a way with words, but we all learned from him." His fingers continued to trace over her. "Why did you speak with Winnifred? I thought you had become adept at avoiding her."

She snuggled forward, resting on his chest, her fingers playing with his. "She saw me standing by the Missouri. Happy and content. She struck up a conversation and seemed friendly. Now I realize she was conniving." With a sigh, she admitted, "Winnifred resents me. She always will, I fear."

"Why?" he murmured. "You're a wonderful sister to her. You protected her on the boat, while still attempting to give her the freedom she desperately craved."

"She loved a man. A boy, really. Named Emory. He was dashing and charming. He convinced her that he wanted to marry her, but she admitted to me that he didn't have the money for a wife and family. He hoped that she would come to the marriage with a large dowry and that they'd live in a grand house from her money."

Eamon sighed, kissing her head. "Her desire for appearances trapped her, aye?"

"Yes," Phoebe whispered. "She didn't know what to do. We had little saved, and Uncle Harvey had just died, leaving his money to our cousins. Although he did leave us each $1,000. But, with how my sisters wanted to live, that money wouldn't have lasted long."

"One thousand dollars?" Eamon asked.

She nodded. "I don't have much of it left. I spent most of

my share on my fare here and on expenses since my mother died last summer." Her eyes clouded.

"I wonder if your other uncle, Uriah, learned about it. I wonder if he wanted it."

She shrugged. "I don't know. He never mentioned it. And it wouldn't do him much good now as it's been spent." Phoebe pressed into his embrace, in need of his comforting arms around her.

He ran a hand through her tangled hair. "I still don't understand, love. Why does Winnie resent you? Why won't Lorena defend you, like a big sister should?"

"Mother found out that Emory was poorer than a chimney sweep and looking to Winnifred to climb the social ladder of respectability and financial success. Mother ensured he understood our financial predicament. She also informed him of our parentage and intimated we would most likely take after our mother."

"Your own mother told you this?" Eamon asked, incredulous.

Phoebe shook her head. "I overhead Mother's discussion with Emory in our sitting room. And I was as shocked as you are now. For Winnie was her favorite." Bee sighed. "Or maybe *because* Winnie was her favorite."

Eamon frowned, his gaze considering all she said and inferred. "You mean, your mother implied you'd act like prostitutes?" He rolled her onto her back, earning a gasp from her. "Why?"

"In her misguided way, Mama believed she was protecting Winnifred from profound disappointment, and she hoped a better man would sweep Winnie off her feet." Flushing, Phoebe murmured, "Somehow Winnie believes I'm the one who told Emory about our family. That I told him that she was not much better than a prostitute. That I forced him away because he was poor. And she won't forgive me."

277

Studying her, Eamon murmured, "Because she's so blinded by keeping up the facade of gentility, she believes that would be your only goal too." At her nod, he let out a huff of frustration. "She should know you better."

"She's heartbroken and angry and needs someone to blame."

His blue eyes glowed with a fierce fervency. "Perhaps, but I will never agree with her having the right to make you feel worse so she feels better. You are too precious and too fine a woman to ever have to suffer her abuse."

She traced a hand over his cheek and smiled. "One day she'll understand what occurred. She'll find a better man. And then she'll believe me."

Eamon kissed her brow and then her nose. "Her lies are not your truth, beloved Bee." At her nod, he smiled. "I imagine Lorena has a similar tale of woe." She nodded soberly. "It's unfortunate Declan's away, for I believe they would have been perfect for each other."

"Why do you say that?" she whispered, her luminous eyes shining with love and adoration.

"Because they both yearn for love," he whispered, lowering his head to kiss her lips. "I'd hope Declan could be who she needed, but I fear I'll barely recognize the brother I left behind when he finally returns to us."

Eamon leaned forward, kissing Phoebe softly. "I was afraid you were disappointed in me. That you couldn't see me as a man who could protect you because I cannot force the saloon owner, Bell, to leave town."

"Eamon," she breathed, as she ran her fingers over his strong chest. "No. Although he terrifies me, I think he's an opportunist. And I was an easy mark for him. Now that I'm with you, I doubt he'll even acknowledge that he ever met me. He'd never risk your wrath. He might be strong, but he could never match the combined force of the O'Rourke men." She met his worried gaze with a reassuring smile. "I have faith in you. I trust that you will always protect me, my love."

He let out a sigh of relief, kissing her again.

She ran her fingers over his cheek. "Forgive me?" she whispered. At his questioning stare, she murmured, "Forgive me for doubting? For giving credence to my fears, rather than having faith in you? In us?"

He nodded, kissing her softly. "Aye, my precious Bee. I forgive you." He nibbled at her throat, before leaning back and meeting her gaze. "We'll have misunderstandings to work through during the many years of our marriage, but I will forgive you anything as long as you always love me."

She smiled luminously at him. "You should ask something more difficult, love. For I'll love you forever."

~

I hope you enjoyed Pioneer Longing- *order the next book in the series*- Pioneer Bliss- *now! Available January 2021!*

COMING SOON! PIONEER BLISS!

A sneak peek at a scene from the upcoming book!

A week later, the steamboat docked in Fort Benton on a hot, dry day in early June. Declan stood at the railing, searching for any sign of his brothers or father. However, no one had come to meet this boat as it approached in the early evening hours. Whatever O'Rourke supplies that were on this boat would be set aside for retrieval tomorrow.

"Don't worry about our things," he murmured to Samantha as they disembarked. "They'll be delivered." He motioned for her to follow him as he made his way across the muddy, wagon and rut filled Front Street, cutting down a side street away from the main thoroughfare that hugged the Missouri River. Instead, he focused on an area away from the thriving, boisterous town.

"Home," he murmured when he saw the large, two story residence with chicken coop in the back. An addition off the rear of the home ruined the precise symmetry of the house, but afforded more space inside for the residents. "We're a large family, Samantha," he murmured. "But they'll accept you." He saw the much younger woman shiver before forcing a look of bored interest. "There's no need to be terrified."

He approached the rear porch. Memories of chasing his brothers up the stairs assailed him. Of sitting beside his youngest sister, Maggie, and chatting with her. Of watching his niece, Maura play as she chased a chicken. How much had everyone changed in his absence? Would they truly want him back?

With a deep breath to ease his own doubts, Declan eased open the kitchen door, his gaze alert and head cocked to one side as he listened for the usual family chatter. When he heard the cacophony of conversation that heralded a typical O'Rourke family dinner, his hold on the bundle in his arms tightened and he stood rocking in place. Familiar voices washed over him as though a siren's call, urging him to take the last few steps and to finally be home. Instead, he closed his eyes, hearing his father's strong, cheerful voice as he called out loving words to his mum. A quieter voice that sounded like mum, but he suspected was his sister Maggie, as it was youthful and not as heavily redolent of Ireland. His brothers's loud voices as they joked and jabbed at each other. Laughter, always laughter and joy.

He took a deep breath. How had he borne the years apart from them? Would they be eager to see him?

Gathering his courage he forced himself to take the final steps into his parent's house. He walked soundlessly, stilling as he watched his family duck their heads for their Da to say grace.

"May we always be fortunate enough to have plentiful work and food and a home to shelter us all. May we never forget the blessings of family and the joy of Mary and Maggie's return. And may we see Declan returned to us sometime this year."

At the solemn 'Amen', he watched as his family dug into

the meal and the controlled chaos as an O'Rourke meal commenced. Battling tears, he swallowed to clear a thickness in his throat before he rasped, "I'm home, Da." His blue eyes shone with pain and relief as he met his da's startled gaze.

"Declan!" Seamus yelled out, dropping his spoon and leaping up. He knocked his chair to the floor in his haste to reach his son who'd been absent nearly two years. "Is it truly you? Have you come back to us?" He clasped Declan's shoulders in a bruising grip as though afraid he were a ghost or that he would disappear again so soon after returning home.

Declan nodded, a tear leaking out of each eye as he met his father's incredulous stare. "Aye," he whispered. "I'm finally home."

"But you look nothin' like Declan," Ardan, his eldest brother whispered as he gaped at him.

Declan shrugged, knowing he appeared much altered since the last time anyone in his family had seen him. Gone were the shaggy hair and the unkempt beard. Instead, he had a genteel appearance about him with a close- cropped haircut and a trimmed beard. His suit was finely styled and nothing like the backwoodsmen clothes he had favored. "'Tis I, Ardan."

～

Order Pioneer Bliss (The O'Rourke Family Montana Saga, Book Five) Now! Available to Read in January 2021!

DON'T MISS A RAMONA FLIGHTNER UPDATE!

Thank you for reading *Pioneer Longing*! I hope you enjoyed it as much as I enjoyed writing it.

I love hearing from you, so please feel free to write me and let me know what you think!

You can reach me at: ramona@ramonaflightner.com

Join My Newsletter For Updates, and Sneak Peeks about the series you love!

Want new release alerts, access to bonus materials and exclusive giveaways, and all my announcements first? Subscribe to my weekly newsletter!

Want to be notified about freebies and sales? Try Bookbub!

Want to stay up to date on new releases, my life in beautiful Montana, and research trip adventures? Follow my hashtag

#ramonasmontanalife to follow along with my adventures as I post gorgeous pictures and videos of my life in Montana. Find Me On Facebook! Or Find Me On Instagram!

ALSO BY RAMONA FLIGHTNER

The O'Rourke Family Montana Saga

Follow the O'Rourke Family as they settle in Fort Benton, Montana Territory in 1865. Coming in 2020!

Sign up here to receive the prequel, *Pioneer Adventure* to the new Saga as a thank you for subscribing to my newsletter!

Pioneer Dream (OFMS, Book 1)- Kevin and Aileen

Pioneer Desire- (OFMS, Book 2)- Ardan and Deirdre

Pioneer Yearning- (OFMS, Book 3) Niamh and Cormac

Pioneer Longing (OFMS, Book 4)- August 2020! Eamon's story!

Pioner Bliss (OFMS, Book 5) Coming Soon! Declan's story!

Pioneer Devotion (OFMS, Book 6) Maggie's story! Coming in 2021!

Bear Grass Springs Series

Never fear, I am busy at work on the next book in the series! If you want to make sure you never miss a release, a special, a cover reveal, or a short story just for my fans, sign up for my newsletter!

Immerse yourself in 1880's Montana as the MacKinnon siblings and their extended family find love!

Montana Untamed (BGS, Book 1)- Cailean and Annabelle

Montana Grit (BGS, Book 2)- Alistair and Leticia

Montana Maverick (BGS, Book 3) Ewan and Jessamine

Montana Renegade(BGS, Book 4) Warren and Helen

Jubilant Montana Christmas (BGS, Book 5) Leena and Karl

Montana Wrangler (BGS, Book 6) Sorcha and Frederick

Unbridled Montana Passion (BGS, Book 7) Fidelia and Bears

Montana Vagabond (BGS, Book 8) Ben and Jane

Exultant Montana Christmas (BGS, Book 9) Ewan and Jessamine

Lassoing a Montana Heart (BGS, Book 10) Slims and Davina

Healing Montana Love (BGS, Book 11) Coming in September 2020!

Runaway Montana Groom (BGS, Book 12) Coming in 2021!

The Banished Saga

Follow the McLeod, Sullivan and Russell families as they find love, their loyalties are tested, and they overcome the challenges of their time. A sweeping saga set between Boston and Montana in early 1900's America. Finally, the Saga is complete!

The Banished Saga: (In Order)

Love's First Flames (Prequel)

Banished Love

Reclaimed Love

Undaunted Love (Part One)

Undaunted Love (Part Two)

Tenacious Love

Unrelenting Love

Escape To Love

Resilient Love

Abiding Love

Triumphant Love

ABOUT THE AUTHOR

Ramona is a historical romance author who loves to immerse herself in research as much as she loves writing. A native of Montana, every day she marvels that she gets to live in such a beautiful place. When she's not writing, her favorite pastimes are fly fishing the cool clear streams of a Montana river, hiking in the mountains, and spending time with family and friends.

Ramona's heroines are strong, resilient women, the type of women you'd love to have as your best friend. Her heroes are loyal and honorable, men you'd love to meet or bring home to introduce to your family for Sunday dinner. She hopes her stories bring the past alive and allow you to forget the outside world for a while

bookbub.com/authors/ramona-flightner

facebook.com/authorramonaflightner

instagram.com/rflightner

pinterest.com/Ramonaauthor

www.ingramcontent.com/pod-product-compliance
Lightning Source LLC
Chambersburg PA
CBHW052028240626
47153CB00006B/2003